New France

①

⑫

②

③

Hurons

Adirondack Mts

Georgian Bay

⑬

⑭ Iroquois Hunting Grounds

Lake Ontario

⑥ Senecas ⑦ Onondagas ⑧ Oneidas Mohawks Cayugas

The Five Nations

English

Lake Erie

Lands of the

DRUMS IN THE FOREST

By ALLAN DWIGHT

Linn Dickson, Confederate

Spaniards' Mark

Drums in the Forest

*

DRUMS IN THE FOREST

By ALLAN DWIGHT

Illustrated by GEORGE L. CARLSON

NEW YORK
THE MACMILLAN COMPANY
1945

To
C. W. C. and K. S. C.

825813

FOREWORD

ALTHOUGH nearly a hundred and eighty years have passed since the banner of France was seen on the ramparts of Quebec, the spirit of the sturdy pioneers who planted it there still lives in their French-speaking descendants along the St. Lawrence. The memory of their exploits remains, too, preserved in place names from Cape Breton to the western prairies. Our pride in Anglo-Saxon exploration and colonization naturally emphasizes the accomplishments of our ancestors, but such names as Detroit, Duluth, St. Louis, Des Moines, Cadillac and many others are reminders that the sons of French Canada played a part no less noteworthy than that of the English in the history of North America.

They were the first pioneers in the vast region of the Great Lakes and Upper Mississippi, for French woodsmen, traders and missionaries had established outposts there long before English colonists ventured across the Appalachians. In the main, they got on well with the natives of that part of the continent, for they sought to develop commerce and spread Christianity rather than to colonize, as the English were doing. That policy was finally fatal to France. The English colonies, settling their people on the land, grew in population and power, while the French remained few in numbers and relatively weak in resources.

Among the officials, coureurs de bois and priests who held this great domain for a century and a half were many remarkable men in whom ability, intelligence, daring were commonplace qualities. French Canada had its share of capable leaders in the contest against the English and their Iroquois allies or it could never have held out so long against increasing odds.

"Drums in the Forest" deals with one of the critical periods in the long struggle between the adversaries, when such qualities came to the fore, a time when, actually as well as figuratively, Indian tomtoms and the drums of the French and the English beat their challenges in the forests of the New World. Life along the St. Lawrence and in the west as pictured here is based on accounts of those who participated in these events and knew stout old Governor Frontenac, the coureur Nicolas Perrot and other historical characters of the story. Indian life, too, as Denis saw it, is recreated from contemporary reports, many of which show sympathetic understanding of the Indian viewpoint, as well as keen observation.

In acknowledging aid from secondary sources especial tribute should be rendered to the monumental works of Francis Parkman. Such histories of the times as those of Becqueville de la Potherie and Father Charlevoix were also used. But much of the material was drawn from invaluable original sources. Among these authentic, colorful documents are the memoirs of the coureur Nicolas Perrot (one of the principal characters of this book); La Hontan's "Voyages"; the lengthy "Jesuit Relations"; the journals of Fathers Marquette, Allouez and Hennepin; the accounts left by Tonty and DuLhut; the historical works of the Abbé Belmont and of C. Le Clercq; the "Documentary History of New York," and the anonymous "Recueil de ce qui c'est passé en Canada." Most helpful in supplying information on Indian life were the works of La Fitau, Loskiel, Heckwelder, Lewis Morgan, Beauchamp, Clark, and Hodge's "Handbook of American Indians." Thanks are due to Dr. Arthur C. Parker, curator of the Rochester, N. Y. museum and an authority on the Iroquois, for his aid.

ALLAN DWIGHT.

CONTENTS

DRUMS IN THE FOREST

Chapter I

CITY OF THE ROCK

THE dull boom of a saluting gun sent Denis de Lornay bounding up the companionway into the bright morning sunlight. With a rattle of iron links the anchor chain slipped into the water, and the ship *Le Glorieux,* sixty-two days out of Le Havre, bearing messages from King Louis XIV to his Royal Governor of New France, came to rest on the broad St. Lawrence. It was late in August of the year 1686.

On the yards sailors began to sing as they furled the canvas. A gunner grinned as he passed Denis. "Quebec at last, my young friend," he called cheerfully.

Denis hurried to the rail. A roar from one of the ship's guns answered the city's greetings. A small sloop came about with flapping sails, and its crew began a shouted conversation with the new arrivals. Two of the odd-looking white boats called canoes were tearing across the water at a fine speed. In the first was one of the red natives of the country. In the second were two men, one Indian, one white. It looked like a race, for all three were wielding their paddles furiously.

As they came nearer Denis realized that something was amiss. The lone Indian swept his craft alongside the ship and began to scramble up the rope ladder, terror staring from his eyes. As he gained the rail, the second canoe reached the foot of the ladder. The pursued man raised a despairing cry of "Captain! Captain!" as he ran across the deck.

What followed took place so quickly that the sailors of the merchantman were too startled, for a moment, to act. The second Indian, his face streaked with green and black paint, a long knife gripped in his teeth, slipped over the rail and darted after the stumbling fugitive, who dodged around a cask. Up the ladder came the white man. He paused for an instant as his feet touched the deck, and Denis saw that he was a tall, powerful, swarthy fellow, with broad shoulders and long muscular arms. He was clad in shirt and breeches of fringed buckskin. A drooping eyelid beneath the scar of an old wound across brow and temple gave his face a sinister expression. He leaped forward, as though to intercept the fleeing Indian.

Denis awoke from his daze and, throwing out his foot, tripped the fellow headlong to the deck. Instantly two sailors were on the man. From the high stern came Captain Marsollet's bellow: "Pierre, Alain, stop those savages! Grab them!"

Denis heard a thin high scream and whirled to see the Indian who had first reached the ship drop with a long knife in his back. At the same instant the white man sprang up and threw off the sailors like a wild boar ridding himself of terriers. "You young whelp!" he snarled, and aimed a blow at Denis, who dodged just in time. Half a dozen of the crew flung themselves at him and bore him back against the mast.

"Hold that Indian!" roared Captain Marsollet, thumping down the steps to the main deck. But it was too late. A figure arched over the rail and hit the water with a splash. Someone fired a pistol.

The Captain's face was red with anger. "Zounds!"

he exclaimed, stooping over the dead man. "It's my old boy, Ockola, the Abenaki. I left him last year with the young clerk, Raoul Mersan. Now what the devil is the meaning of this?"

He whipped out his cutlass and turned to the stranger. "I said, sirrah, what is the meaning of this?"

"How should I know?" replied the other coolly. Although he was still breathing hard, his voice was suave. "It is an outrageous thing to seize a man when he is trying to stop a killing. I'd have, too, if that young fool hadn't tripped me."

The fellow's black eyes flicked a glance at Denis. "You don't seem to remember me," he told the Captain. "My name's Marcel Loutray. I have furs to sell. To be first on the ship I hired a Huron to bring me out as soon as I sighted your sails. As we were launching the boat the Abenaki dashed past us and jumped into his canoe. My Huron went after him. I didn't know why until we reached the ship. Some Indian feud, likely."

Captain Marsollet looked first at the man who called himself Loutray, then at Denis, and finally out over the gleaming St. Lawrence toward the city. He scratched his chin.

"He was paddling just as hard as the Huron," put in one of the sailors. "Why was he doing that if he wasn't after the Abenaki?"

"Because I thought he was sent out by another trader," replied Loutray promptly.

"A pretty tale," commented Captain Marsollet, "and yet I do not like it."

"What do you mean?" blustered Loutray.

Marsollet flushed angrily. "I say your story doesn't satisfy me, smooth as it is. I wish I could order you a good flogging. Now get off my ship. Pierre, bundle him over the side. Mordi! As if I haven't plenty to do without this!"

The man with the drooping eyelid scowled and turned toward the rail. Denis drew back with a shiver as he passed, for he perceived, in the moment their glances met, something in the eyes of the other that boded him ill if their paths should ever cross. But as the fellow began to descend the ladder he lost the scowl and his expression became smug, as though he were striving to hide a secret amusement.

Quickly Captain Marsollet gave directions for disposal of the Indian's body. Then he strode below to prepare himself for his visit to the Governor.

Denis's bright anticipations had been banished by the murder of the Indian. Truly this Canada where he had chosen to seek his fortune was a harsh land. For the first time since he had met Captain Marsollet beside the stream in far-off Normandy he began to have forebodings about the future. It was clear that one must be very careful. He turned his hazel eyes toward the city and stared thoughtfully.

Less than half a mile away across the water stood the lofty rock of Quebec. About its base clustered the lower settlement, spread along the footing between the plateau and the water, a jumble of gray, dormered, stone houses with steep slate roofs that glistened in the sunlight. Above the huddle of roofs rose the cliff, broken at one place by a slope gentle enough for a narrow twisting street, bordered by a single row of houses, to climb precariously toward the gray dwellings, monasteries and churches that formed what was known as the upper town. The buildings perched at different levels on the plateau, which mounted by an easy incline toward the culminating heights of Cape Diamond.

Beyond the estuary of a small river that rounded the nearer end of the rock lay brown marshes against a background of dark forests and distant hills. On the other side of the ship, opposite the city, stood the wooded heights of Levis. Narrowing between the two headlands, the mighty St. Lawrence stretched westward into the wilderness of New France, with its wild animals and Indians, its promise of wealth and adventure.

Far up the river two small boats like those used by the Indians were pushing upstream into the unknown. Perhaps the tiny figures in them were woodsmen, who, Marsollet had said, set out at this season for the farther wilderness to trap the beaver. This thought, coupled with the cheerful sounds around him, somewhat restored Denis's spirits.

Behind him Captain Marsollet's voice was ordering the longboat made ready. The Captain had changed to a long blue coat frogged with designs in silver thread, a crimson waistcoat and a freshly powdered wig. He cocked an eye up the river, then, spying Denis, pointed to the distant canoes. "See, lad," he rumbled. "There go some coureurs de bois now. A thousand miles they'll voyage, like as not, before they settle for the winter. Next summer they'll be back laden with skins. You'll be one of these woodsmen before long, with plenty of gold in your pocket. But here comes a boat. It's Maître Pezzard himself. Quick, look to your appearance."

Hastily Denis smoothed his brown hair, pulled down

the cuffs of his shirt and buttoned his coat. Maître
Pezzard, a merchant, might give him employment,
the Captain had said.

The boat, paddled by two Indians, came nearer,
touched the ship's side. A moment later a stocky figure
clad in a suit of fine black broadcloth clambered over
the rail.

"Welcome, Master Pezzard," boomed the Captain.

The merchant was a man of medium height, with a
full clean-shaven face. A pair of small observant eyes
of palest gray, set rather closely together, gave him
an expression of shrewdness. He wore a broad-
brimmed black hat, and the buckles on his square-toed
shoes were of silver.

"Good day, Captain, good day," he replied in a
high-pitched voice. "A pleasure indeed, sir. I trust
your voyage was easy?"

"A bit stormy for this time of year, sir, but otherwise good."

"And the merchandise, Captain?"

"All in order, good Maître. But, before we go below . . . You spoke last fall of needing a bright boy
for your errands. Denis de Lornay here is just the
one for you. He is strong, capable and honest. He has
been my cabin boy on this trip."

Denis, gaping at the pudgy man he hoped would be
his future master, hastily collected his wits and bowed.
He straightened to find the pale eyes regarding him
with chilly interest.

"Yes, yes. I remember," said the other. "How old
are you?"

"Sixteen—nearly seventeen, sir."

The merchant looked him up and down and felt his
muscles, as though, thought Denis, he were a draft

horse. "How is it that your parents have let you come to Canada?" he inquired.

Denis, stammering a little in self-consciousness, explained that he had no parents. He had been brought up by old Giles, who owned a little farm back in Normandy. But times were hard and taxes high. During the last year or so his benefactor had grown so poor that Denis felt he could no longer be a burden on him. He had decided to seek his own fortune, hoping to make money so Giles could have comforts in his old age. Then he had met Captain Marsollet, who had told him of wealth to be gained in Canada. When the Captain had seen how the wind lay he had offered him passage in exchange for work. It had seemed providential.

To all of which Pezzard listened without comment. "How will you do without the boy on your return?" he asked.

"Oh, I'll make out," replied Marsollet, throwing an arm around Denis. "It was mainly to help the lad."

It seemed to Denis that the Captain had been made uncomfortable by the question, but before he had time to wonder at this Pezzard wanted to know if he could read and figure. Denis replied that he could and that he had some Latin and history as well. The answer seemed to satisfy the merchant, for he said, "Very well, I think you'll do. Get your things together."

Denis hurried to his tiny cabin where he began to cram his few shirts and pairs of hose into a cloth bag. His luck was holding. He would learn much about skins from the good merchant; and that would be invaluable when the time came for him to launch out on his own as a fur trader. He snatched up his bundle and made sure that his knife sheath was securely attached to his belt. The sheath held a slender dagger that had belonged to his father. It was his one possession of value. Old Giles had given it to him only last year, saying that he must never let it out of his sight. The blade, now dimmed by the tarnish of years, was of fine steel from the East. The hilt, which he kept wrapped in a rag lest some sailor covet the weapon, was of beautifully wrought silver.

With a last look around, he shouldered his bag and took post outside the Captain's cabin. Although Marsollet had been a kind master, he was eager to get ashore and begin his new life, and every moment that he had to wait seemed like an hour. At last the two men appeared, both apparently in the best of spirits. The merchant proceeded at once to the deck, but Marsollet paused.

"You've been a good boy," he said. "I hope you'll like your new berth."

"Oh, sir, I'm sure I will. I can't thank you enough for all you've done for me."

"It was nothing, my boy," said Marsollet gruffly. "Nothing. But have you any money?"

"Two louis, from selling my school prizes," answered Denis proudly.

The Captain produced a large linen handkerchief, blew his nose and, staring at Denis, reached into his pocket. "Here are two more. Don't be spending them on foolishness."

Denis was too overcome by this magnificent gift to thank the Captain properly. Marsollet put an end to his struggles with a pat on the back. "There, run along now. I will see the message you are sending to your Giles reaches him safely. We will meet next summer, I trust."

With this brief farewell Denis took his leave and followed his new employer down the ladder to the boat, where two Indian rowers sat motionless as statues. The moment he was settled they pushed off, and almost before he realized it *Le Glorieux* was growing smaller, slipping away from him as the coast of France had slipped away that afternoon two months ago.

The Indians brought the craft expertly alongside a dock, and Denis sprang out to hold the boat while the merchant landed. His intention was good, but he lingered overlong about the business, fascinated by what he saw. Beached along the neighboring shore, beneath the cliff that shadowed this part of the city, were a dozen or so frail canoes. Bearded men in leathern shirts strode among the boats, laughing and jesting as they loaded them with sacks and bundles, kegs and muskets. They were so blithe and jaunty at their labors, with such an air of devil-may-care independence, that Denis could not help gaping.

The merchant was not pleased. "Ho, addle wit, wake up," he said curtly. "This is no time to gawk at coureurs de bois. Come."

Reddening, Denis hastily obeyed.

Their route led along a narrow thoroughfare between closely packed stone houses so similar to the houses of Normandy that Denis had a comforting feeling of being at home. There were many people in the street, some of them as familiar in appearance as the houses, others as strange as men from the moon. A brown Franciscan monk pattered by, smiling greetings to respectful working men. A shopkeeper displayed a bolt of green cloth to two admiring habitants, peasants from the country, clad in woolen clothes and red stocking caps. An aproned apprentice dodged nimbly around a dignified notary and fetched up short just in time to avoid two savages, haughty in paint and feathers, who stalked by with scarce a glance to right or left. With slow tread a black-gowned Jesuit passed, fingering the leaves of a breviary.

The street widened into a small square paved with cobblestones. At one side of it stood an unfinished church. In its center was a tiny plot of grass surrounded by an iron fence. The merchant led the way across it and halted in the middle of the next block before a door set between two barred windows. Denis followed him into a dark hall filled with the stuffy smell of skins and furs. Stairs led up in the gloom to the second story. On the left was a storeroom filled with boxes and bales.

Pezzard, whose manner seemed less cordial than on the ship, clumped up the stairs. After a moment of hesitation Denis followed. The merchant halted before a door near the stairhead and, throwing it open, motioned Denis inside. "It is your room," he explained. "Make haste and join me downstairs in my office. It is across from the store."

Denis looked about him doubtfully. There were three pieces of furniture, a bed with a straw mattress, a table and a stool. The room was poorly lighted by a narrow window which was separated into two parts by an iron bar set upright in the masonry. The place better deserved the name cell than room, he thought.

He found Pezzard seated at a massive mahogany desk before a litter of papers. "Now then, young man, take yonder high stool at the counter and call me this list of goods while I check the ship's invoices. We shall soon see how good you are at figures."

And so it was that Denis began his duties by reading aloud an interminable catalogue of goods—axes, knives, shoemakers' awls, needles, Venice beads, sewing thread, pack thread, cakes of vermilion, fishhooks of all sizes, cocked hats, boots. It seemed scarcely the stuff of romance.

Noon had passed before the job was done. At last Pezzard put the papers in a drawer and, fishing a silver box out of his coat pocket, helped himself to a small pinch of snuff.

"Marie, in the kitchen, will give you your dinner," he said as soon as he had finished sneezing. "Eat in your room today, then report to Joseph, my helper in the store, who will teach you the prices of the trade goods. But stay a moment! In addition to such clerkly duties as this you will have errands to run. Some of them will be—important." He shot Denis a sidelong look. "I am but a humble merchant," he continued, a trifle pompously, "but Monsieur de Champigny, the Intendant, does me the honor to consult me on matters touching trade, and Governor Denonville himself thinks well of my judgment. Hence, in the course of your duties, you will be called on to carry confidential messages, and perhaps you will overhear some things better forgotten or at least kept to yourself. Silence, as the saying goes, is golden. Do you understand?"

"Yes, sir," replied Denis uncertainly.

"Very good. You may go."

Denis hesitated, at a loss to bring up a subject which, he remembered, had not been discussed on shipboard. "Please, sir," he blurted, "how much are you going to pay me?"

Pezzard's eyebrows raised themselves a good inch. "Pay?" he repeated. "What effrontery is this, jacka-

napes? Apprentices are not paid. I have to bear the
cost of your food and clothing and lodging. That is
more than your services are worth."

Denis felt sick and breathless, as if he had been
struck in the pit of his stomach. Somehow he con-
trolled his voice. "I must have money for my friend,
sir," he said quietly. "That is why I came to Canada.
I told you on the ship."

"Silence," snapped the merchant. "Plainly you know
nothing of trade matters. Be glad you have a home. I
will decide when the time comes for paying you. Now
go."

The boy's eyes dropped before the cold gaze of the
other. He turned and was stumbling blindly toward
the door when it opened. He took a backward step out
of the way and stood motionless, as though turned to
stone. The man who entered the room was the fellow
of the drooping eyelid, who called himself Loutray!

"It turned out very well, Maître." Loutray's tone
was gleeful.

Pezzard frowned and gestured toward Denis. "I
know," he replied. "This is the new errand boy," he
added meaningly.

Loutray turned his head and saw Denis. He gave an
almost imperceptible start of surprise. His mouth
tightened.

Denis shrank back against the wall. "Maître," he
gasped. "This man is—"

"Is my assistant, M'sieur Marcel Loutray, from
whom you are to take orders," interrupted Pezzard.
"I had best tell you, to begin with, that though he has
a kind heart, he has been a soldier and believes in discipline. The Huron warrior behind him is called Black

Fox. I am sure," he added softly, "that you will get along splendidly with them."

It was the Indian who had murdered the Abenaki. His garments were still damp from his swim in the river. He looked at Denis impassively. His small eyes were like two black pebbles set above his broad cheek-bones.

The silence was broken by Pezzard. "I think you had best go and get your dinner."

Denis gathered his wits together. White-faced he walked past the two, trying not to show fear. The door closed behind him and at once he heard the rumble of Loutray's voice. He could not distinguish the words but he knew that Loutray was telling what had happened on the ship.

He walked slowly to the foot of the stairs. He was not hungry any more. Nevertheless, he sought the kitchen, for it might be a long time before supper.

Marie, the sullen, slatternly cook, was plainly displeased at having an addition to the household. Grudgingly she gave him a slice of dark bread, a piece of strong cheese, a pitcher of water, a towel. He accepted them dully and mounted the stairs to his room. There he placed the tray on the table and sat down on the bed, his chin between his fists, to stare at the blank wall.

He got up after a bit and washed his face and hands. Then he began munching his bread and cheese. But for once food was tasteless. Being bound to a man who would pay him nothing was bad enough, but much worse the thought of being under Loutray's orders. What was the real reason for the stabbing? Was Pezzard involved in it? He could not believe that, little as he liked his new master. After all, Marsollet seemed to have high regard for him. Bitterly he regretted having come to New France. Only the thought of Giles kept him from going to the Captain and begging return passage. He could endure a lot if it finally meant security for his old friend. Perhaps a better job would turn up before long. But in the meantime Loutray would make his life a hell.

Despondently he finished the bread and cheese. He resisted an impulse to fling himself on the bed and sob. That wouldn't do any good. Better to go down and get to work. But the more his head cleared the worse grew his forebodings. A knowledge deeper than reason told him that there was a mystery here. "I do not like this place," he murmured.

As he shut his lips on the last word he heard above him a faint moan.

CHAPTER II

DEEP WATERS

DENIS sprang up and listened. He fancied he heard a slight movement in the attic overhead. Then, unmistakably, the groan was repeated. He hesitated, wondering what to do, while dark suspicions began to take shape in his mind. An hour ago he would have gone to the merchant. But now he trusted none of them.

Cautiously he opened the door. Looking up, he peered into the gloom of the corridor and saw a trapdoor in the ceiling. By mounting his stool he was able to reach it and, after a stout heave, to push it open. He grasped the edge of the opening and quietly drew himself up.

A single dormer window with dirt-incrusted panes admitted enough light to the attic for him to see the outlines of rafters slanting up to meet overhead in the gray murk of cobwebs. Softly he rose to his feet. In one corner a man, bound hand and foot, lay on the dusty floor. By his side spread a great dark stain.

Heart hammering at his ribs, Denis tiptoed to the figure. The man was young. His face was pale and drawn. Fearfully Denis touched him.

The man shivered and opened his eyes. There was desperation, and pain, and fear in the look he fixed on Denis. With great effort he gasped, "Who are you?"

"The new errand boy," Denis managed to whisper. "What has happened? Can't I help you?"

The man shrank from him. "No," he said.

"Shall I fetch Maître Pezzard?"

"No! No!"

The vehemence and horror in the other's tone threw new light on the matter. Bending low, Denis whispered, "Sir, I am your friend. If Pezzard or Loutray or that red fiend have done aught to you I will try to set it right."

The fevered eyes stared searchingly. Gradually their expression changed.

"Unbind me," he begged. "Water."

Denis's fingers shook as he cut the cords, for he saw that there was a great knife wound in the man's side. Quickly he swung down through the trapdoor. He snatched up his pitcher of water and filled a pewter mug that stood on the table. Tiptoeing back to the corridor, he regained the attic as quietly as possible. The stranger drank while Denis supported his shoulders.

"You are kind," he murmured, his voice somewhat stronger now. "Why are you in this house?"

Denis hastily explained, impatient to help the man and get to the bottom of the mystery. The other gave a sigh of relief. "I think you have been sent by the Saints," he said. "But I warn you . . . danger . . . to help me." He closed his eyes. His features were like wax. "I'm done for," he whispered.

"My name," he went on, opening his eyes after a moment, "is Raoul Mersan. . . . Why do you start?"

"I have heard it before, sir," replied Denis, and told of Captain Marsollet's mention of the name as he stood over the murdered Indian.

In his agitation Mersan made a pitiful attempt to raise himself on his elbow. "Ockola," he gasped. "Poor, loyal Ockola. He escaped last night. He turned to the only one he could trust. Now we are undone. . . . Unless . . ."

"Tell me what to do."

"Listen . . . carefully."

In labored gasps Mersan told a story that Denis would have found well-nigh incredible had it not been for Loutray's part in the murder on the ship. He said that he had been sworn to secret work for the good of New France, work which made it necessary for him to act as a clerk in the office of the Intendant. He had come recently to lodge with Pezzard to learn more of his activities, for Pezzard was involved in treason. He had found proof that the merchant had committed crimes against the country and against Count Frontenac, the former Governor. But Pezzard had grown suspicious of him. Last night Loutray and Black Fox had trapped him in his room. They had tortured him. Unable to make him tell what he knew, they had dragged him to this attic. Loutray, enraged, had stabbed him and left him for dead.

"They are black villains. I beg you for aid against them. . . . Not for me—for Frontenac and Canada." His voice was tense with emotion.

"Aye, sir," said Denis hotly.

"Go to the middle room of the three below," the man directed huskily. "The third board from the left as you enter . . . Press the left edge—a pace from the farther wall. It tilts. Under it a packet wrapped in oiled silk. Take it at once to Alexandre LeRoux, lawyer in the upper town—Rue St. Louis, near the garden of the Jesuits. . . . The door has a brass

knocker shaped like a quill. . . . Give him this ring.
. . . Quickly."

"But you, sir. What is to become of you?"

"There is nothing you can do but this. . . . In
heaven's name, go!"

Denis pocketed the ring, dropped through the trapdoor, and slipped like a shadow into the stranger's
room. It took him but a moment to open the secret
cache and button the papers securely beneath his jacket.
He listened at the doorway, but all was quiet below
save for a faint hum of women's voices in the kitchen.
He tiptoed down the stairs and through the empty hall.
Quietly he opened the door and stepped into the street.

It was not hard to find the narrow steep road he
had seen from the river. Near the top of the hill a
kindly Recollect priest gave him directions.

A thin, gray-haired man opened the door of the
house with the goose-quill knocker. He peered at Denis
over square spectacles.

"I seek M'sieur LeRoux. Raoul Mersan sent me."

"I am the avocat LeRoux," said the old man in some
surprise, darting a quick look up and down the deserted
street. "Come in."

He showed Denis into a room lined with well-filled
bookshelves and dark massive furniture. A window
opened onto a walled garden.

"Why does Mersan send *you?*" he asked sharply as
he shut the door.

"He has been stabbed," blurted Denis, plunging his
hand into the front of his jacket. "He sent you his ring
and this packet of papers. I found him in the attic of
the house of Pezzard, the merchant."

With an exclamation the old man seized the parcel.
His hands trembled as he opened it and adjusted his

spectacles. Denis waited anxiously. At last the lawyer put the papers down and sank into a chair. "How did you learn this?" he demanded.

Denis told him of all that had happened since the ship had dropped anchor. LeRoux listened with grim attention, interrupting only to ask about Mersan's wound.

"I am afraid he cannot live," replied Denis. "I wanted to help him, but he said there was nothing I could do. He said this was more important."

"True. And I fear you are right, or he would not have employed such desperate means. Ah, those devils! They'll pay for this some day."

To Denis the events of the morning, now that he had marshaled them in order, were as unreal as the memory of a bad dream. LeRoux sensed what was passing in the boy's mind. "It is a strange thing that has happened to you," he said. "Tell me more about yourself, where you come from and why you are in Quebec. First, your name?"

"Denis de Lornay, sir."

The lawyer knit his brows and muttered the name to himself as if trying to place it.

Denis explained that he had no people in Canada, so the name did not matter. "I landed only this morning. I come from Cailly, near Rouen."

"Ah, Normandy," said the lawyer with a nod. "Go on."

So Denis told him about Giles and the little farm where he had been reared.

His first memory had been of holding fast to Giles's strong hand as he trotted down the lane that led from the farmhouse toward the old castle where no one lived. In time he had learned that Giles was not his father. He had wanted, then, to know about his parents, and Giles had told him that his father had been a brave soldier and loyal friend and that his mother had been as beautiful as she was good. Of course Denis asked other questions from time to time, but he had been told that such matters were not for young lads to worry about. Some day he would learn more. In the meantime he was to go to the school kept by the good curé and study hard. Better than his studies, though, had been the lessons in fencing with the rapier, the epée, and the saber, taught by Giles, who, like his father, had been a soldier.

Later years had not been so happy as those earlier ones. Giles had a son named Armand who thought of nothing but the farm. As the family had grown poorer and the taxes higher Armand had begun to object to Denis's continued schooling. It would be better, he had said, to put the boy to work in the fields so that he could earn his keep. Giles had curtly refused. Denis had tried to help with the work at night after lessons, but Armand had not been satisfied. As Giles grew more feeble Armand's demands had become more insistent. At last there had been a stormy scene between the old man and his son.

The day after that Denis had been coming back through the forest from market where he had sold a fowl when he met a hunting party. One of the nobles, a thin man dressed in green velvet, had asked him if he knew where the wild boars could best be found. Denis had told him of an oak grove where the mast would be thick. The gentleman had asked his name and complimented him on his knowledge.

Denis remembered the incident clearly because of the trouble with Armand and because the talk with the noble had opened vistas of a strange and splendid life. A few days later he had met Captain Marsollet, who had told him that even a common man, such as he was destined to be, could become rich in New France in the fur trade. Fascinated by the Captain's stories, Denis had suddenly decided that he would go to Canada. Marsollet had carelessly offered him a chance to work his passage. Denis had known better than to broach the matter to Giles. With some last-moment misgivings, he had slipped away one night and walked to Rouen, where the Captain had met him at an inn.

For some moments LeRoux, his long fingers tapping the arm of his chair, gazed at Denis without speaking. "And so you are pitched neck and crop to the tender mercies of Pezzard," he mused at last. "You are evidently an honest and quick-witted lad. Do you believe what Mersan told you?"

Under the other's intent gaze Denis hesitated. "I saw Loutray and the Indian, Black Fox, murder the Abenaki," he replied. "Pezzard hinted I had better hold my tongue about his dealings with the Intendant. I think these things fit in with Monsieur Mersan's story."

"Good," said the lawyer. "You have an old head on your shoulders. So I am going to take you into my confidence. You'd be better off not involved in all this; but now you are in it you should know more, so you may realize how necessary it is to guard the secret of this packet. I need not tell you that you are in danger. To save their own skins Pezzard and his crew would not hesitate to strip off yours. There is explosive stuff in these papers. Do you know of Count Frontenac?"

"I believe Monsieur Mersan mentioned his name," replied Denis.

"He is a great and wise man," explained the law-yer. "He was sent out in 1673 as Governor. We never had a better one. He ruled with a firm hand for the good of the colony. There are selfish, greedy people here who would not hesitate to ruin the country if thereby they could add to their purse or power. Other governors have ignored such evils, but Frontenac would have none of them. So he made many enemies, some of them traitors, others honest, perhaps, but jealous. They united against him, and three years ago, in 1683, were at last able, through their friends at court, to persuade the King to recall the Count to France. That was the worst thing that ever happened to Canada.

"You will learn soon enough," continued the law-yer, "why we must have a strong ruler here. We are but a small colony, strung out along the St. Lawrence and surrounded on all sides by perils. On the south we are beset by the fierce Iroquois. They are constantly raiding our farms, burning and murdering. To the west the Hurons and our allies of the farther lakes are fickle, as hard to hold as water. At the first sign of weakness they would league against us. Behind the Iroquois are the English of New York and New Eng-land. Just now we are officially at peace with them, but they are ever urging the savages against us. New France is like a bear surrounded by wolves: as long as the bear keeps his back to the cliff he is safe; if he turns tail the wolves will be on him in a flash."

Denis listened wide-eyed. This was not like the pic-ture of Canada Captain Marsollet had painted.

"You see, then, that we Canadians must stand to-gether. Our fate hangs in the balance. Here—" he clapped his hand on the packet—"is proof that Pezzard, who is not the most powerful of Frontenac's enemies, but dangerous enough, has been in treasonable correspondence with the English. Also there are lists gathered by Mersan of men Frontenac can trust and of those who secretly hated him and plotted against him. What they did once they will do again. . . . You have served the King well today.

"Mersan and I, among others, have been working to have Count Frontenac returned as Governor," the lawyer went on. "His friends in France are also active in his behalf." He shook his head and sighed. "But I do not know. The odds are great."

"Couldn't you send the papers to the new Governor?" ventured Denis. "Maybe he would punish Pezzard."

Again the lawyer shook his head. "Governor Denonville is well meaning but weak. The Intendant, who administers the civil laws and regulates trade, listens to Pezzard and his kind, and Denonville listens to the Intendant, whose office, indeed, gives him almost as much power as the Governor. Nor can I send this to France, for I doubt if it would ever reach the King. It is better to hide it here until Frontenac returns, if he does. I must work for that in other ways."

He rose and went to the large stone fireplace at one end of the room. "I am going to trust you with the secret," he said. "The rest of us may be marked men now, but you would hardly be suspected. If the worst happens you should know where this is. Look. Here, inside the hood, is a handle which opens the draft for the fire. If, instead of pulling it up or down for the draft, one pushes it to the right, thus, the sooty stone here at the back of the chimney may be moved, for the handle has withdrawn a bolt that anchors it. So we pull it out, and we find behind it a little iron door with a knob that turns to the right fourteen times, fourteen for our good King Louis. Try it."

Denis obeyed. After the last turn the door swung out, revealing a small compartment. LeRoux put the packet and Mersan's ring in a black box in the hiding place, replaced the door and the stone and jerked the handle to the left.

"Remember the directions," he cautioned. "It is unlikely that you need concern yourself with this, but Fate can play queer pranks." He wiped his hands delicately on a large linen handkerchief. "You had best go now. I do not like it that you are staying with Pezzard, but it would not be safe to leave him immediately. Explain your absence by saying you wished to see something of the city. At the end of a week come to me and I will try to find something better for you. Remember," he added, taking Denis's hand in his own, "you must keep your wits about you."

Regretfully Denis bade him good-by and turned his lagging steps toward the lower town. He was terribly afraid to return, but he did not know what else to do.

He passed the gardens and emerged on the open square called the Place d'Armes. Here the low stone houses were crowded tightly as if striving with one another for their narrow frontages on this, the principal center of life in the upper town. To the right was a church with a tall spire. Across the Place at the very edge of the cliff and overlooking the houses of the lower town, stood a low, steep-roofed, somewhat dilapidated stone building. Before its entrance two soldiers paced slowly back and forth. This was the Fort, or Chateau, St. Louis, residence of the Governor of New France.

In spite of his worries and the secret that lay heavily on his mind, Denis found much to look at on his way down the winding Rue de la Montaigne. One side of the street was lined with small shops. Through the open doors he could see holy images and gaudy blankets, glass beads for trade with Indians, bolts of cloth, knives, and kettles and sabers. Ascending or descending the narrow street were soldiers in white uniforms, priests in broad-brimmed hats and black gowns, Indians from the southern missions. Stolid peasants made way for two young seigneurs in plumed hats and velvet suits who strode past Denis arrogantly, their swords slapping their high boots at every step.

At the foot of the descent he came to the Rue Notre Dame and stopped cautiously to inspect Pezzard's house from a safe distance. It was well he did so, for at that moment the door opened and Loutray came out. Having no mind for explanations just then, Denis darted around a corner and ran squarely into a hard-framed stranger.

"Mordi! But watch where you go, young whelp," growled a fierce bass voice. "Dashing about blindly as a mole! In the Iroquois country you would have your gizzard slit before you knew it."

"Your pardon, sir," gulped Denis.

The man was clad in tunic and trousers of soft tanned buckskin. About his middle was twisted a huge sash of brilliant orange from which protruded the haft of a long and efficient-looking knife. He was of medium height and had a curly red beard. His fur cap, set jauntily on one side of his head, revealed a mop of hair of the same resplendent color. As he saw the astonishment on Denis's face his brown eyes began to twinkle.

"Open mouths catch flies," he observed.

"Are you a voyageur, a coureur from the great woods, sir?" asked Denis, the twinkle giving him courage.

The bearded face cracked into a smile, then frowned portentously. "Where do you come from that you do not recognize François de Chastaignac, known through the length and breadth of Canada as Miscoue Scoute, the Red Fire?"

"From France, sir, only this morning. I want to be a coureur, too."

A great laugh boomed from the red beard. "What would you do if the Iroquois were about to put you in the kettle, little man? Would you knock their thick heads together as Chastaignac did with the Illinois chieftains? Could you take prisoner a whole tribe of Miamis? Could you make such magic that the Assiniboines would fall on their faces?"

"No, sir," said Denis, awed.

"I did such things and many more," said the other calmly. "I am, in brief, the greatest man in New France, with one possible exception. So now, maybe you will know me next time, eh?"

"And who is the possible exception, Miscoue?" drawled an amused voice.

Denis turned to see a tall, brown-bearded man, dressed much like the other save that he wore a black leather belt instead of a sash. His steady blue eyes shone against his bronzed face as he smiled.

"Who else but you, Nicolas Perrot," grinned Chastaignac. "Our young friend here is as ignorant as a Kickapoo."

"I am a stranger, sir," Denis explained defensively.

The tall man studied him briefly. "Miscoue is a Gascon," he said. "That breed runs to brag and bluster and tall stories. The devil of it is, most of his tales are true."

Redbeard laughed aloud. Denis smiled a trifle uncertainly. Chastaignac clapped him on the back. "You're all right, young one." He took his pipe and a leather pouch from his pocket, filled the pipe with a dark tobacco and lighted it.

The man named Perrot said something in his deep pleasant voice about loading the canoes, and added that he was awaiting delivery of the last of the goods. "We should be able to start by ten o'clock tonight," he added.

"To the forests?" asked Denis eagerly.

"Yes," said Perrot.

"Past the great lake of the Hurons, many leagues to the west," supplied Chastaignac. "Come, you may watch, my would-be coureur. Only don't get in the way of the work."

Joyfully Denis followed the pair to the waterfront where he had seen the canoes that morning. Some twenty-five or thirty brown lithe men were busily loading the fragile boats, moving about noiselessly in their moccasins. Some were carelessly dressed, as dour and savage-seeming as Indians. Others were gay and light-hearted and neat as His Majesty's soldiers. But all alike had a certain loose-jointed, swaggering, hawk-like look that the wilderness stamps upon the faces of her children.

Denis, who had been left by his companions in the midst of a group of townspeople, decided that the canoes were not so frail as they looked, for they were being packed full of heavy bundles and bales. As he watched, one of the boats was launched. Three men stepped into it and, digging their wooden paddles in the water, set off upstream. The others paused in their work to shout rough jests.

"We'll help you over La Chine rapids if we haven't passed you long before," cried one. For reply the man in the bow gave a derisive wave of his paddle.

Bright-eyed, Denis watched until the canoe rounded Cape Diamond. Even after it had disappeared he accompanied it in imagination through perils of river and forest and savage ambush. Another set off and then another, while he fairly danced with envy and excitement. How boldly these men jested as they turned their backs on civilization! How wonderful if he, too, were going!

But at last the shadow of the great cliff lengthening across the blue St. Lawrence warned him that the afternoon was nearly gone. Reluctantly he waved good-by to his two friends and turned toward the house of Maître Pezzard.

CHAPTER III

TERROR IN THE NIGHT

DENIS slipped quietly into the hall. Joseph was busy with a customer. The door to Pezzard's office was shut, but behind it Denis heard voices. Softly he climbed the stairs.

At the top he peered toward the trapdoor. It was closed. He could not remember if he had shut it. The question suddenly assumed a great importance. He tiptoed to the stairhead and listened, then darted into his room, seized the stool and, mounting it, pushed up the door.

There had been little enough light in the attic even at midday. Now that the sun was hidden by the Rock the place was so dark he had to feel his way inch by inch.

"M'sieur Mersan," he whispered.

There was no answer. The attic was empty.

In panic he groped his way to the trapdoor and swung down. As his foot touched the stool his arms were seized from behind. "So, the young cockerel is a spy," growled the harsh voice of Loutray.

Terror lent Denis strength. He fought desperately, but he could do nothing against the man's vicious grip. Kicking and squirming, he was dragged to the stairhead.

"Maître Pezzard!" shouted Loutray. "Here is a

matter for you. . . . Be still you young devil. . . . Maître Pezzard!"

Light flashed into the hall as a door was opened. Pezzard came out of his office, holding a candle above his head. As he turned and peered up the stairs, his face, by a trick of the light, resembled that of the murderous Punchinello in the puppet shows.

"What do you want?" he demanded.

"I've caught this young spy coming out of the attic."

For the space of two seconds there was dead silence, then Pezzard was bounding up the stairs.

"If he'd got away . . ."

"Quiet, you fool," rapped Pezzard. He held the candle close to Denis's face. There was a flicker of something like fear in his eyes, but his voice was smooth. "It was only innocent curiosity, eh, Denis, lad? You wanted to see what it was like up there? You should have asked permission."

"Curiosity!" snorted Loutray. "I heard him call a name."

Pezzard drew his breath with a hiss. "What name?" he asked softly, while the candle jerked in his hand.

"The name of Mersan," said Loutray.

In the quiet that followed Denis could hear the throbbing of his own heart. Suddenly the merchant seized him by the jacket. "What do you know of Mersan?" he shrilled.

In spite of his fright a great anger rose in Denis and he gave his master stare for stare.

"Talk to me," threatened Pezzard, shaking him violently.

Two raps on the front door echoed through the house. The interruption was enough in the merchant's present state of nerves to make him release his hold and turn his head. Loutray clapped a hand over Denis's mouth and dragged him backward away from the stairhead. Denis heard the sound of Joseph's footsteps, a creak as the door opened, a buzz of talk, then Joseph's bleating call of "Maître Pezzard! Oh, Maître Pezzard!"

"Ah, messieurs, good evening," called the merchant. "I will be down in an instant. Be so good as to enter my office."

He turned as though to go into one of the adjacent rooms, but waited until the door had closed behind the visitors and then darted to Loutray's side. "Hold him," he ordered. "Do something with him until I can get rid of these strangers. He'll tell what he knows, or he'll wish he'd never been born."

"But, Maître, it is your custom never to see strangers alone."

"A thousand devils! You're right. Into his room with him, then, and come along."

"That is best," growled Loutray. "He'll be safe until we can get back. I've got the key."

"He might raise an outcry."

Loutray laughed softly. "Let him yell his head off; the walls are thick and no one who matters would hear him from the alley. Black Fox will be back soon. Then we'll find out."

"All right. Hurry."

Denis was thrown into his room so violently that he crashed against the wall and fell to the floor half stunned. He heard the key turn in the lock and saw the crack under the door grow dark. He got to his feet and stumbled to the bed, while the walls swirled about him. But the thought of torture cleared his head as nothing else could have. He had to escape! At once!

The door was securely locked, as he knew it would be. It was too thick and well built to be broken down. Frantically he examined the window. The bar was firmly set into the masonry and the space between bar and frame was too small for a man to squeeze through. But a boy—

It was a close business even to get his head through. The dim light from the kitchen window showed a courtyard bounded by a low fence. There was a gate in the fence leading to a dark alley between the backs of neighboring houses. He would have to risk passing the lighted window. He could only hope the alley was not a blind one.

There were two worn blankets on the bed. Fumbling in his haste, he tied them together and knotted one end around the bar. Now came the real test! With his bundle of clothes in one hand he swung his legs over the sill, turned sidewise and began to squirm his way out, feet foremost. It was hard work. He had a moment of rib-cracking panic when he thought he was hopelessly stuck. Then, somehow, he wriggled through. He was out and sliding down the blanket past the lighted window. He darted off as his feet touched the ground. The gate was unlocked. The alley turned at right angles and led into a street. He stopped in a shadow to consider what he should do next.

He remembered Captain Marsollet's tales of men who took to the deep woods and stayed hidden for years, but he did not have the equipment or knowledge for that. It would be much wiser to swim to *Le Glorieux* and ask the Captain to take him back to France. At as quick a pace as he dared he headed through the dusk toward the river.

But the more he turned the plan over in his mind

the less he liked it. It meant going back to Giles with no money in his pocket. It had an element of danger, too, for Captain Marsollet was involved with Pezzard in trading ventures and he might feel it his duty to return him to the merchant. The ship would be the first place Pezzard would look. And, somehow, he did not like leaving the country because of the papers he had taken to LeRoux. Sometime the lawyer might need him. No, he could not leave New France. But flee Quebec he must.

Lights moved on the beach ahead of him. As he drew nearer he saw they were pine torches. He heard the buzz of coureur talk, oaths, jests, orders. Loaded canoes backed into deeper water, gleamed whitely as they turned broadside and disappeared into the moonless night. He hurried toward a bearded man who loomed gigantic in the wavering torchlight. Behind him he thought he heard a shout.

"May I buy a passage with you, sir?"

"No," the man replied brusquely, after a glance. "No room."

"As far as Montreal. See, here is a gold louis."

"That would take you only to Three Rivers."

"I might find more. . . ." clinking the gold in his belt.

"In that case—" said the man doubtfully. Denis wished he could see his face, his eyes. "Well, get in there. Here, Thomé, show this one where to sit. He goes with us—to Three Rivers."

In a moment Denis was wedged between two knobby bales. There was a soft slither as the canoe was pushed off into the water. Someone climbed in behind him, another man in front. Slowly the shore drew away. The lights disappeared. He started to turn his head for a last look at the town, but the man behind ordered him not to move. He hugged his knees tighter and stared ahead to where a pale star hung over the blackness of the river.

He must have slept, for the next thing he knew was a sudden jar and a voice growling for him to get out of the boat. He started to get up, but the voice informed him with a torrent of curses that that was no way to leave a canoe. He bit his lip and watched while the black-bearded man cautiously rose, poising himself in the exact center of the boat, and put one moccasined foot overside into the shallow water. Gingerly Denis followed suit. A blackness deeper than that of the sky lay ahead. Somewhere in it, seemingly a long way off, a tiny light glimmered. Then in a flash his surroundings settled into normal order, and he realized that the light was the beginnings of a fire kindled by a shadowy figure only a few paces away. Solid land was beneath him.

"Is this Three Rivers?" he asked.

A burst of rough laughter answered him. "We'll be lucky if we see Three Rivers in four days, with this current strong against us. We sleep here tonight. Find yourself a place."

Hesitantly Denis drew nearer the fire. By its uncertain light he could distinguish bulky figures, black beards, flashing eyes, but he could not decide which was the man to whom he had paid the louis. Another canoe was beached.

"That will be Michel," someone grunted. "All the canoes will reach here tonight."

Denis gave up trying to learn more about his companions. He was too sleepy and tired to be curious.

He found a comparatively flat piece of ground a little way from the fire and was asleep in two minutes.

He awakened stiff and cold and very hungry. It was gray dawn. The branches above his head stood out sharply black. He sat up quickly, forgetting for an instant where he was. A bank of mist blotted out river and shore. The fire had died to a tiny heap of white ashes. He shivered in the dank air and drew his woolen jacket closer about him, discovering as he did so that his belt was unbuckled. That was odd. In quick alarm his fingers felt the small pockets inside the belt where he kept his louis. The three gold pieces were gone.

He jumped to his feet with a cry. Only then did he realize that he was alone. That the beach was empty. They couldn't take his money and leave him. . . . But they had. **825813**

He began to run up the shore, peering wildly into the fog, hoping the coureurs had overlooked him, that they were playing a joke on him. He called out hoarsely, stumbled over a log, got up with a sob and rushed on. At last he stopped and called again with all his strength.

"Who's there?" shouted a voice through the mist.

"Wait," cried Denis. "Oh, wait, please." He started running toward the sound. A gust of wind parted the fog and he found himself on the shore of a little bay. Half a dozen men squatted around a fire near three laden canoes. Coming toward him was a solitary figure.

"Give me back my money," he entreated.

"What babble is this?" demanded the figure.

Dazedly Denis recognized the man as his tall brown-bearded acquaintance of Quebec, Nicolas Perrot.

"Hello!" cried Perrot, equally surprised. "It's our young friend who wanted to be a coureur. What are you doing here?" His face grew stern. "A runaway, eh?"

"May I go with you, sir?" begged Denis breathlessly. "I'll work my way. I'll work hard. I must get away from Quebec. They stole my money."

Perrot reached him in a stride. "Steady now." A strong hand grasped his arm. "Why must you leave Quebec, and who stole your money?"

"I had to get away, sir. I was going to work for Maître Pezzard. He wouldn't give me wages. Then something else happened, something I can't tell you except that it was about Maître Pezzard and that man called Loutray. They would have killed me. I *had* to come. I left last night. A man said he would take me to Three Rivers. They ran away with the rest of my money."

Perrot watched him gravely. His blue eyes, so quick to light with laughter, were impersonal as he weighed the story. "Describe the men who took your money."

Denis could remember little but the size of the leader and the number of men in the party.

"That would be Jacques Dubec," muttered Perrot. "He drives his canoes hard, but we will try to catch him."

"Then I am to go with you?"

"At least until we can get your money back. To Three Rivers, perhaps. I know something of your Maître Pezzard. Truly you were in bad company." He called to the others. "Jean, Yves, some bacon on

the fire for the new voyageur. Miscoue, it is the lad
who had never heard of you."

Out of the huddle about the fire rose a flaming red
head. Chastaignac stared at Denis. "Ventre St. Gris!"
he rumbled. "Has he sprouted wings?"

"From his story I think it likely he would have if
he had stayed longer in Quebec," said Perrot, laughing
at Chastaignac's astonishment. "Come, infant, get
some breakfast into you."

Chapter IV

SEIGNEUR OF THE WILDERNESS

To Denis the first stage of the river journey was a blur of sliding blue waters, green wooded shores and flickering fires in the night. These were scarcely more than pictures seen dully through a haze of weariness. The only real thing was the agony of forcing the paddle forever against the stubborn water—that and the unobtrusive kindness of Sieur Perrot.

Anxious to be of help, he had begged one of the extra paddles. Perrot had shown him how to grasp it just above the blade with one hand and cover the flat top with the other, how to draw it back with steady pull of arm and shoulder and back and sweep it forward quickly through the air. All this had to be done while kneeling, balanced precariously so as not to tip the boat. It called for muscles that Denis had never used in fencing or farm work, muscles that soon began to shriek their protest.

It might not have gone so hard with him if he had been able to take his time in a canoe by himself. As it was, he felt that he had to keep to the swift rhythm set by the tireless voyageurs. Pride made him go on, but Perrot knew when he had reached the limit of his strength. He would suggest a rest, and Denis would slump forward gratefully.

That night they camped within sight of a hamlet on the north shore of the river. Denis was too tired to be hungry. He fell asleep before the fire in the midst of a long story about the Huron chieftain Songuitehe whose shrewish wife was the sister of a famous wizard and so was able to frighten Songuitehe half out of his wits with charms and bad dreams. It must have been very amusing, for the others laughed frequently, but Denis heard little of it.

By the middle of the next afternoon he was able to take an interest in his surroundings. That night he had a wolfish appetite. After filling himself with dried deer meat and corn cakes he was preparing to roll up in the blanket he had been given when he heard his name spoken. Perrot stood over him.

"If you can stay awake a little while I would like you to walk with me on the beach," requested the leader.

A dash of cold river water on his face wakened Denis thoroughly. He was uneasily aware that he was expected to tell why he had run away from Quebec. Certainly some explanation was due his benefactor, but such talk could be dangerous. What more could he say without saying too much?

For a time Perrot spoke easily in his pleasant deep voice of incidents of the day's journey, of the need for rain to lessen the danger of forest fires. At length he stopped and, leaning against a tree, regarded Denis quietly.

"You are wondering how much to tell me, and whether I may be trusted," he observed. "You don't have to tell me anything, but in fairness to yourself you should realize that a boy who runs away from his master in the night is not above suspicion of dishon-

esty. If your master were to send after you I would
have to give you up to him."

"I didn't steal anything, sir, if that's what you
mean," said Denis.

"I don't believe you did, or I wouldn't have taken
you with me," said Perrot. He waited.

"It was an accident, sir," blurted Denis. "I found
out something—something Pezzard didn't want me to
know. He and Loutray are dangerous. They were going to kill me. . . . I can't help it if you don't believe it."

"I never said I did not believe it," returned the
other. "I know something of that pair. In my business
I have to discover what goes on behind the scenes in
Quebec as well as in the councils of the Ottawas. I
know, for example, that Pezzard and the Intendant
are thick as thieves. Which," he added dryly, "is a
good word for them. And that Pezzard hates Count
Frontenac. Ah, you start at that name, eh? Now,
maybe, we are on the trail of something. You are over-
young to be mixed in politics."

Denis was thinking fast.

"Again I say, do as you like," continued Perrot.
"But if your leaving Pezzard has anything to do with
his enmity for Frontenac, rest assured that I will not
betray you. I have long been eager to see the Count
return to New France. I am very proud to remember
that he has called me friend."

The words lifted a weight from Denis's mind. He
was calmly certain, of a sudden, that he could depend
upon anything this man promised. "I will tell you, sir,"
he said and launched again into the story of his adventures. Perrot listened silently, a comforting presence in the darkness.

When Denis described the interview with LeRoux and told of what the lawyer had said about Pezzard being in communication with the English, Perrot showed his surprise by a grunt.

"Then he took the papers and put them—"

"Nay," interrupted the woodsman. "Where they are hidden is a matter between you and the lawyer. Leave out that part."

When Denis had finished Perrot said it was a strange tale. "You can't go back to Quebec, that's certain," he added thoughtfully.

They walked back without further speech until, a few paces from the fire, Perrot halted. "Would you like to go to the west with me, lad?" he asked in an undertone. "I can promise you little but hardship, but I would be glad to have you."

Denis barely stifled a cry of joy. "Do you really mean it?" he begged. "I haven't any money."

"Who is asking for money?" demanded the other gruffly. "You can keep accounts. You will be useful, never fear. We'll consider it settled. Get your sleep now."

But tired as he was, Denis was too excited to sleep at once. For a long time he lay looking at the embers of the fire, picturing scenes in which he and Perrot and Chastaignac captured whole tribes of Miamis and made such magic that Assiniboines, whatever they were, fell on their faces in awe.

Late the next afternoon, in the midst of a cold rain, they arrived at Three Rivers. The little town huddled along the bank of the St. Lawrence, its small houses clustering about the church as though for protection from the encompassing forest. They ate their supper in a smoky log cabin not far from shore. And Denis slept under a roof for the first time since leaving the ship.

Toward the middle of the following morning, when the mist lifted, he saw they were following a shore grown marshy and that away to the left was a wide expanse of tumbling waters, gray beneath the scudding clouds.

"Are we at the western lakes already?" he asked.

"Not yet," replied Perrot. "This is only Lake St. Peter, a part of the St. Lawrence itself. We must go the length of it, all of six leagues. And let us hope," he muttered to himself, "that when we get there we don't meet a war party of Iroquois in search of our scalps."

"Scalps?"

Perrot explained about scalping.

"Why do the Iroquois hate us so?"

"Because the great Champlain, founder of the colony, aided the Montaignais Indians around Quebec against the Iroquois," replied the leader. "The Sieur Champlain thought it best to make an alliance with the neighboring Indians to assure peace for the settlers. So he marched against their enemies. Down by Lake Champlain he defeated the Iroquois, who had no firearms then. They swore eternal hatred, for they are a brave proud lot. Afterwards the Dutch came to the Hudson River and traded them guns, and for fifty years they have been a menace to New France. I often think if Champlain had made peace with them how much better it would be for us. When they wish to be brothers they can be loyal and true. As it is, no St. Lawrence seigneurie is safe from them."

"Seigneuries? Here?"

"They are called that, though they are not exactly

like the estates of the nobles back in France. They are
grants to gentlemen, who lease much of their land to
settlers."

"Where, sir," asked Denis timidly, "is your seigneurie?"

Perrot laughed. "The wilderness," he answered,
"though the Indians might dispute me. A seigneurie
larger than all of France."

But in spite of Perrot's misgivings they passed the
end of the lake without signs of enemies. Three days
later they sighted the hump of Mont Royal and soon
afterwards saw the stone buildings of the Sulpitian
priests, founders of Montreal. Thankfully they moored
their canoes that evening at wharfs along St. Paul
Street near the square stone fort that protected the
town.

Montreal was much larger than Three Rivers. After
so many days of wild forest in which the presence of a
lonely stockade was an event, the city seemed a great
and bustling place. The tidy row of houses paralleling
the river and the loopholed stone windmill which stood
on a little hill nearby looked permanent and homelike.

They camped overnight, sleeping in the open near
the canoes. In the morning Perrot had to attend to
last-minute preparations. He told Denis to meet him
at noon at the shop of the merchant Hertel.

In the dark shop, filled with fascinatingly strange
smells, Perrot bought him a complete outfit. There
was a fur cap, round and brown, a long buckskin shirt
to go over his woolen jacket, buckskin trousers, heavy
woolen socks and high moccasins so soft it was a pleasure to run his fingers over them. He did not understand Hertel's laughing remark that they would be
easy to eat until it was explained that sometimes

coureurs, lost in the woods and without food, had eaten their moccasins to keep alive. Perrot promised Denis that the cost of his clothes would be deducted from the price he should receive for his own furs. That sounded as though he was already fully accepted into the brotherhood. When they left the store he tried to swing his shoulders just as Perrot did so no one would suspect he was but newly come to Canada.

As they turned toward the canoes a naked Indian slid from around the corner of the shop and disappeared behind a neighboring house. Something in the stealthy movement recalled Black Fox. Denis caught Perrot's arm.

"Do you suppose Pezzard could have found where I went and sent word ahead of us?"

A troubled look came into the other's blue eyes. "No, I do not think so. We have come quickly. Now no canoe will catch up with us for many months. Our accounting with those two must wait for a long time, I think. Come along, the others will be ready."

But they were not to leave so quickly. A sudden gust of wind had blown one of the canoes against a sharp rock and torn a wide gap in the frail bark. When Perrot and Denis reached the shore they found Chastaignac bent over a newly kindled fire, stirring something in an iron pot. Denis peered into the pot and saw a sticky black mass from which arose a fragrant aroma of spruce woods. Chastaignac, ever willing to share his knowledge as long as the pupil showed the proper amount of awe, explained that the concoction was a mixture of wood gums and that when it came to the right temperature it made a fine glue to hold a bark patch.

"Others make gums of sorts, but mine is superior," he said proudly. "I make it better even than the Indians. Though when you think about it, that isn't so surprising."

While the mess came to a boil, Chastaignac, between stirrings, cut a piece of bark from a roll carried for such emergencies and, fitting it over the tear, trimmed it to the proper size. The sticky stuff was smeared around the rent, the patch was applied and pressed tightly to the canoe. "Now we must wait for it to harden," he explained.

The hardening took some time. Perrot glanced at the sun and then at the canoe, lying on its side on the beach. "I had hoped to reach the La Chine by dusk," he announced gently.

Denis remembered hearing the word. It meant river rapids around which unloaded canoes must often be carried, though sometimes they were poled or dragged against the current.

"Perrot, mon brave, if you wish your canoe you must be patient," Chastaignac replied decisively. "Even I can't perform miracles."

"What? Do you mean to say you're only human, after all?" jeered one of his companions.

Perrot turned away with a smile that quickly faded as he stared across the water. "That canoe is in a hurry," he remarked. "Something must have happened across the river."

To Denis it seemed an unusually peaceful scene. The river stretched, broad and placid, to the green of the opposite shore. Over the trees on the little island of Ste. Hélène rose a tiny thread of gray smoke from the distant seigneurie of Longueuil. The canoe Perrot spoke of was rounding the southern end of the island. Behind him the sounds of the town, the barking of dogs, the cries of children at play, the mellow tones

of the bell in the Sulpitian chapel, seemed muted, like
the drowsy hum of insects on a summer day. The sky
was bright blue; the sunlight slanting and golden.

"It looks like Gauvin," someone said. "Something's
wrong at Longueuil."

The lone paddler beached his canoe below the fort
and dashed for the open gateway, oblivious of hails
from the voyageurs.

"Iroquois," said Chastaignac softly.

Denis concealed his excitement, for he saw that the
others, though curious to hear the news, were taking
the matter calmly.

A file of Indians carrying canoes bottom side up on
their heads came out of the fort and trotted to the
river bank. They tossed the canoes into the water,
climbed in and began paddling for the southern shore.
Three white men followed in another boat. After them
came Hertel.

"Mohawks," he announced. "Probably the same war
party that burned Foubert's place last week. They fell
on Crèvier's farm this morning. Caught him and his
eldest son in the fields, but the younger son got back
to the blockhouse in time to close the gates. As soon
as it was safe the boy slipped out and ran to Longueuil."

"Crèvier and the other boy, were they taken?" asked
Perrot.

"No," answered the merchant grimly, "only their
scalps."

The others heard the news in silence. Denis summoned courage to speak. "Why don't we go after
them?" he asked.

"Those Indians you saw, Hurons and Mohawks
who have accepted the teachings of our Church and

have settled in nearby villages, will track the raiders better than any white man," replied Perrot. "Some soldiers from the fort will follow, but they can't do much. The Iroquois slip in like ghosts, strike any farmhouse that seems ill defended and are gone before help can arrive. The habitants cannot band together to follow, for they must think of their own families. We are not callous, Denis; if it would help any we would go, but the people hereabouts are best served by these Indians, who hate their savage brethren. Each to his own task. If we took the trail we would delay to no purpose, and we have work to do in the west."

He lifted his expressive hands as though to free his shoulders of a burden. "If only we could throw off the Iroquois threat!" he growled. "Come, François, let us try the boat."

A small crowd of townspeople collected as the canoes were launched. A gray-robed priest scattered drops of holy water on the craft and blessed them. The crew of one broke into a snatch of song. Denis thought of the man and his son lying in the field near the dark forest and wondered if all deaths were forgotten so soon in this wild country. Kneeling in front of Perrot, he dug his paddle thoughtfully into the water as they headed once more up the mighty river.

CHAPTER V

A DAGGER FOR A LIFE

There followed weeks of grueling, backbreaking labor, bending over the paddles or struggling waist-deep through icy rapids while the canoes at the end of the towropes bobbed and curvetted like skittish horses. For several days after passing the Saut St. Louis above Montreal the travelers moved cautiously, lest they attract the attention of raiding Iroquois. But as soon as they were well up the Ottawa River into Huron territory vigilance was relaxed, and once more they gathered nightly about big campfires to sing songs and tell jokes. They were a friendly crew, though a bit quicktempered and rough of speech. Some had come out from France only a year or so before, others were veterans, but Perrot was the only one who could boast of twenty years passed in the wilderness.

In time the paddling came to be fun and so did the towing. Portaging was a more wearing business, for then it was necessary to unload the boats and carry both them and their freight through the woods until the unnavigable stretch was passed. But Denis did not greatly mind any of the hardships except the insects. There were mosquitoes and midges and monstrous flies that seemed determined to eat him alive. Only in the smoke of campfires or smudges was there any relief. Perrot said the first frost would settle things, but Chas-

48

taignac told cheerfully of the ferocity of black flies in June. He gravely advised the growing of a beard, whereat Denis blushed and the others laughed.

It was on the Ottawa above the Lake of the Two Mountains, shortly before they reached the portages of the Chaudière, that something happened to make Denis realize on what a slender thread their lives might depend. They were wading up the rapids dragging the canoes. The third canoe, jerked by a cross current, caught on a rock and snapped the rawhide line. The men who were towing it pitched forward and were swept from their feet by the rush of water. The free canoe poised momentarily, turned broadside and was about to whirl off to destruction when Perrot threw himself into the sweep of the current and, catching the end of the parted line, breasted the foaming rapids until the others could come to his aid.

Nothing was said until the boats were in calm waters again, then Michel LeSueur, wiping the sweat from his forehead, muttered, "Most of the powder was in that canoe, and a lot of the trade goods. How long would we last unarmed and empty-handed among some of our dear red friends?"

Denis did not wonder that every suggestion Perrot made was at once obeyed.

The leaves had begun to turn soon after they had left Montreal. By the time they reached the black rock pinnacles of the Portage of the Cats, the forest was a riot of colors. Against the somber darkness of pine and spruce and hemlock flared the scarlet of maple and the clear yellows of birch and beech. A bluish haze, impalpable as a dream, softened the vivid hues of the trees and, growing deeper in the distance, shrouded the low hills in a veil of mystery.

As they pushed farther and farther into the land of Huronia the leaves turned brighter and brighter and began to flutter down to lie like bits of stained glass on the smooth black water. Overhead arrows of wild geese flew south, honking mournfully. All of one day Denis gazed in amazement as millions of wild pigeons passed, darkening the sky on their way toward warmer lands. By the time the voyageurs had made the short carry over the divide separating the Ottawa waterway from Lake Nipissing the trees, save for some oaks and birches, were bare, and the nights were growing cold. They must hurry now, lest winter catch them short of their destination, Perrot's fort on the great river the Indians called the Mississippi.

Camp was made late one afternoon on the winding, island-choked French River. Denis stood on the shore watching the sunset glow like molten gold between the dark spruces. The still air was sharp with the promise of frost. He stretched his arms above his head and breathed it deeply, savoring the tang of it.

He was about to return to his job of gathering spruce boughs for a bed when he heard a faint sound of chanting. He listened curiously as it grew louder. It was a young voice. He could not understand the words, but he could tell from the sound that the song was proud and defiant. Chastaignac, who had been collecting driftwood for the fire, joined him as six canoes swept around the bend of the river. They were manned by Huron braves, fierce in black and red war paint. In the prow of the leading canoe, his arms bound to his sides, knelt a slender young Indian. It was he who was chanting.

Chastaignac raised his right arm. The Huron warriors howled greetings and made fierce faces in sign of victory.

"A lot of noise about very little," said Chastaignac sardonically. "They have one prisoner and there is only one scalp on that paddle propped behind him. Ah, well, Indians are ever braggarts."

"Where are they going?" Denis asked.

"To their village, which we passed half a league back, you remember."

As he ate his supper of venison Denis wondered what was to become of the boy in the canoe. At the end of the meal Perrot rose, saying that he and Chastaignac would pay a call on the Huron village, lest the warriors consider themselves insulted. No one else was to leave camp.

Denis spoke quickly. "Please, may I come, too?" he begged.

Perrot hesitated, then nodded curtly. "Stick close to Miscoue and do as he does," he ordered.

They had paddled for a time in silence when Denis ventured to ask a question that had puzzled him ever since the Indians had passed. "Why was the Indian boy singing?"

"That was his death song," replied Chastaignac. "Each warrior has his own particular song, which he makes up out of his head as he chants. He tells his deeds of bravery and those of his forefathers. It's a sort of brag to put his captors to shame and to keep up his own courage. This one seemed young for the warpath."

"Are they going to kill him?" asked Denis in a small voice.

"Very likely. After they tire of crowing over their victory."

Night had fallen when they arrived. The wavering firelight revealed the outlines of a dozen bark huts and a few skin tepees. The village was obviously a temporary summer headquarters. As they drew near dogs began to bark, women looked up from their cooking, and children stopped their play. Warriors lounged in front of their lodges, apparently indifferent to the sudden commotion. The canoe was beached. Perrot exchanged guttural greetings with the tall chieftain.

The captive Indian boy was lashed to a stout post in the middle of the village. Around his feet was heaped a mound of dry spruce branches. He stared disdainfully into the night, showing no sign of fear or weariness.

A horrible fascination drew Denis nearer while Perrot and Chastaignac exchanged the customary compliments and speeches of greeting with the chief and his warriors. For a moment the captive's black eyes encountered Denis's pitying gaze, then the Indian returned to his stoical contemplation of the dark forest.

After the savages had feasted their fill on the dubious contents of their kettles and the tobacco pipe had passed twice from hand to hand, the warriors conversed with the white men for a proper interval about weather portents, hunting and other such topics of casual Indian talk. The squaws and children looked on with an air of suppressed excitement. The amenities came to a close with a period of dignified silence as all waited politely to see if anyone wished to say more. Then the chief pointed toward the prisoner and barked the single word, *"Houna."*

A little Indian boy whooped and, snatching a stick from the fire, laid the blazing end against the captive's thigh. If he had expected an outcry he was disappointed, for the prisoner bore the pain without a tremor. But Denis flinched as though he had suffered the burn. "Sieur Perrot—Miscoue," he whispered, beginning to feel sick, "don't let them do that."

Chastaignac frowned. "Hush. They will despise you for a weakling. He'll be hurt more before he's dead. One must get used to such things. We'd never have come had we thought they were going to torture him so soon. Now we're here we've got to stay."

Another child rubbed a blazing stick against the captive's chest. A woman brought hot coals and laid them among the spruce sticks. The prisoner began to chant in a clear defiant voice. A little flame darted up the outer edge of the pile of boughs.

Denis sprang up and bounded to the stake. He scattered the burning faggots with furious kicks, stamped with moccasined feet on the tongues of flame. He had no thought of the consequences. Amid sudden deathly silence he planted himself in front of the bound Indian.

The Hurons jumped to their feet. A sullen muttering, like the rising sough of wind through pine trees, swelled among them. Perrot's face was a grave mask. Chastaignac's eyes were narrowed. The two got up quietly and ranged themselves beside Denis. The chief began to speak angrily, gesticulating with both hands. White-faced, shaken, Denis clutched his dagger.

Perrot's voice rang out sternly. He spoke to the warriors, decisively but without heat. The chief replied with a long harangue. Again Perrot spoke. When he ended the Indians argued among themselves. Then the chief grunted and extended his hand toward Denis.

"He agrees to a ransom," said Perrot.

Denis hesitated, while the Hurons waited expectantly. He had nothing of value since he had lost his gold. Then he realized he was still clutching his dagger. Hastily he slid the sheath from his belt, tore off the covering rags, held the weapon aloft. The chief watched avidly as the firelight shimmered on the silver hilt. There was an appreciative murmur from the warriors.

With rigid arm Denis extended the knife. The chief took it, pulled it from its sheath and tested the edge on his palm. He was barely able to conceal his joy as he stuck it in his own belt. The prisoner was freed. Stoically he marched between the woodsmen to their canoe.

There was little talk on the return. In the silence of Perrot and Chastaignac Denis felt a strong disapproval. No doubt they would have plenty to say later. But he had no regrets.

The coureurs were asleep when they arrived, save for Michel, who stood guard beside the fire. "You're a young fool," he said when he had heard the story. "D'ye want to get us all killed?"

Under Chastaignac's direction Denis applied grease to the prisoner's burns and brought him food and water. Perrot began to question him in Huron. The answers were evidently in another dialect, for Perrot, who spoke Huron fluently, seemed not quite sure of all the words.

"He is a Mohawk, a warrior of one of the five tribes of the Iroquois league," he explained at last.

Denis suppressed an exclamation. He stared, half expecting to discover horns peeping from beneath the captive's black hair. From what he had heard of them he had imagined Iroquois warriors to be like fiends, with wolf fangs and horrible bestial faces. But this lad sitting so quietly before him in no way resembled the picture Denis had formed. There was strength in his face, and intelligence and breeding. His eyes were large and dark. He had an aquiline nose, slightly humped, and thin firm lips. Had it not been for his copper color he might have passed for a European. Slowly Denis's mind revised its conception of the Iroquois.

"His name is Skonakoa," continued Perrot, "which means, I believe, 'he of good strength.' He is seventeen. Belongs to the Turtle Clan. This was his first raid. A small band had been summering here doing all the damage they can, which, no doubt, has been plenty. He and a friend, whose scalp you saw in the canoe, left the main party to hunt. They were ambushed. He asks your name and tribe. He says he is grateful and will not forget what you have done."

He dismissed the young warrior, who raised his arms stiffly in salute and stalked away to lie down near Chastaignac. The red-haired man pointedly rolled over so as to face him.

Denis started unrolling his blanket. Over his pipe Perrot watched him thoughtfully. "You prized the knife, didn't you?" he asked.

"It was my father's." Denis spoke gruffly to hide his emotion.

"No doubt yonder young savage is puzzled by what you did," mused Perrot. "To Indians such a thing is very strange. . . . You acted rashly tonight."

Denis hung his head. "I did it before I thought," he said. "But I just couldn't stand to see—that. I guess," he added honestly, "I'd do it again."

Perrot nodded. "That is why you must listen to what I have to say. I admire your motive, but I can't say much for your judgment. Sit down."

He smoked for a while in silence. "It is a harsh life

you have adopted," he said at last. "You might as
well begin to get used to it. We coureurs have to understand and accept Indian ways. Pity is alien to them.
They can be kindly and humane to their own tribesmen—no member of a tribe ever starves so long as
any of his fellows have food—but they do such things
out of a sense of reason and proportion and justice
rather than from pity. In war they follow a harsh
logic: your enemy seeks to do you harm, so destroy
him. The matter of torturing prisoners is one of the
rules of the game. All self-respecting warriors try to
endure torture without flinching. They know their
enemies honor them for it. They prize honor—their
sort of honor—more than we do, I fear."

Michel threw another log on the fire. Perrot
watched the sparks fly up into the night. When he resumed his voice was lower.

"I have seen many things so dreadful that I shut
them out of my mind. Why? Because I can do little or
nothing about them. There have been times when I
would have given all I possessed to stop some burning or torture, but I have had to remember that these
deaths, sickening though they may be as individual incidents, are but tiny threads in an old pattern, the pattern of Indian life. We cannot change the pattern
greatly. If we try to change it, other than through the
teachings of the priests, we get nowhere, and we fail
in our duty because we risk the loss of France's hold
over these tribes.

"We have set up the arms of King Louis and taken
the lands in his name, but our claims are hollow unless
we can keep the Indians our allies. So, knowing what
I do of our plans and policies and the situation between the Indian nations, I ask myself, 'For the sake

of France and Canada is it better that this man live
or die?' "

"What difference does one prisoner make?" asked
Denis stubbornly.

"It might make a great deal," replied the other.
"Let us say the Pottawattomies and the Crees, after
years of enmity, are ready to declare peace. Then the
Pottawattomies catch a young Cree in some villainy
on their lands. According to custom they have the right
to kill him. If they do the war will continue. Other
tribes may be dragged in, the Miamis and the Mascoutens on the side of the Pottawattomies, and the
Sauks and Foxes on the side of the Crees. A dozen
tribes might become involved. Our enemies the Iroquois would ask for nothing better. Their war parties
could burn and pillage as they willed. The woods would
no longer be safe for the French. Our trading posts
would be burned and our furs destroyed. That, in
turn, would affect the lives of all in Montreal and
Quebec, for the fur trade is indispensable to Canada.
So, in such a case, the life of the Cree prisoner is valuable to us.

"On the other hand, let us say that the Hurons are
thinking of making an alliance with the Iroquois, blowing now hot now cold. Such a treaty might be fatal to
many of the western tribes and would certainly cause
us much trouble. But if the Hurons were to kill a captive Iroquois—such a one as this lad here—the treaty
would not be made and we would gain a few more
years of peace. Hence the death of the prisoner might
save the lives of many Frenchmen."

He paused and regarded Denis quizzically. "I think
you suspect that in spite of certain admirable qualities
we coureurs lack decent regard for polite ways, even

for human life. No doubt you'll hear from others that
we are violent, unprincipled, lawless. That is true of
some. But remember that without us New France
would still be one or two poor villages on the St. Lawrence. We endure cold and starvation and death at the
hands of savages to open up this wilderness to the
Black Robes, the soldiers and the traders. We take
some profit out of the business, it is true, but scarcely
enough to pay us for the risk—the merchants and the
politicians skim the cream. But each of us carries with
him the fate of Canada. To the Indians we are each
a representative of Onontio, the Great Father at Quebec, as they call our Governor, and are held account-
able accordingly. Some are not worthy of their trust,
I grant. But others, such as de la Forêt, La Durantaye,
Tonty, DuLhut have made the name coureur as honor-
able as any in the world.

"I have talked overlong," he said, putting his hand
on Denis's shoulder. "It is a subject on which I have
strong feelings. I am not sorry you acted as you did
since we came out of it whole, but think twice next time.
The Indians judge our actions by their own lights."

Four days later the river emptied into a vast gray
sea that stretched away to the west seemingly without
end. "Is this the passageway to China?" asked Denis
innocently.

His companions laughed. "Did you learn that in
school or from some follower of the Chevalier de la
Salle?" gibed Chastaignac. "In spite of the Chevalier
I do not believe there is any waterway to China. This
is the Lake of the Hurons."

On a wooded point of land the Mohawk boy, who
had scarcely spoken since his rescue, was put ashore

with flints, a bag of corn, a hatchet and a knife. Despite his youth he had been treated with courtesy by the voyageurs. Any representative of the dreaded Five Nations deserved respect. They had been rather surprised that he had not escaped during the nights, but that, too, was in keeping with the dignity of a warrior. He had told Perrot that he was sure he could find some of his people, or, failing that, reach his own distant land in safety.

Equipped with his gifts, he ceremoniously saluted Denis, then Perrot. He spoke briefly and disappeared among the bushes without a backward glance.

"What did he say?" asked Denis.

"He said," replied Perrot, "that you are his brother. He also said to tell the Hurons that he and his people are coming back and wipe up the earth with them, or words to that effect."

From the mouth of the French River they followed the north shore of the lake, past Manitoulin Island with its Ottawa refugees, and turned southward across the straits which led to yet another great lake and so came to the mission of Michilimackinac, principal French trading post of the region.

After weeks in the wilderness, the station of Michilimackinac seemed a fine and comfortable place. The Jesuit Fathers, called the Black Robes by the Indians, had built their own house, church and workshop, all surrounded by a palisade. Along the shore were storehouses and cabins of the traders. On the other side of the church stood a palisaded fort built by the Hurons, and farther away, beyond fields of corn, stood the lodges of the Huron and Ottawa villages.

Within the palisade of the Jesuits Father Engelran,

his worn black habit flapping in the wind, made the travelers welcome. He told them the news and inquired eagerly of happenings in Quebec. The good priest's dark eyes glowed in his thin weather-beaten face as he listened. In turn he informed Perrot that Sieur DuLhut had gone that summer, under orders from Governor Denonville, to build a fort at the straits of Detroit to keep the English from the western lakes. Sieur de la Durantaye, commander at Michilimackinac, had left only the day before on the rumor that there was trouble again between the Miamis and the Illinois at the lower end of Lake Michigan. . . . Winter would come early this year; already ice was forming on the ponds.

Perrot was disappointed. "I had hoped to see both DuLhut and La Durantaye before next summer. I bring him letters from the Governor. Will you see that Sieur DuLhut's is sent after him, Father, and the other held for the return of La Durantaye?" He placed two parchment-covered packets in the Jesuit's hands and lowered his voice. Denis could not help hearing the words "war" and "Senecas."

"I expected," continued the leader, "to rest here a few days, but if we are to reach our post before the lakes are frozen we must leave at once."

An hour later, blessed by Father Engelran and watched by a few jesting coureurs and a crowd of stolid Indians, the travel-worn party pushed off, heading toward the southwest.

Chapter VI

THE MAKING OF A WOODSMAN

AFTER he had grown accustomed to the harsh cold and heavy snows, the winter began to pass all too quickly for Denis at Fort St. Nicolas. That was the lower of Perrot's two trading posts. It lay on the east bank of the Mississippi River just above the mouth of the Wisconsin. Protected by a palisade of pointed logs planted upright in the ground and backed on the inner side by a bank of earth, it was a snug shelter in the icy wilderness. Within the palisade were log cabins, a large one in which the men cooked and ate, two smaller ones for storage of supplies and furs and three others where the coureurs slept.

Each day Denis learned more of the thousand and one things a proper coureur de bois should know. He learned how to shoot with musket and with bow and arrow, and how to make traps for fox, muskrat, marten and otter. Chastaignac taught him how to make snowshoes such as the Indians wore and how to travel on them over the white prairies and through the dark woods. He learned to tell the prized *castor gras* from the four lesser types of beaver skins, though he never fully understood why such a fur should be prized after some unwashed Indian had been wearing it for months.

He began to pick up something of the Algonquin language, which was partially understood by most of

61

the tribes of the Great Lakes region. He was reminded of his schooldays and his struggles over Latin verbs, for he found to his dismay that Algonquin verbs were also conjugated. The nouns, however, were not declined, and to make plurals of them one merely added *k* or *ik*. The language was not hard to pronounce, as each syllable was accented equally.

Later, when he took up Huron under Chastaignac's teaching, he had more difficulty, for all Huron words were pronounced without shutting the lips, as though, thought Denis, the Hurons were too lazy to bother. LeSueur, the third in command of the post, told him that Huron and Iroquois dialects were somewhat similar. Both nations had ridiculous difficulty with some of the French sounds. They said *ouon* for *bon, rils* for *fils,* and *caounsieur* for *monsieur.* Denis was thankful that foreign tongues came to him easily.

Perrot taught him many things, too—bits of forest lore such as how to make fire without flints, how to have a warm sleeping place by raking the coals of the campfire away and lying down on the spot where the fire had burned, how to imitate the calls of wildfowl. Most valuable of all his lessons was that a coureur must always be brave and cool-headed and resourceful.

And all this time Denis had the comforting assurance that pelts marked to his account were being stored for sale when they returned to Montreal. Perrot had advanced him credit for his equipment, but even when that account was paid there should be many louis to send to Giles. It was indeed a pleasant life.

The week after the first heavy snowfall Denis learned one of Perrot's methods of dealing with Indians. Only seven men were at the fort, the others having gone hunting or to trade at the northern post on the shores of Lake Pepin, some fifty leagues up the river. Unexpectedly a band of Crees arrived with a large number of fox and marten skins. They pitched their tents in the snow and settled down to camp, watching the Frenchmen with beady-eyed wonder.

The second morning after their arrival Chastaignac came storming into the storehouse where Perrot was counting skins. "My ax is gone!" he bellowed. "My favorite. The finest ax west of Montreal. Trade or no trade, this is too much. Those Indians . . ."

"Softly, François," interrupted Perrot, rising and dusting off his knees. "You left it outside last night, eh?" he smiled. "I'm surprised even a Cree would take it, with its nicked blade and broken handle. But we'll get it back," he added hastily, as Chastaignac opened his mouth again. "Not for the ax, but to keep them from taking the roof from over our heads. Tell everybody to come to the gate at dusk."

That evening, as the last red glow faded in the west and the snow turned from white to blue, a solemn circle, the French behind Perrot, the Crees behind their chief, Kisskusis, formed at the gate. Perrot spoke, recalling the years of friendship between the French and the Crees. He told of joint hunts, of smoking the calumet in Cree lodges. But now—he paused dramatically —the friendship had been broken. An ax had been stolen. . . . The Crees looked politely bored.

With a sweeping gesture Chastaignac handed him a cup of melted snow. Perrot offered it first to the chief, then to three warriors. All tasted it, and all agreed it was water. Perrot made a series of passes over the cup with his right hand, and Denis was amused to see that he managed to pour a little brandy into it from a tiny flask hidden in his sleeve. He called for a blazing stick and touched it to the cup. Up went his arms above his head as the brandy flared into blue and yellow flames. The Indians swayed like a field of corn beneath the wind.

"If the ax is not returned the French will come among the lakes and streams of the Crees and set them on fire as this cup of water has been set on fire," he solemnly promised. "I have spoken."

Next morning the ax, together with a hind quarter of venison, was found at the gate of the palisade.

Occasionally independent coureurs, not attached to any post, stopped to rest as they journeyed north to the Chippewas or south to the Mascoutens. At first Denis feared that each new arrival might be Loutray or an agent of the Intendant with authority to arrest him. Even Perrot's stout arm might not be able to protect him against the Intendant. But as his fears proved unfounded he grew less nervous about the visitors and soon was able to join in each lively welcome.

Best of all were the gatherings in the evenings about the roaring fireplace. While their deft fingers fashioned moccasins, snowshoes, pipes or paddles, the coureurs talked. Sometimes they spoke of France; more often they told tales about the Indians.

One evening LeSueur mentioned a bad dream he had had the night before. He had dreamed that a bear was chasing him around and around a pond. He had awakened, he said, just in time.

"If I were a Huron I'd put on a bearskin and chase you around a bit," said Chastaignac with a grin. "The Indians are great believers in dreams," he explained to Denis. "First time I ever saw this dream business working out was in a Huron village. Seven young bucks were prancing around one of their friends they'd tied to a stake. They were making a great to-do of torturing him with sticks. Had even kindled a small fire not too near his feet. I thought they'd gone crazy. But no. He had dreamed he'd been captured and tortured by enemies. Since every one of them devoutly believed the thing must come true some way or another, his friends were stealing a march on the devils by making it come to pass as painlessly as possible."

"A superstitious lot," said young Jacques Gruaud, who had never before been west of Montreal. He spoke with an air of superiority. "That story about the ghost drum that is heard near that square rock on Green Bay when danger threatens the Pottawattomies. Silly, I call it."

"I know a chief who swears he heard it in '71 before the great Iroquois raid," said one of the coureurs reprovingly.

"And anyway," added Chastaignac, "what about Hertel's black cat at Montreal? I saw you walk a good thirty paces to avoid crossing its path."

Jacques hung his head and muttered something about that being different, while the men laughed.

"But is it really true about the ghost drum?" asked Denis, his flesh creeping at the thought.

"It is an old legend," replied Perrot. "The Pottawattomies say that many years ago one of their warriors, captured by raiding Hurons, sacrificed his life for his village. He managed to escape from the Hurons, but rather than save himself he fled to this rock where the tribe kept a war drum to warn of danger. There he tapped out the message, was recaptured in consequence and died of torture. When any danger threatens the tribe his spirit returns to sound the drum and warn his people. That is their belief."

But Jacques was only temporarily silenced. He returned to the subject of the oddity of Indian behavior with the remark that he couldn't understand why Indians were so willing to give away everything they possessed and at the same time were such thieves.

"It's not strange," replied Perrot. "They haven't our sense of private property. Once when I was staying in a Huron village a warrior lost his rifle overboard in deep water while making a canoe trip. No sooner had he told of his loss than eight warriors offered him their own guns. He accepted the one he liked best as a matter of course, and everybody was satisfied. No one thought of the guns as personal belongings; they belonged to the tribe. Indians steal for the same reason," he continued. "It isn't thievery to them; it is simply taking something they need out of the common store. To us they seem foolishly hospitable because they may eat up half a winter's supply of food in a feast of welcome and give the stranger the best of everything. But the visitor is expected to do the same. If I accept gifts I see that they are returned before I leave, or else I give others of equal value. If I didn't I would be very rude."

"That's why he gets on so well with them," spoke up Chastaignac. "Hark ye, Jacques. If you want to keep your hair tight on your head you'd best learn to respect Indian customs. I recollect a fool English trader among the Shawanoes back in '81. He'd had a good thing of it with them if he'd minded his own business. But no, he must be telling them what was wrong with their way of doing things. Instructed the elders how to run the village. Wanted to put the warriors into pants. They're polite people, the Indians, but they'd gotten a bellyful of this fellow. I happened along just in time to save him. I don't know why I bothered; if ever a man deserved getting his empty skull cracked he did."

Perrot remarked that while the Indians had many admirable qualities he wished the Great Hare had made them a bit more steadfast in their undertakings. Of course Denis at once wanted to know about the Great Hare. Perrot replied that the Ottawas believed he was the creator of all things. Chastaignac suggested that he tell the Ottawa legend of how the Great Hare made the earth. So, between puffs at his pipe, Perrot told the story as he had heard it from the Indians.

A long time ago, before the Great Hare made man, there was no land anywhere. All the birds and beasts lived on a raft that floated on endless waters. The Great Hare had made the raft, but he saw, as time passed, that it was too small, for the lesser beasts were always being stepped on. He thought of a better plan, and sent the beaver, a good diver, down to see if he could find land under the waters. The beaver couldn't. Next the otter was sent, but he, too, came back without succeeding. Then the little muskrat volunteered. He was gone so long they thought him drowned, but after two days he came up, nearly dead, with a single grain of sand clutched in his paw.

The Great Hare dropped the grain of sand at one end of the raft. There it multiplied into countless grains and grew and grew until at last it became the earth. Then the Great Hare sent the fox to run about the land and see if it was large enough to hold all the animals. The fox is a selfish beast. As soon as he saw it was large enough for him he returned and reported that there was plenty of space for all. So the animals trooped off the raft, and the raft sank beneath the waters.

But it was not long before the Great Hare saw his mistake in believing the fox, for the animals, who had gotten along peaceably on the crowded raft, now began to fight among themselves, each wanting more and more land. Because of this the Hare has never trusted any of the animals since. And he is still going around the world trying to make it bigger. That is the reason for earthquakes and landslides.

"Why, that is like the story of Noah and the Flood," exclaimed Denis.

Perrot smiled. "The likeness has helped the good Fathers at Michilimackinac in their efforts to convert the Ottawas. When the Indians heard the account of the Flood they agreed that the Black Robes spoke truly, though they had gotten the story somewhat garbled, they said, since Noah, being a man, could not have been alive then."

Denis was still thinking of the Great Hare and of the ghost drum of the Pottawattomies when he dropped off to sleep that night.

As the winter wore on, Perrot's journeys to visit neighboring Indian villages became more frequent, which meant that either LeSueur or Chastaignac was left in charge of the post. LeSueur was content to remain, but Chastaignac's restlessness made the duty of command irksome, and he could scarcely wait for Perrot's return. His wanderlust might seize him at any hour. He would drop the paddle or moccasin he was making and stand up, stretching his hands above his head, while the firelight glinted on his red beard.

"Me, I am suffocating here," he would proclaim. "Nicolas, I am taking the trail. I don't know how you'll do without me, but I must go."

And go he would, as likely as not that very night. In a week or so he would return, perhaps drawing a sled loaded with skins, perhaps empty-handed, but always with some tale of adventure to which the coureurs listened with grins, believing less than half of what he said. But, as Perrot had observed back in Quebec, Chastaignac's boasts had a way of being true more often than not. It might be a month later that some coureur would appear with sheepish reports of stories that went the rounds of Indian campfires concerning a red-haired Frenchman who, it might be, had defeated a war band of Sioux singlehanded, or demonstrated to the wise medicine men that he was, beyond all doubt, a magician.

Late in January the band of Crees returned, blandly certain of welcome. One morning, after the trading was done, their chief, Kisskusis, his face blackened with charcoal, presented himself at the gate and announced a bear hunt. He had observed the ritual that insured success. He had given a feast and had fasted for four days. At last the proper dream had come to him. The spirit of his grandfather had appeared and told him that it was necessary for the man with red hair to accompany the warriors.

Chastaignac winked at Denis. He told the chief that he, too, had dreamed of the hunt, and the spirit had told him that it was well for him to go with the Crees, but that it was equally important to take along the young man with hazel eyes and no beard.

So Denis and Chastaignac journeyed with the Crees into the woods of the northwest, and Denis learned how the sleeping bears were hunted. It was the Cree custom to blacken their faces anew each morning and to go without food until the end of the day, for fasting was believed to sharpen their wits. The band would spread out in a great circle a mile across and close in toward the center, each man as he went tapping certain hollow logs or trees where bears might be holed up. Not often did they make mistakes. Denis could not help being sorry for the blundering beasts, bewildered and helpless when aroused from their winter sleep. There was a feast at the end of the hunt which, true to portents, had been very successful.

After the feast Chastaignac and Denis bade their companions good-by and set off for the fort at Lake Pepin. On their way they passed a band of Outagamis, or Foxes, on a beaver hunt. These people ordinarily had little love for the French. They suffered the strangers to watch them, however, as they chopped holes in the ice of a small pond and pounded on the humped beaver house to drive the inhabitants forth. Soon a sleek head, rather like that of a dog, appeared at one of the holes, and the Indian watcher promptly stunned the animal with a club. It was not sport, nor did the Indians so regard it. Unlike white men, they did not kill for fun. When they hunted they sought food, or skins to keep them warm or to exchange for things they needed. Chastaignac said they always left three pairs of beaver to a pond so the supply would not be exhausted.

Later Denis visited the Pottawattomies and saw a game of Indian ball played between two neighboring villages. It was called by the French lacrosse. It was played with a ball covered with rawhide and with crude racquets made of a webbing of rawhide strips

stretched over a hoop on the end of a long handle. A
pair of goal posts was set up at each end of the field.
The game began with the ball being tossed up in the
center. A player caught it on his racquet and ran toward the rivals' goal. The ball might be either carried
or tossed from one to another; and a score was made
when one side threw the ball between the other's goal
posts. All the warriors in the two villages played. The
game quickly turned into a melee of scrambling, yell-
ing savages, thwacking one another enthusiastically
with their stout racquets. When players were injured
they dropped out to recover, but the fierce game went
on without pause.

Denis played for a time and managed to score one
goal, though his triumph hardly repaid him for his
aching shins. By the end of the afternoon fully half
the warriors were on the sidelines, nursing lame legs
or broken heads. Everyone was betting freely on the
outcome. But in spite of the injuries and the high
stakes, Denis never heard an angry word. The rough
play was taken good-naturedly as part of the game.
In this, as in many other things, the Indians were good
sportsmen.

In early March three Frenchmen arrived from
Michilimackinac. When Denis learned they had made
a detour on their way to Tonty's fort, St. Louis, on
the Illinois River in order to bring Perrot the latest
dispatches from Governor Denonville, he shook in his
boots. Surely the packet of parchment they delivered
contained the fateful order for his arrest. But Perrot
soon reassured him.

"It is about the war against the Senecas," he explained. "We set out at the beginning of summer. But

first I am to go to the Miamis and other tribes and try to persuade them to join us."

"The Senecas—they are Iroquois, aren't they?" Denis asked, not really caring at the moment, so happy was he that trouble had passed him by.

"Yes," said Perrot, with a strange gleam in his blue eyes. "You'd best learn more about these enemies of ours. The Iroquois call themselves the *Hodenosaunee,* or People of the Long House. The nation is composed of five tribes, the Mohawks—the young warrior you saved from the Hurons was one of those, you remember—the Oneidas, the Onondagas, the Cayugas, and the Senecas. They live westward from Albany to the great falls of Niagara in the English land of New York. The Senecas are called the Keepers of the Western Door of the Long House. According to their legends, the tribes were first formed into a confederation by a chief named Hiawatha, who persuaded them, a long time ago, to stop fighting among themselves. Much of their strength lies in their union, though each tribe may make war and peace by itself. They have lost all respect for us since Frontenac left Canada. Now, maybe, we will teach them a lesson. It is high time."

"It seems a long way to go for a fight," said Denis doubtfully.

"It wouldn't to an Iroquois," replied Perrot dryly. "For years they have scourged a vast territory, from Quebec to the Illinois country, from the northern Huron lands south to the Beautiful River, which the Indians call the Ohio. If we can stop that we'll do a good day's work."

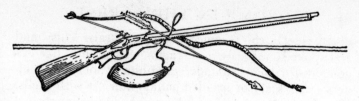

CHAPTER VII

DIPLOMACY

THE snow had melted and the Mississippi was jammed with slowly moving masses of ice when Perrot, Chastaignac and Denis set out, toward the last of March, on the Governor's mission to gather the tribes for war against their ancient enemies. They went first to the land of the Miamis, nine days' journey overland from Perrot's fort.

It was the middle of a bright morning when they struck a well-beaten trail that led them to a clearing in which stood a large palisaded village. At the edge of the forest Perrot halted and sent out a ringing call. Amid furious barking by the village dogs a warrior appeared at the gate. Perrot raised aloft the calumet of peace, a pipe with a bowl of red sandstone and a two-foot stem decked with white eagle feathers. A band of warriors issued from the palisade. Perrot led the way at a slow pace to meet them.

The Miamis were well built and slender, with handsome features. In comparison with the heavy, ungainly men of some of the more northern tribes they looked like aristocrats. They wore their hair in two long locks over their ears. Some bore designs tattooed on their faces and bodies. Others had achieved similar but less lasting decoration with daubs of yellow or blue or green paint.

An elderly chief named Choppatee raised his hand and spoke sonorously in a language sufficiently like Algonquin for Denis to understand him. About his shoulders was a scarf of braided buffalo hair set with shells. Bracelets of small bones at his wrists and knees clicked as he moved. His greeting was couched in the poetic form of speech dear to the Indian.

"How beautiful the sun is, O Frenchmen, when you come to visit us! I thank you for having taken the trouble to make the journey. Never has the earth been so beautiful or the sun so bright as today. Never have our trails been so smooth, for the rocks have vanished under your tread. Our corn will sprout better for your coming, and our hunting will be good. Our tobacco will taste better smoked with you. Our lodges are open to you. We are full of joy."

Perrot's reply was equally extravagant. The warriors then led them inside the palisade to the open space in the middle of the huts where councils and dances were held. There they seated themselves in a circle around their guests.

The calumet of peace was first offered, amid profound silence, to the sun, which the Miamis worshiped. Then the members of the council each took a puff, breathing the smoke out slowly and gravely. Those who bore the peace calumet were respected and safe to go anywhere they wished, for it was used to strengthen alliances and settle disputes, and its bearer was sacred. Perrot was one of the few Frenchmen on whom it had been conferred.

Denis expected him to get to the matter in hand at once, but nothing was said about the Iroquois, nor did their hosts show curiosity about the purpose of the visit. The forms of hospitality must come first.

Accordingly a great feast was held. The first course was sagamite, corn meal boiled to a pulp and seasoned with bits of fat and rancid fish oil. The chief himself fed the guests the first mouthfuls from the platter. Denis did not like the taste, for it was entirely without salt, which the Indians never used. Next squaws brought three fish, boiled whole. The third course consisted of two large animals which Denis, after a doubtful inspection, recognized as dogs. He nearly refused his portion, but under Perrot's warning glance he managed to choke down a few mouthfuls. The fourth course was venison. The remainder of the dishes Denis did not try to recognize. He decided that under the circumstances ignorance, if not exactly bliss, was at least the lesser of two evils.

The capacity of the Indians amazed him. It was a point of honor with them to continue stuffing themselves as long as they could hold another bite. Toward the end of the afternoon, replete to the point of suffocation, they stopped and listened groggily to a series of orations that Denis thought would never end. After nightfall, recovering a little from the effects of their meal, they began to dance and to beat the drums. To their delight Chastaignac joined them, prancing and grimacing and making gestures as ferocious as any his hosts could produce. Long after the Frenchmen had withdrawn to their own camp they could still hear the throbbing drums and the warriors' monotonous chant of *"Ninahani, ninahani, ninahani, naniongo."*

The next day, in solemn council attended by the whole tribe, Perrot presented four gifts. The first was a musket. This, he told the council, assured the Miamis that the French King had their welfare ever in his heart. The second, half a dozen strings of beads and two cakes of vermilion, would dry their tears over any of their people who had died during the past year. The third, an ax, was to show that the French regarded the Miamis as their most trusted friends. The fourth, a belt of the prized purple wampum, sight of which brought forth admiring grunts, was—and here Perrot came to the point—to seal an agreement that the Miamis would join their brothers against the Senecas. Together, said Perrot, they would go that summer to the Seneca villages and destroy them as a buffalo crushes an anthill.

As each present was flung to the ground in front of the chief the warriors murmured, "That is reasonable," though their response to the last proposal was noticeably less enthusiastic. Choppatee replied that an answer would be made in two days. Deep thought would be given the matter. With that the three Frenchmen withdrew to their camp, glad to escape the smells, the swarms of dogs and the dubious food.

At the appointed time another feast was held. In a long speech the chief informed the visitors that the Miamis were grateful to the French King for his love; that they cherished the friendship of their brothers. Truly they would join with them against the Senecas. Perrot received the news with a dignified show of pleasure. He told them to meet him at Michilimackinac in one moon and bade them farewell.

But once they were free of the guard of honor sent by Choppatee to see them on their way Perrot shook his head doubtfully. "I do not expect them. They are easily swayed by the last words they hear. I saw some of the Sokokis in the village. That is bad. They are friends of the Iroquois."

They were but a day's journey from the fort when

they encountered a warrior of the Malhominie tribe.
The two coureurs recognized him as a friend and
stopped to talk. At length the Indian remarked, as if
it were a matter of no particular importance, that it
would be advisable for them to hasten on to their post.
He said a thousand warriors of the Foxes, Mascoutens and Kickapoos were on their way to war with the
Sioux beyond the Mississippi and, knowing that Metaminens was absent, had agreed to kill the Frenchmen
at the post, hide the skins stored there and take the
arms for their campaign. "Metaminens," meaning
"Little Corn," was the name by which Perrot was
known to all the western peoples. Perrot thanked the
Indian and gave him a hunting knife. Chastaignac fell
to cursing the faithless allies.

Perrot tightened the straps of his pack and started
ahead at a steady lope. At sunset they stopped for
water and a handful of dried corn. Dusk came down
as they began to cross a prairie. By the time they were
in the woods again the moon had risen, lighting the
forest with an eerie glow that confused rocks and
shadows, but the pace never slackened.

A wisp of smoke crept lazily upward from the main
cabin into the clear dawn. From the bare hill behind
the fort they could see the gate was barred.

"Either we are in time or it was a false alarm,"
growled Chastaignac.

Denis was too tired to care greatly.

LeSueur, yawning mightily, opened the gates. No,
there had been no sign of Indians for several days,
he said. Perrot ordered Denis to get some sleep.

It was nearly noon when he was shaken awake by
Jules Malot. "Quick, go to the storehouse. The hills
are alive with savages."

Denis tumbled out of the cabin just as LeSueur opened the gates to admit eight chieftains. Chastaignac disarmed each as he entered. Denis recognized the Foxes by the daubs of red on their faces, the Kicka- poos by the blue lines about their chins, the Mascou- tens by their girdles of buffalo tails. In lordly fashion the chiefs advanced toward the main cabin. Suddenly Perrot opened the door and confronted them. Not even by the flicker of an eyelid did they show their astonishment.

Chastaignac beckoned to Denis from the storehouse. "Grab a deer robe," he whispered. "Put on this hat. Walk slowly to the lower cabin. Change inside it to some other clothes. Then come out and go to the kitchen and repeat the change. We've got to make them think there are a lot of men here."

Denis obeyed while Chastaignac took off his own shirt and donned a spare coat of LeSueur's. On his way to the lower cabin he passed as near the circle of Indians as he dared. A pipe was making its slow round. Behind Perrot a row of loaded muskets leaned against the cabin wall.

Chastaignac came in the cabin laughing. "Perrot told them there are forty men here. Can you look like eight different fellows? This is the only time I've ever regretted my red beard. Give me that shawl. Maybe they'll think one of me has a toothache."

As Denis emerged without a coat and with buffalo tails tied to his cap he heard one of the Foxes ask scornfully, "Is Metaminens displeased?"

Perrot's answer came quick and harsh. "Yes, and with good reason. You have listened to the words of fools. You have thought to trick me. But the Great Spirit has told me what is in your hearts. You would kill my men and take my guns to fight the Sioux."

For the first time Denis saw Indians show consternation. They sprang up and started toward the gate. At the same moment the guard signaled frantically to Perrot. A shrill war whoop rose beyond the wall.

Perrot snatched a musket. "Stop!" he ordered. "Tell your young men to go in peace or I will break your heads and send your scalps to the Sioux."

The chiefs halted uncertainly. Though they had seemed unaware of the Frenchmen passing and repassing before them, Perrot's stratagem had been successful. They were puzzled and somewhat awed by a thing that seemed supernatural.

"Do not shoot," one of them muttered. "We cannot fight one who is protected by the Great Spirit. Our young men will go away."

Escorted by LeSueur, the chief who had spoken mounted the turf rampart near the gate and shouted over the palisade that the Great Spirit had warned Metaminens. The shouting died away to sullen murmurs while Denis, squinting along the barrel of a musket, watched anxiously. The slope before the fort was thick with warriors. He knew if they chose to storm the palisade nothing could stop them. But the chief's words fell on their ears like a thunderclap. Convinced that his own life depended on his success, he harangued them, vowing that the Great Spirit had transported Perrot and his scattered men back to the fort by magic. It was evidently madness to oppose such a one.

The warriors gradually dispersed. When the last of them had retired beyond gunshot the chief returned to Perrot. "Now will you give us presents?" he demanded blandly.

"Only if you will give up this war against the Sioux," was the stern reply. "If you want fighting I will lead you to it. Come to Michilimackinac by the next moon and join us against the Senecas. All the western nations are taking the warpath. Are you women to stay at home?"

One of the other chiefs spoke up. "If you will give us powder and shot we will go with you."

Perrot gave them a liberal supply of ammunition in return for some beaver skins of doubtful quality and added two kettles and five fishhooks to close the doors of the country of the Sioux.

The next morning the horde had disappeared.

Perrot, Chastaignac, Denis and fifteen coureurs started a week later for Michilimackinac. Perrot had been averse to taking Denis, not only because of the danger from the Iroquois but also because he feared trouble through the presence of some of Pezzard's friends among the levies from Quebec, but Denis had begged so hard that Perrot at last had yielded.

Their way lay first through villages of the Foxes, Kickapoos and Mascoutens. There, to Perrot's secret amusement, the elders praised him for being in such close partnership with the Great Spirit and for so easily outwitting their young men. As Chastaignac pointed out, this was one of the likable qualities of the Indians, that they regarded all life as a game and honestly admired a skillful opponent.

On the western shore of Green Bay they were given a grave welcome by a large band of Pottawattomies. These trusted friends ordinarily were overjoyed to see Metaminens, but now they were ill at ease. Something, it seemed, had frightened them, and they were of two minds about the war. Perrot and Chastaignac set themselves to learn the reason.

The Pottawattomies told them the tribesmen who had been tricked at Perrot's fort and had promised to give up the Sioux war and join against the Senecas had instead gone south to the Miamis. Here the Sokoki spies Perrot had seen had persuaded them that the French meant treachery. So these raiders, together with the Miamis, had turned westward to pick up the quarrel with the Sioux. No help was to be expected from any of them.

"Can't something be done?" asked Denis indignantly.

Perrot shook his head. "There is no time. I am not surprised. They promised too easily."

"And we wore out our moccasins for nothing," grumbled Chastaignac. "I haven't your patience, Nicolas. I wasn't cut out for a diplomat."

"We've got to be diplomats, and skillful ones," replied the other with a wry smile. "We must have the Pottawattomies, at least. Something else, something more serious, is the matter here."

Circuitous questioning revealed the reason. The ghost drum had been heard throbbing out its message of disaster. The guardian spirit of the old warrior was again warning his people. . . . Perrot's brow cleared at the news.

He rose and began an oration of praise for the steadfastness and courage of his hosts. When he had them in a better mood he spoke of the drum. He had no doubt, he said, that they had heard the drum. The question was what it meant. The old warrior of the legend had not been a coward. He had warned their ancestors so they could fight, not flee. The ghost drum spoke to warriors, not to timid squaws. If they did not take part in this war to stamp out the Iroquois the spirit would be angry.

The Indians looked at one another out of the corners of their eyes, ashamed of their fears. Truly Metaminens was wise.

At dawn the following morning the whole Pottawattomie band set out eagerly by canoe with the three voyageurs for the meeting of the western allies.

CHAPTER VIII

SPARKS AT MICHILIMACKINAC

SHRILL yells. A spatter of musket shots. Leaping warriors. Michilimackinac!

The violence of their welcome by the Indian hordes was fairly bloodcurdling. The Pottawattomies, exulting in the uproar, dug in their paddles furiously, raising their own war cries in answer to the Ottawa screams of "Sassakouie! Sassakouie!" Racing into the shallow water, Hurons and Ottawas seized the canoes as the Pottawattomies sprang out and, raising them aloft, dashed for the beach.

Denis waded ashore with the rest, tautly watchful for the spark that might turn the welcome into a battle. An accidental injury would be enough. As if sensing the danger, a tall Indian raised his arms and advanced toward Perrot shouting, "My brother! Metaminens!" A lone eagle feather rose from the band around his head. His face was streaked with zigzag lines of red and green. He wore his necklace of bear claws as proudly as though it were the order of St. Michael.

"That's the Pottawattomie, Mesheketeno, the best chief of all," explained Chastaignac in answer to Denis's inquiring look. He stamped the water from his moccasins. "Let's go to the fort and get the news."

At the fort they found a young lieutenant in charge of a garrison of twenty men. The officer failed at first

to recognize Denis. "Ma foi!" he exclaimed after a
puzzled inspection, "it is the lad Perrot took in tow.
But what a change since the fall. You have filled out
and grown so brown I would scarce know you. And
you are going too, eh?" he asked enviously.

He was much disgruntled at being left behind. Only
this morning the Sieur de la Durantaye had started
for the Straits of Detroit with some hundred Frenchmen, soldiers and coureurs, and a mixed band of Chippewas, Ojibways and Hurons. Father Engelran had
gone with him. They were to meet Tonty with the Illinois allies at Detroit and would join the army from
the St. Lawrence somewhere on Lake Ontario.

Chastaignac pursed his lips. "Then why are so many
Indians here?"

"The tribes have been divided among themselves
over this business. Most of the Hurons remained. The
Ottawas have been backing and filling for two weeks,
changing their minds hourly, claiming they need more
time to mend their canoes. Sieur de la Durantaye at
last lost patience. Maybe Sieur Perrot can persuade
them."

"Hmp!" snorted Chastaignac.

That night on the slope beside the fort the French
gave a great feast. Perrot spoke eloquently, while the
firelight flickered on painted faces and brown bodies.
Alternately cajoling and flattering, he delighted the
Indians with praise and fired their imaginations by de-
scribing the deeds they would perform against the
Senecas. With one shout they agreed to start the very
next morning.

But when morning came the Ottawa canoes still
needed patching; and the Hurons said the signs were
unfavorable.

For five days Denis wandered among the Algonquin tribes, improving his knowledge of the dialects and observing with interest the difference between the squat, ungainly Ottawas, the affable, cleanly built Pottawattomies, the insinuating Hurons and the proud Crees. On the afternoon of the sixth day he and Chastaignac were coming down from the fort when they spied a solitary canoe headed in from the straits. As they neared the shore and saw the craft more plainly Chastaignac stopped and beckoned to a young Pottawattomie.

"We would know who the stranger is before showing ourselves, O Nayonsay. Go listen and tell us, and we will speak your name before Metaminens." He continued to peer at the approaching craft as the Indian sauntered to the beach. "There is something queer about yonder crew," he murmured. "They were paddling slowly at first, then they stopped. Now they are coming in at a fast pace. Why?"

A circle of curious Indians hid the occupants of the canoe as they landed. In about ten minutes Nayonsay returned.

"The sun is bright but the sky will soon be hung with clouds," he began in the usual oblique Indian fashion. "They are three Hurons with one Frenchman. I do not believe they expected to find so many here."

He paused, plucked a twig and chewed on it reflectively.

"Speak, my comrade," urged Chastaignac.

"They say English are coming up the lake bringing many presents and much rum. They will pay higher prices for our furs. They say we should be friends with the English and not the French. The Ottawas listen and say that is reasonable." He sniffed. "I believe

Mesheketeno, who says the French are our brothers."

"Ventre Saint Gris!" swore Chastaignac. "Come, Denis, let us get out of here before they see us. I, Miscoue, will not forget this, O Nayonsay."

The two companions stole behind some neighboring lodges and made their way around the foot of the hill. "Last year an English trading expedition won the hearts of some of the Hurons with cheap trade goods and a lot of rum," explained Chastaignac. "Now they are back, determined to make favorable treaties. If they succeed, they will shut us out of the west." Once safely out of sight of the beach he broke into a trot. Five minutes later Perrot and the young lieutenant were hearing the news.

Quickly the garrison was turned out, and the gathering word was sent to the coureurs. With military precision the soldiers, Perrot and their commander in the lead, filed to the shore. Silent and apprehensive, the Ottawas parted before them. Denis saw the strangers. His heart missed a beat. The white man was Loutray. One of the Hurons was Black Fox.

He stepped quickly behind Chastaignac's broad back, though too late to avoid being seen. He was sure, too, that he had been recognized in spite of his changed appearance, for a flash of surprise had passed across the face of the man with the drooping eyelid. But Loutray was not one to let down his guard.

"How fortunate that you are here, Sieur Perrot," he was saying affably. "I was afraid the post was left undefended. Two weeks ago I and my Hurons were captured by a party of English led by a Dutch trader from Albany. They are on their way to seize this place and win over the western tribes. This morning at risk of our lives we got away from them to warn—"

"Canoes!" cried a coureur, pointing toward distant Mackinac Island. All eyes turned toward the lake.

"It is the English," said Loutray.

Denis managed at last to make out a number of tiny black spots on the sunlit waters.

Perrot's level gaze returned to Loutray. "We will remember what you have done," he said. "Lieutenant, I think we had better go to meet them." He turned to the waiting Indians. "Let those who have not forgotten the French are their allies come with us."

Denis bent low over his paddle as he knelt in the bow of Chastaignac's canoe. The enemy craft were nearer now; he counted fourteen of them, low in the water from the weight of their cargoes. Over his shoulder he glimpsed the Pottawattomie canoes following steadily. In the stern Chastaignac kept up a running fire of comment, as he was apt to do when stirred.

"Good old Mesheketeno. He's the one to count on in a tight place. . . . Those Hurons will bear watching. They are circling to the north, paddling as hard as they can. Fifty canoes of them. Trying to reach the English first, the lice. Mille tonnerres! If they join the English we are lost. Put your back into it, lad!"

"Where are the Ottawas?" gasped Denis, laboring with all his might.

"Arguing on the shore. No, they are launching their canoes. . . . They aren't following us. They're circling south. They'll wait to see what happens and then take the winning side. A thousand sacred pigs! Bend that paddle, my boy, or I'll bend mine over your head."

The sweat rolled down Denis's face. His arms weighed tons. Out of the corner of his eye he saw half of the Pottawattomie canoes under the furious drive of the warriors draw slowly ahead toward a point that would place them between the English and the racing Hurons. The remainder sheered off to watch the Ottawas. The French plowed on steadily.

With a deft sweep Chastaignac stopped the canoe in line with the others, barring the way to Michilimackinac. From the center canoe Perrot's voice rang out. He was leaning forward, his strong hands clenched on the thwart, his hair blowing in the wind.

"In the name of King Louis of France, I summon you to surrender," he shouted.

The English shipped their paddles. Denis went cold at the thought that one of them might shoot Perrot.

"Resistance is useless," he continued. "You can see that you are surrounded. Surrender peacefully and save your lives."

"If they only knew it, they are far from surrounded," muttered Chastaignac. "Now we'll see if they are gamblers."

The Englishmen looked at the two lines of Pottawattomies, at the Hurons, slowing to a stop, then at the hovering Ottawas. Their leader, a stocky, red-faced man, slowly raised his hands above his head.

"We give up ourselves," he said sullenly in broken French. "No shooting."

Escorted by the French and the Pottawattomies, the English canoes headed for shore. Denis felt suddenly exhilarated. He stared at the strange craft, observing the heavy loads of goods, watching the occupants and wondering what sort of men they were. Outwardly they differed little from the coureurs.

Halfway to the beach the Hurons and Ottawas with a great burst of speed and fierce shouts of "Sassakouie" dashed between the convoy and the shore, then, swerving like gulls, charged, all flashing paddles and threshing arms, straight at the prisoners. Two boat lengths away the savage flotilla swerved again while the English recovered their breath. Chastaignac chuckled. "Our faithful allies are claiming the credit," he observed sardonically. "If they'd got there first and made a deal we'd be at the bottom of the lake now."

As he stepped ashore the red-faced leader, who proved to be a Dutchman from Albany, looked so crestfallen that Perrot was moved to say he should not blame himself for the fortunes of war.

"Things might have been different but for treachery," was the reply.

"You mean the Frenchman who guided you here and promised you the fort," said Perrot grimly. "That one is not to be trusted by either side, M'sieur."

The prisoners were marched to the stockade under escort of the soldiers while Perrot supervised the distribution of their goods which, as contraband, could be confiscated. Although the Hurons looked black and the Ottawas sulked when some of the largest kettles, finest hatchets, and longest sticks of tobacco went to the Pottawattomies, they made no protest. In one of the packs Chastaignac found a handsome gun and a horn full of powder. With an obvious effort of the will he turned to Nayonsay.

"Here, my brother, I haven't forgotten." He looked at the weapon lovingly as the young Pottawattomie grasped it with a satisfied grunt.

Part of the cargo consisted of twelve small kegs of rum. Perrot ordered them taken to the storehouse in the fort. The Hurons began to clamor for their portion of the prized firewater at once. Perrot's sorely tried patience cracked. "When the Hurons take the warpath and prove they are men then let them ask for strong drink," he growled. It was one of the few times Denis ever saw him show temper.

"Nay, my children," he continued, regaining control of himself. "The English, brothers of the Iroquois, send you the drink that makes one stupid. They would have you drink it and become foolish. Then they would take your furs and laugh." He waved them back. Disconsolately the Hurons watched the kegs disappear into the fort.

When all the captured goods were distributed Denis followed Perrot toward the palisade. On the way they met Loutray. At sight of him Denis instinctively started to shrink behind Perrot.

"Steady, lad, remember you are a coureur de bois now, not a friendless cabin boy new to the country," urged Perrot softly.

Denis was ashamed. "I will not forget again, sir," he muttered, raising his chin and staring straight at the approaching figure.

"Ah, Sieur Perrot, I have been waiting for you at the fort," said Loutray. "Things have turned out well, it seems. It's a good thing I arrived in time."

"Yes," said Perrot gravely.

Loutray's eyes turned to Denis. "You have grown taller," he said, "but I recognized you at once."

Perrot waited silently.

"Is this boy of your company?" asked Loutray.

Perrot nodded.

"He's a rascal—a runaway from the shop of Master Pezzard in Quebec. He broke his contract as apprentice and stole a silver mug. You're lucky to be warned about him. I'll take him back to answer the charges."

"I never stole—" began Denis hotly, but stopped at the touch of his companion's hand.

There was a look of bright anger in Perrot's eyes. "I have heard something of this. The matter will be adjusted in good time, but not now."

The scar over Loutray's drooping eyelid grew livid. "There is a law about runaway apprentices," he said.

A faint smile hovered around the corners of Perrot's mouth. "In my own country and among my own men I am the law," he replied softly. Suddenly his voice grew harsh. "Denis de Lornay stays with me, despite your orders from Pezzard. Whoever attempts anything against him—anything, you understand—will answer to me."

Loutray's eyes blazed. His hand slipped to his knife, then he wheeled and strode away.

Perrot watched him. "That man is a mad wolf at heart," he observed. "You will do well to stay close to me or to Chastaignac while he is around."

The coureurs and soldiers ate supper at the fort. As he elbowed his way to the steaming kettles Denis kept a sharp watch for his enemy. Once he thought he saw him in the midst of a group near the gate, but it was growing dark and he could not be sure.

With the dusk a fine mist drifted in from the lake, and the men retreated to the barracks where they were soon engaged in gesticulating argument as to the value, conduct and possible results of the Seneca war. Most of them were impatient to be off. A man from Kamalastigouia, Sieur DuLhut's post on the northern shore of Lake Superior, was talking with Perrot about the attitude of the Crees toward the war. Across the room Chastaignac had secured attention by the simple means of shouting down all opposition and was telling the story of an old fight with the Iroquois. An hour of clamor in the smoke-filled room made Denis long for fresh air. He slipped out of the door. He would have liked to visit his friends the Pottawattomies, but, remembering Perrot's warning, he decided to stay within the palisade.

The gate of the fort was directly opposite the barracks. On the right, dimly bulking through the mist, were the storehouses. Denis had started toward the gate to speak with the guard when he heard a faint scraping at the cabin where the rum had been stored. Some coureur was probably improving the opportunity to help himself to a dram, he thought, smiling at the notion of surprising the man. He crossed to the nearest cabin, edged cautiously around it and tiptoed toward the sound. It was very dark between the buildings, a darkness all the more intense because of the glow of Indian fires beyond the palisade. As he felt his way around the corner of the storehouse Denis saw silhouetted against the glow the figure of an Indian astride the log wall. The savage bent down, took something in his arms and, lifting it with difficulty across the wall, lowered it to someone outside. As he repeated the performance Denis saw that the objects were kegs.

His foot slipped in the mud and he staggered against the cabin. The sound, soft as it was, must have reached the Indian, for he disappeared beyond the wall. An instant later another figure, by his clothes a white man, quickly mounted into the glow and likewise dropped on the other side of the barrier. Denis fumbled his way to the wall and found a wooden ladder leaning against it. He clambered to the top. Hurrying toward the Indian camp were four men, each carrying a keg. He dropped to the ground and felt his way to the front of the storehouse. The door was open. The lock and chain that had secured it lay on the ground.

Perrot caught his eye as he reentered the barracks, rose and, not too hastily, strolled toward the door. He drew Denis outside. "By the looks of you something is wrong. What is it?"

Denis led the way to the rifled cabin. As well as they could tell in the darkness only eight of the twelve kegs remained. Without a word Perrot made for the gate.

Two great fires flared against the dark background of field and forest, casting a fitful light far over the cornfield. Hundreds of bronze figures clustered around the leaping flames. As they drew nearer the two could see that there were three distinct groups of Indians, all intently watching three or four men near one of the fires. Perrot circled to the rear of the crowd and halted in the shadows.

One of the four stooped, seized a keg of rum, and balancing it on his shoulder, turned slowly around so that all could see. For a moment the firelight shone on his face, giving it an odd masklike look. It was Loutray.

"See, my brothers," he cried. "It is the rum Meta-minens would not give you. The night is cold and damp, my brothers. Drink and be merry and forget how you have been treated."

The Ottawas shrieked approval. A tall Indian Denis recognized as Mesheketeno rose in the forefront of the Pottawattomies. "We do not drink English rum," he announced. His words were drowned by jeers.

Loutray lowered the keg to the ground and knocked it open with his hatchet. Indians fought to dip their hands in the rum. Only the Pottawattomies stood unmoved.

Suddenly one of Loutray's three companions leaped on top of one of the unbroken kegs. "The rum is good," he howled. "There is more at the fort. Are we dogs that we are glad to get the bones the French throw away? Let us be men and take what is ours."

"That is Black Fox," whispered Denis excitedly.

A circle of leaping warriors formed as if by magic about the fire, brandishing tomahawks and knives. Another Huron, rising from the mass about the keg, drained a bark cup. *"Ahirrha!"* He screamed. "I will show my brothers how to fight. To the fort! Plunder! Kill!"

In a bound Perrot was beside the savage. With one blow he knocked him spinning to the ground.

"That is the way your brother fights, like a pig rooting in the earth," he shouted, and his laughter boomed above the howls. "Is that the way he would fight the Iroquois? This is how Metaminens greets his enemies." He pulled his hatchet from his belt and in two clean strokes staved in the heads of the remaining kegs.

The dance stopped. The yells died away to murmurs. In the confusion Denis lost sight of Loutray and Black Fox. But the moment of surprise was short-lived. The Indians broke into an angry clamor. Fortunately they had not had time to become inflamed by the rum, or Perrot's audacity would have been the end of him. But he pressed the attack, giving the storm no time to gather. He kicked over the kegs. The rum streamed toward the fires. As it burst into blue flame the warriors backed away, leaving Perrot, Denis and Mesheketeno in command of the wreckage.

"The French are coming to the lakes with many soldiers," Perrot proclaimed. "Would you have them burn your villages?"

He looked around the circle of warriors. "Where is the man who gave you the rum?" he asked and his voice had the chill of steel.

There was no reply.

A Pottawattomie slipped away into the shadows. In a moment he was back. "They have run off like foxes, O Metaminens," he said loudly enough for all to hear. "They have taken a canoe. I could see them on the water but I had no gun."

Mesheketeno started toward the lake.

"No, my comrade, let them go," said Perrot. "They are cowards and cannot harm us." He turned to the Hurons. "Go to your lodges and sleep, my children. Tomorrow we take the warpath. Too long have we delayed. I have spoken."

Without waiting to hear the Ottawa protests he placidly returned his hatchet to his belt and with Denis on one side and Mesheketeno on the other he stalked toward the fort.

The next morning the fleet of canoes headed across the straits. The Ottawas, who had begged for only one more day to mend their canoes, watched from the shore. There had been no further sign of Loutray, for which Denis, as he stroked the bow paddle in Chastaignac's canoe, was heartily thankful.

Chapter IX

DENONVILLE BUILDS A FORT

ONE July day, six weeks after Perrot's band had left Michilimackinac, the combined canoe fleets of the western forces crept slowly over the sparkling waters of Lake Ontario. The long journey was nearly over. Somewhere beyond the low headlands of the southern shore lay the villages of the Senecas, Keepers of the Western Door of the Iroquois Long House.

For six days since leaving the mouth of the Niagara River the French and their Indian allies had forged steadily eastward, camping at night on the beaches and tossing on the rough waters by day. Word had come to them at Niagara that Governor Denonville's army was setting out from Fort Frontenac and would join them at Irrondequoit Bay. In addition to the forces from the north under La Durantaye, Perrot and Du-Lhut, the fleet now included Tonty's Illinois warriors and even the Ottawas from Michilimackinac, who at last had made up their minds and had come overland from Lake Huron.

Chastaignac spoke excitedly. "Look, there is the rendezvous. Irrondequoit." Scarce a league ahead the shore curved to the south. "Now if our tortoise of a governor will only show up, we will have the business over at last."

Hardly were the words out of his mouth when there

came a shout from one of the leading canoes. "There they are, the levies from the St. Lawrence. It's an omen—a good omen. We meet at the rendezvous at the same hour."

Denis stood up, balancing himself expertly in the bobbing craft. Far away where sky and water met in dazzling brightness he could see a multitude of black specks.

The cry was taken up all down the line, only to be drowned out by the wild yells of the Indians. Paddlers struck their blades into the water with renewed energy, eager to be the first to land.

The canoes were beached on a low sandy spit which separated the lake from Irrondequoit Bay, a marsh-choked estuary that extended back some miles to the south and was bordered on either side by steep rugged little hills.

While the coureurs unloaded their boats and pre-pared a makeshift camp and the Indians began busily to deck themselves in their wildest array of paints, the four leaders of the expedition gathered to await the Governor. Beside the soldierly figure of La Durantaye stood Perrot, his hand resting in friendly fashion on the shoulder of the small supple Tonty, the staunch friend of the Chevalier de la Salle, the great ex-plorer, seeker for the way to China, who was now attempting to plant a colony at the mouth of the Mis-sissippi. During the weeks since Tonty had joined the expedition at Detroit Denis had grown to admire him for his gaiety, bravery, wisdom and steadfast devotion. The preceding winter he had made a fruitless journey to the lower Mississippi to try to find his chief and had returned to his fort on the Illinois just in time to muster his Indians for this expedition. He was of

Italian blood and had the black hair and sparkling eyes of his race. His famous iron hand, which replaced the one he had lost in a Sicilian battle, was incased in a kid glove. He cheerfully admitted that an unbreakable fist was an advantage in dealing with Indians.

The fourth of the group was Daniel Greysolon DuLhut, lean ex-member of the King's Guard. A thorough gentleman, kindly and courteous in manner, he was equally at home in the court circles of Versailles or in the council lodges of the Sioux. Like Perrot he was held in highest respect by the western tribes for his fair dealing and unflinching courage. Strangely enough, in view of his outdoor life, he was a chronic sufferer from gout.

The Governor's flotilla had now drawn close enough for Denis to see that the black specks were flatboats filled with regulars, militia and Christian Mohawks from the mission settlements around Montreal. Standing erect in the leading boat were three men dressed in full regimental uniforms.

Chastaignac shaded his eyes to peer at them. "The one on the left is de Callières, Governor of Montreal," he told Denis. "In the center is our Governor of New France, the Marquis de Denonville. I don't know the other chap."

"That's the Marquis de Vaudreuil," supplied the messenger from Fort Frontenac who had brought news of the Governor's plans. "He's just over from France with a new regiment that's been left behind to guard the towns."

Chastaignac's eyes were amused. "They look pretty," he said. "De Callières is all right, but the other two will probably learn some things about war that aren't in their textbooks."

A final sweep of the long oars drove the boat to the beach. The three leaders, smiling with satisfaction at sight of the coureurs and their Indian horde, stepped ashore. To Denis they seemed splendid in their plumed hats, their white sashes and topboots. Certainly they were a contrast to the four woodsmen who advanced to meet them. Though perhaps Chastaignac was right; lace jabots and dainty rapiers suspended from yellow baldricks were of little use in the forests.

La Durantaye bowed and presented his buckskin-clad companions, and the group moved into the nearby beech grove where the tents were to be pitched. The western Indians, grunting with astonishment, crowded close to stare at the finery of the officers, who, in turn, could scarcely help showing a faint dismay on a closer inspection of their savage allies. Most of the Indians wore little but ornaments—horns on their heads or the tails of beasts behind their backs. Iron rings hung from their noses and ears, and their faces were grotesque masks of paint, in red and green circles, spots of black and white, or jagged streaks of ocher.

Never had Canada witnessed such a military scene as that which now took place on the sandy shores by Irrondequoit. The Governor's fleet of four hundred batteaux and canoes lined the two-mile stretch of sand spit. Four battalions of regular troops, accoutered as if for review by the King, and four additional battalions of Canadian militia in the garb of farmers or huntsmen and led by the feudal seigneurs of the St. Lawrence, formed the backbone of the army. Added to these were scores of Christian Iroquois, led by black-gowned Jesuits, a hundred and eighty coureurs from the west and their four hundred pagan allies—Pottawattomies, Hurons, Ottawas and Illinois. In all,

Governor Denonville had a force of nearly three thousand men.

While supper was being prepared there came a spatter of musket shots from the camp of the Christian
Indians. Word was passed that some Seneca scouts had
hailed their fellow tribesmen from the edge of the
forest, demanding to know the meaning of the expedition. The Montreal Mohawks had replied, "To fight
you, you blockheads," and suiting the action to the
words, had blazed away at their kinsmen. The Senecas
had disappeared into their forests, shouting defiance.

When he had filled his bowl with venison stew Denis
contrived to find a place near the fire where Perrot,
La Durantaye, DuLhut and Father Engelran, the
priest from Michilimackinac, were engaged in low-
voiced discussion. Around their own campfires the Indians pranced and boasted. In a few minutes Tonty
appeared out of the gloom.

"Heard the news, my friends?" he inquired in his
soft voice.

"What news?" grunted La Durantaye.

"We are to give the Senecas plenty of time to get
ready for us," replied the Italian sarcastically. "Instead of cleaning them up at once and turning on the
Oneidas and Onondagas we are going to spend the
next three days fortifying this place. We are going
to have as grand a base of operations as if we were
setting out to besiege a fortress in the Low Countries.
It is our good Governor's idea. Bah!" He glared
fiercely at La Durantaye, as if he were in some way
responsible.

"There is no need to grow excited, Henri," said
DuLhut coolly. "We can't surprise them anyway, perhaps a day or so won't make much difference."

Tonty snorted. "If you are going to catch a bird you don't wait until it is on the wing."

"True, cousin, but you know as well as I how little weight the words of coureurs have with Governor Denonville. He would listen politely and then do as his Quebec friends advise. That crafty rascal of an Intendant has poisoned his mind against us. We'd be wasting our breath."

"Oh, if only Frontenac were here!" mourned Tonty. Perrot shot him a warning glance.

A brown shadow slipped between DuLhut and his cousin and settled beside Perrot. Denis recognized Nayonsay. The young Pottawattomie whispered something in Perrot's ear. As he listened Perrot's face grew grim. Nayonsay disappeared as silently as he had come.

"What now, Nicolas?" asked La Durantaye.

"Treachery," replied Perrot, rising. He looked at Denis. "You recall, Sieur de la Durantaye, my tale of the Frenchman who arrived at Michilimackinac in advance of the English and tried to make the savages drunk so they would attack the fort? He has turned up again. Our young friend, who was on sentry duty at his camp, saw two Indians skulking among the trees. They stole toward the camp of the Hurons and hid in a nearby gully. He followed them. After a time they came out and mingled with the Huron warriors. Nayonsay says he recognized them. One was the Frenchman, Loutray, in disguise. The other was his henchman, a Huron named Black Fox."

In spite of himself Denis shivered.

"Canaille," muttered Chastaignac. "We should have shot them."

"I'm going to the Governor," said Perrot. "Loutray is working for the English and the Iroquois."

"Much good it will do you," grumbled Tonty.

DuLhut threw his arm around his kinsman's shoulders. "You speak before you think, Henri. That is not wise."

"You are right, Daniel," agreed the other. "But I am much annoyed. We have come a long way for this job. I'd like it done properly."

It was nearly two hours before Perrot returned. Chastaignac had rolled up in his blanket, but Denis waited beside the leaders, for sleep was out of the question.

Perrot sat down moodily. "The Governor was very busy," he said. "When I finally was received by him I told him what happened at Michilimackinac and what Nayonsay saw tonight."

"And then?" prompted Tonty.

"He laughed," said Perrot quietly, his mouth tightening at the corners. "He said I had misinterpreted Loutray's actions throughout. He said Loutray had come to him well recommended by the merchant Pezzard, that he had put him to work spying among the English and Iroquois, that he has brought in much valuable information. It is evident I have been in danger of underestimating our friend with the drooping eyelid."

"And of overestimating our worthy Governor's intelligence," added Tonty bitterly. "Wait. Here comes the Pottawattomie again."

Nayonsay stepped noiselessly into the firelit circle. At a gesture from Perrot he spoke. "I took some of my people to find the men as Metaminens ordered. They were gone. We looked, but it is too dark. We lost the trail."

"Nayonsay has done well," replied Perrot with a sigh.

When the Indian had gone DuLhut rose, wincing as his gouty foot touched the ground. "I am going to bed," he announced. "Gentlemen, I bid you good evening." The others followed. When they were out of hearing Perrot turned to Denis. "Don't worry," he said, "but stay close to us. I would that you were back beside the Mississippi."

For three days the coureurs, aided by the militia and the regulars, labored in the heat to build a fort that would satisfy the Governor. Hundreds of trees were felled and planted upright in the sandy soil. Blockhouses were erected at the four corners. A great abatis of branches was made. Four hundred men were to be left behind to guard the boats.

The Indians looked on, refusing to raise a hand. They had come to fight the Senecas, they said, not to build houses. They watched, at first with amused curiosity, then with growing contempt.

"The white man fights like a beaver," they said among themselves, and laughed, for it was well known that, though the beaver builds, he does not fight at all.

CHAPTER X

DRUMS THROUGH THE FOREST

BUT all things, even the snaillike preparations of the Marquis, must have an end, as Chastaignac cheerfully observed. On the morning of the third day the fort was finished to Denonville's liking. Soldiers and woodsmen laid aside their tools and took up their muskets. At three o'clock that afternoon the vanguard, under the command of de Callières, set out on the broad trail that led to the Seneca town of Gannagaro, seven leagues to the south.

This first section of the army was a motley aggregation which appeared to have no sense of order or discipline. But in reality it was more formidable in woods fighting than the soldiers and militia behind it. In the center were the coureurs de bois from the west. On the left, ranging fanlike through the woodlands, were the Christian Iroquois under dashing young Sainte-Hélène, one of the nine sons of Charles Le Moyne of Montreal. On the right flank were the naked savages from the upper lakes, flitting like painted specters among the trees, rushing ahead or pausing to rest as the whim of the moment dictated. Perrot, assisted by Chastaignac, had been given the unenviable job of trying to keep them in hand. Knowing that they could not be depended upon to obey the orders even of their own chiefs, he let them range as they would. They

104

were wise in their own kind of warfare; it would have been a mistake to try to change their habits.

Behind came the main body of regulars and militia, with Denonville and de Vaudreuil at their head. Each trooper bore his own provisions and ammunition; other supplies were left with the four hundred guardians of the boats.

Denis trod the springy forest turf as eagerly as a dog let off the leash. He was excited, a little uncertain and determined to give a good account of himself. He wondered how Giles had felt before a battle.

But there were too many things to do and see for thinking overlong about what lay ahead. He followed Perrot for a time, then was dispatched to Chastaignac with a message. Chastaignac was in high good humor again and was keeping everyone about him laughing.

It was a pleasant country. The trees were oak, walnut and chestnut, and the ground was free of underbrush. Overhead the branches met in continuous arches, and the sunlight, filtered and dimmed by the leaves, formed constantly changing patterns on the ground. It seemed to Denis that they were passing through some vast crypt whose green roof was supported by sturdy gray trunks. Except for the low-voiced talk and the laughter, the advance was quiet, muffled by the turf. The Indians, watchful for an expected ambush, had lost their bravado now that they were approaching the enemy.

From time to time a disquieting sound was heard— a sharp but distant throb, like the beat of a tomtom except that it was more liquid. It came, Denis learned, from a Seneca water drum, a small wooden vessel half filled with water and covered with taut skin.

Sometime before sunset the Governor ordered a halt.

The army bivouacked under the trees, without camp-fires.

The dawn was sultry. The day blanched quickly into stifling heat. For breakfast Denis had a hard biscuit and a drink of tepid water from his canteen.

The march was resumed, with some Mohawks of the colony of Saut St. Louis, near Montreal, as scouts. The tribes from Michilimackinac and the Illinois moved forward silently, Perrot in their midst. Farther to the west the Hurons kept pace, prancing when they thought they were observed, skulking if left to themselves. On the flank the Ottawas were occasionally glimpsed, warily watchful of their own interests. The Indians had been given red rags to tie about their heads to distinguish them from the Senecas when the fighting began. The black robe of Father Engelran flitted here and there among them, encouraging, exhorting, the wooden beads of his rosary clicking at every step.

They passed cautiously through a defile between two steep hills, an ideal place, Chastaignac noted, for an ambush. But there was still no sign of the Iroquois. As the sun mounted higher the lifeless air under the trees grew more and more oppressive.

Beyond the defile Father Engelran was waiting, wiping the sweat from his forehead with his sleeve, his sunken blue eyes shining with excitement.

"It is hot work," he panted. "These children of mine must perform bravely, for the glory of God and our great King Louis. With my brothers from Montreal looking on from among their converts it would never do for our western people to run."

"The Pottawattomies and the Illinois may be depended upon, Father," said Chastaignac. "The Hurons are less certain, and as for the Ottawas—" he shrugged.

"The cross shall lead them," vowed the Jesuit. "Ah, Denis, lad, I am reminded of something. It comes to me that I may be killed today. I have a letter for my most blessed Superior which I am anxious should reach him. You will oblige me by carrying this packet to Father La Tour who is with the Christian Mohawks from the Montagne. He will see that it is delivered."

Gladly Denis set off. . . . It took him some time to find the band from La Montagne, for the Mohawks had been slowed by difficult ground and had fallen somewhat behind. On his return to the trail he found that the last of the coureurs had passed. In a moment the main army, with Governor Denonville marching in the lead, came in sight. The Marquis had shed his long coat and was mopping his sweating face with a limp handkerchief which from time to time he flapped about his head to discourage the hordes of mosquitoes. He was hot and disheveled and very uncomfortable, but he was pushing on at a good pace, laughing and chatting with his companions as though such hardships were everyday occurrences. Watching, Denis felt a dawning respect for him.

Behind came four militia companies led by masters of the St. Lawrence seigneuries—Granville, Longueuil, Berthier, La Valterie, Le Moyne, names well known throughout Canada. Some of the militiamen wore buckskin, others their woolen working clothes, and here and there were to be seen the faded uniforms of veterans of the old Carignan regiment. Scarcely had the last of the levies passed when the head of the column of regulars, led by two drummers, rounded the curve in the trail. White uniforms and gold braid shone bravely in the sunlight, but the pace of the soldiers, though military in its precision, was slow. The sweating red faces of the heavily burdened men showed how terribly they felt the heat.

Denis realized that he had lingered overlong. Cutting through the woods, he repassed the head of the column and soon caught up with the advance guard. He had reached La Durantaye when one of the Mohawk scouts rushed up to the commander.

"See village," exclaimed the Indian in his broken French. "No warriors. Women work in fields. You hurry."

La Durantaye promptly sent messengers to the rear to inform Denonville. It began to look as though the Senecas were not expecting them. Denis dodged through the ranks of the coureurs until he gained the right flank among his own pagan Indians. Behind him he could hear muttered words running from man to man.

They began to descend a long slope, thickly wooded and crowded with bushes that hid all but the nearest Indians. On their right lay a marsh filled with alders and high grass. At the foot of the slope was a narrow swale divided by a swift stream. Beyond the swale the path mounted again through dense underbrush.

Denis was crossing the brook when he heard a shrill yell from the thickets ahead. It began with an ear-piercing high note, slid down the scale, seemed to hesitate, then rose again to a falsetto scream. Instantly it was repeated on all sides until the air was aquiver with the furious sound. Denis stood paralyzed in the rushing water.

Chastaignac's hand jerked him back to the other bank, threw him behind the trunk of an oak. Hundreds of Indians were streaming down the slope. Musket shots cracked around him. He raised his gun and looking down the barrel saw a red rag tied about an Indian's head. He lowered the musket.

"Sacré diable!" growled Chastaignac, and fired. "They have discovered our trick. Red heads everywhere. But their paint is different. Shoot, youngster, if you value your scalp!"

The rush of the warriors had carried them past the stream. Denis and Chastaignac, unashamed, turned and raced for shelter. From the hills on either side rose a pandemonium of yells and shots. Denis could see the coureurs crouching behind any available protection, fighting the Indian in his own way. The Christian Iroquois stood bravely, but the Ottawas had vanished.

As soon as they saw the French were determined to stand, the Senecas took to cover. Suddenly a tall warrior stood forth from behind his tree and shouted something in Iroquois. Denis could just make out the words. "Cowardly dogs of Christians. Come on. Afraid."

One of his Christian Mohawk brethren sprang out and stood, arms folded across his chest, crying, "Shoot, Seneca. We do not fear. But shoot straight, for I will not miss."

The Seneca fired at the last word. The bronze figure of the Mohawk never wavered. The Seneca dropped his gun and waited, erect and unmoving. The Mohawk gun flashed and the Seneca toppled. There was a babble of furious cries, taunts, jeers. . . .

Meanwhile, confusion reigned to the rear where the ambushed Senecas had swept down from their hill coverts to surround the French. They had correctly estimated the advance guard as a force somewhat larger than their own, but had made the serious mistake of thinking it the whole army. From where he stood Denis could see the first companies of militia as they came into the fight. The sight must have surprised the Senecas, but they quickly rallied and drove home a charge that broke the ranks of the St. Lawrence levies. For a moment the militia wavered. Some turned and ran. Denonville appeared among them. His sword rose and fell as he whipped the men back into ranks.

With a ruffle of drums the first line of the regulars topped the rise. They halted in good order and poured a deafening volley into the woods.

Nearby, Perrot's shout rose above the din. "Are we children, to be held by a handful of Iroquois? Forward, Hurons, Pottawattomies, with your white brothers!"

Denis scrambled around a clump of oaks and started for the brook. A puffing, white-shirted figure brushed past, leaped into the water, and struck down a Seneca on the farther bank. It was the Marquis de Denonville—a faulty general, perhaps, but no coward.

A moment before the woods beyond the stream had seemed empty. Now each bush sprouted a warrior. Invaders and defenders were everywhere inextricably mingled in hand-to-hand fighting. Denis shot at a half-glimpsed savage whose face bore the Seneca war paint. As he hastily reloaded a young officer thrust past him to lunge at another enemy. A grinning Iroquois sprang from behind a tree and poised his tomahawk to dash out the officer's brains. Denis hurled his musket, butt foremost. It struck the Seneca an instant before the blow descended. A coureur leaped on the stunned warrior.

The young officer whirled. "Quick work," he approved coolly. "I am under deep obligation you, Sir Woodsman." With a smile he fumbled in his pocket and produced an enameled snuff box. "Pray accept this as a small token of my gratitude. I am the Baron La Hontan." He pressed the box into Denis's hand and was off before Denis could reply.

Denis recovered his musket and dashed on. He sighted Chastaignac's red beard.

"A good eye," panted the Gascon as Denis rejoined him. "I saw your throw. I couldn't have done better myself. But don't forget to have your knife out in such a case." His amused glance rested on Denis's belt where the knife remained snugly in its sheath.

Side by side they ran up the slope. A piercing shout rose ahead of them. Its sound was different from the ferocious cry that had rent the air at the beginning of the fight. They came out of the trees into open fields, and saw the Senecas disappearing into dense woods beyond. On top of a hill less than a mile away stood the charred remnants of a palisade and the blackened skeletons of the huts of the village of Gannagaro. Crowning the summit like squat towers were round bins where the Iroquois stored their corn.

"That ends this fight," remarked Chastaignac. "Look, they carefully burned their village beforehand. They're good scrappers, the Senecas. We've killed a few of them, but we've done them no real harm, thanks to Denonville's fort. Faugh! If only Frontenac had been here! At least we wouldn't have had to fight on a few dry biscuits."

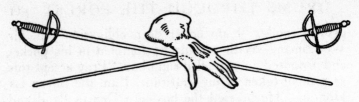

CHAPTER XI

DUEL BY FIRELIGHT

THE work of destruction had been carried out enthusiastically, and the result was somewhat as Denis
imagined the inferno to be. A pall of smoke from heaps
of burning corn hung over everything. Through it the
gaunt remains of the Seneca village loomed black and
jagged on top of the hill. Campfires glowed redly in
the desolate fields. Against the flames were silhouetted
moving figures, red and white, dancing, talking, feast-
ing. A dull murmur like the buzzing of bees, but punctuated continually by yells and laughter, rose from the
encampment. The army was consuming the spoils of
war, gorging itself on green corn plucked from the
fields and fresh pork from the slaughter of Seneca
hogs.

It was dusk of the second day after the fight. The
first had been spent on the battlefield. Cautious to an
extreme, Denonville had refused the Indians permission to follow the defeated Iroquois, for he greatly
feared another ambush. The undisciplined western allies had almost mutinied at his orders, feeling that the
French were failing in their part of the bargain. Fortunately their wrath had turned on the cowardly Ottawas who, having fled the fight, came back shamelessly
to scalp the Seneca dead. The coureurs had all they
could do to keep the peace. Some thirty Senecas had

been killed. French losses were light—ten dead and twenty wounded, among the latter Father Engelran, who had been shot in the side. The Jesuit seemed scarcely to notice his wound, so grieved was he at the conduct of the Ottawas and so proud of the steadiness of his other charges.

Denis wiped his hands on some leaves. He could have eaten much more, but Perrot had warned him that a surfeit of green corn and fresh pork would make a man deathly sick. Chastaignac reluctantly threw aside a half-eaten ear.

"Come, Denis, if we don't move now we won't for hours, after such an ill-advised feeding. Let's go and hear what the chiefs have to say to our dear Marquis de Denonville. They have been conferring for the past hour and are in a rare state of rage. I have no liking for any man who cannot think for himself, but I feel rather sorry for the dolt. He has gotten into deep waters."

Denonville sat on a cross section of a tree trunk by the largest campfire, his officers around him. At a little distance clustered the leaders of the coureurs, rather pointedly ignored by the uniformed group. All talk died away as ten Indian chiefs, one for each nation with the expedition, stalked in front of the fire to stand in a still row before the Governor.

Denonville twisted on his seat, his heavy face flushed with heat and food, his little eyes blinking rapidly. His mouth was petulant. "Perrot. Where is Perrot? I want Perrot to interpret. Tell them their father is glad to see them."

Thus summoned, Perrot, with no perceptible hesitation, complimented the chiefs on the conduct of their warriors.

"We trade no words with our brothers the French," grimly rejoined the Huron chieftain, Taouinet. "We came for war on the promise that the Iroquois would be wiped out. We have come many days' journey only to take a walk with the French among the trees and to burn corn. The Senecas are laughing. It is easy to rebuild their huts. Their kinsmen will send corn. Onontio is afraid. He will not lead us against the Onondagas. He turns away from the war trail while it is fresh. Never again will we trust the words of Onontio. We have roused the Iroquois hornets, but we have not crushed their nest. Soon they will begin to sting. For many summers they will come to our lakes to sting us. Onontio will be to blame. We have spoken."

Denis remembered the ghost drum of the Pottawattomies. Had the warrior spirit, after all, sought to warn his tribe that the expedition would succeed only in stirring the Iroquois to reprisals?

The chiefs stalked away even before Perrot had finished translating. Denonville's head jerked up angrily. "They cannot talk to me in that fashion. . . . No, on second thoughts, let them go. It would be undignified to argue with them."

"But may I point out that their friendship is vital to the well-being of New France," broke in de Callières. "We cannot afford to ignore them. Some of them will be leaving for Montreal to join their tribesmen who are bringing down the fur fleet. I suggest that the Sieur Perrot be sent there immediately to talk to them. We depend on the Indians for our beaver skins, and we owe them our protection."

"An excellent plan," approved Denonville hastily. "Sieur Perrot, you are known as a brave man and a

wise one. Start immediately for Montreal. Take four
of Berthier's habitants and the best canoe at Irrondequoit." With a wave of a white hand Perrot was
dismissed.

At the edge of the forest he paused and turned to
Chastaignac, tugging at the lobe of his ear. "I do not
like to leave, but I have no choice. François, keep
Denis with you. If there is trouble go to DuLhut.
When the forces are dismissed hurry to Michilimacki-
nac and wait for me."

"You do not need to worry about me," Denis assured him earnestly. "I will be very careful."

Perrot smiled. "I know you will try, Denis. But
once I, too, was young." He wheeled and followed the
four habitants into the black tube of the trail.

"A good man, our Perrot," said Chastaignac
thoughtfully. "If you should become one thousandth
as much a man you might count your time on earth
well spent. But come along. We'll stay away from the
Indians lest we meet Loutray and his Hurons. I want
to see Jean-Marie Lariepy, with the habitants of
Grandville at the other end of the clearing. The sound
of his good Gascon will wash this mincing Parisian
talk from my ears."

Jean-Marie turned out to be a stocky little man with
gay brown eyes. He fell into Chastaignac's arms, and
the two walked up and down, gesticulating and shouting, oblivious of all else, while Denis watched the shift-
ing crowds around the popular Grandville fire.

Mindful of the assurance he had given Perrot, Denis
kept near his companion until he noticed a group of
young officers comparing rapiers around the next fire.
His fingers twitched, unexpectedly eager to feel the

chill firmness of a hilt, the delicate strength of the dueling blade. Hesitantly he drew nearer.

One of them looked up, caught his eye and gave him a friendly nod. Denis recognized the officer named La Hontan who had given him the snuff box after the Seneca fight. "So, my friend, you know rapiers as well as tomahawks? Which of these would you prefer?"

Paying no attention to the supercilious glances of some of the officers, Denis eagerly took sword after sword, whipping and bending them until he returned to La Hontan's, a slender blade with a plain guard and graceful quillons. It was so well balanced it seemed to move of its own accord.

"The others are fine," he said diplomatically, "but this one a man could—"

"Could follow through hell," cried La Hontan, clapping his hands delightedly at the choice.

The clank of accouterments and the sounds of new voices caused everyone to look up. "It's the Governor, making his nightly inspection," said one of the officers.

"Pray be at ease, gentlemen," said Denonville ponderously. "I trust, Baron La Hontan, you have posted sentries to watch the Ottawa camp."

"It has been attended to, sir."

Denis waited, the rapier still in his hand, feeling uneasily that his woods outfit made him conspicuous amid the bright uniforms.

A figure moved out of the shadows behind the Governor. Even before he could see the face distinctly Denis recognized the powerful shoulders, the slouching walk of Loutray. A chill ran down his spine. For an instant their eyes met. He saw Loutray glance at the group calculatingly and turn with a veiled look of triumph to whisper something in the Governor's ear.

"What?" Denonville demanded irascibly. "Who's that? Where?"

Loutray's hand swung up and pointed straight at Denis. "There he is, Your Excellency. The runaway apprentice I spoke to you about, the one who stole from Maître Pezzard. With your permission I will take him back with me. Maître Pezzard will be lenient, I know."

"Yes, yes. I remember. Pezzard spoke about it too, some months ago."

Denis found himself looking into the small cold eyes of the Governor.

"What have you to say for yourself, sirrah?"

"I say it is a black lie, sir. I never stole. I left because my life was threatened. That man is a traitor and so is Pezzard—"

"Silence!" bellowed Denonville. "How dare you speak so of your betters! No wonder you sought the woods riffraff! By all means take him, good Loutray. Your work is done here. You may go at once."

Desperation and rage made Denis forget all caution. "So this is your justice, is it?" he cried. "You can't call Perrot riffraff. They're all better men than you'll ever be. I'll die before I go back."

A thunderstruck silence succeeded his words. One of the officers gasped. The Governor's face grew purple.

"Take that young cub and deliver him to Pezzard with my compliments," he barked. "Tell him to give him a sound flogging." Abruptly he wheeled and strode away into the darkness.

Four Hurons moved out of the crowd. Loutray

circled the fire toward Denis, smiling a little. "Come, my boy, and be thankful you're getting off so easily."

Something cold and hard settled in the pit of Denis's stomach. Almost without volition he swung up the rapier. He was ashamed that the blade was shaking. "Don't touch me," he said hoarsely.

With a snarl Loutray snatched out his knife and leaped, quick as a pouncing cat. Denis lunged. The point of his rapier pricked his enemy's shoulder. He sprang aside.

Cursing, Loutray flung down the knife and snatched a sword from one of the officers. In the firelight it whipped across Denis's vision, a thin and terrible flame. The whicker of it against his own weapon steadied him. He was suddenly conscious of the silent circle of staring men. Would he remember all Giles had taught him in the grass-filled moat of the old castle? He would have to, for Loutray was a swordsman.

The blades flickered, clicked, played with each other. Loutray thrust in high quarte, his elbow up and bent slightly. Denis recognized the stroke, parried and lunged almost in a single movement. The point of his rapier tore a jagged hole in Loutray's jacket near the heart.

"The lad is no apprentice," murmured one of the officers.

But Loutray profited by his mistake. He fought more cautiously now, guarding himself well and never giving Denis a moment's rest. Through the two blades Denis could feel the iron strength of his opponent's arm. He kept his gaze fastened on Loutray's narrowed blazing eyes. He circled cautiously, feinted, missed his footing by a fraction of an inch and felt a sudden hot flame in his shoulder. Loutray was smiling again. Denis retreated, on the defensive, tiring a little. How long could he last?

A heavy hand flung him aside. Chastaignac leaped in front of him and engaged Loutray's blade. "When you fight, you pig, pick someone your own size," he growled.

Denis attempted to push him away, but La Hontan's grip restrained him.

"Let's see what you can do against a Gascon." There was a joyous ring in Chastaignac's voice. "Your father," he continued conversationally, "swept out stables, and your mother was not as good as she might have been. And as for you, you are gallows' meat, but I am going to save the King's hemp by spitting you like a roasting fowl."

Inexorably he was pushing Loutray back, maneuvering him so the light was in his eyes. All the time he kept up a running fire of talk so gaily insulting that the officers, despite their fear of the Governor, began to chuckle. Loutray fought, tight-lipped, grimly, his breath whistling through his nostrils.

Denonville, unfortunately returning by way of a neighboring campfire, heard the commotion.

"What's this?" he demanded, pushing his way angrily through the crowd. The officers paled. The Governor had issued explicit orders against dueling.

One of the staff knocked up the swords. Others seized the combatants.

"My faith!" roared the Marquis. "Do you want to go to the galleys?"

"Ah, but we were not fighting, Your Excellency," protested Chastaignac. "We were merely exercising—settling a wager. Was it not so, gentlemen?"

"That's a lie," panted Loutray. "When I attempted to take that boy he sprang at me sword in hand. I was forced to defend myself. Then this *sale chien* took his part. They tried to kill me."

The Governor's little eyes darted from one to the other. "Captain St. Aubin, is this true? Why did you allow it?"

The abashed officer admitted that Denis had menaced Loutray with the rapier.

"Guards," bawled Denonville. "Take that red-haired man away. Tie him up. If he escapes, your lives will be forfeit. Do you, Loutray, proceed as I directed."

There was a wild melee of flailing fists and tumbling forms as half a dozen guards dived at Chastaignac. Two soldiers seized Denis and held him despite his struggles. Chastaignac, overcome by numbers, was dragged before the Marquis.

"Coureurs to the rescue!" he shouted. "DuLhut! La Durantaye!"

With cold deliberation a soldier struck him over the head with the butt of his musket. He swayed, then tumbled to the ground.

Denonville looked down at him coldly. "By all the Saints!" he gritted. "Do they think they rule Canada? Loutray, take your prisoner. Gentlemen, let us go."

La Hontan's fingers gently removed the rapier from Denis's grasp. "I'll find the Sieur DuLhut," he whispered. "It's best to go now, quietly. We'll do all we can."

Rough hands jerked Denis's wrists behind him, bound them tightly with rawhide thongs. Loutray permitted himself a smile. "I'm only sorry," he murmured, "that I must take you all the way to Quebec before—" He left the rest unsaid.

Surrounded by the Hurons, Denis was dragged, stumbling, across the fields toward the trail to Irrondequoit.

CHAPTER XII

THE MAGIC BOX

AT THE head of Irrondequoit Bay Denis's captors left the broad trail and plunged into the forest. From occasional glimpses of the North Star he knew they were holding steadily eastward. Toward dawn they halted for a brief rest, and the Hurons, making sure that Denis was securely bound to them, went promptly to sleep. Loutray propped himself against a tree trunk and dozed. But exhausted as he was, Denis found sleep impossible. He lay as tense as a trapped rabbit, straining his ears for sounds of pursuit and hearing only the early morning twitter of sleepy birds or the scuttle of small woods creatures.

Five days passed, and still the nightmare journey continued. Denis estimated that they must have come well over a hundred miles. The pace grew somewhat more normal as the chance of pursuit by friends of DuLhut lessened. During all this time Denis and Loutray had not exchanged so much as a word. Sometimes Denis felt his enemy's narrowed eyes upon him and was moved to give stare for stare, but what was the use of talking? Always he was kept tied to two of the Indians. Sometimes the other two Hurons would disappear, to return later with a brace of ducks or some rabbits.

Late on the afternoon of the fifth day Black Fox,

who had been examining the ground with attention, suddenly stopped in a little glade and threw up his hands in warning. Denis was jerked to a halt.

"A small party passed not long ago," the Huron explained in a whisper. "I think we are catching up with them."

Loutray scowled. "Better sneak ahead and have a look."

Black Fox disappeared noiselessly. Loutray and the other three Hurons waited. Denis was torn between hope and fear—hope that the strangers were coureurs, fear that they were Iroquois. Though even if they were the latter, he reflected, his lot could scarcely be much worse. Fifteen minutes passed.

There came the pad of moccasins, and Black Fox burst from the spruce thicket ahead, running for all he was worth. Behind him came five Indians, racing silently after their quarry. Loutray raised his musket and fired. The five figures kept on.

Swiftly Loutray slashed the two Hurons loose from Denis so they would have the use of both hands. But they had no intention of facing the Iroquois. They paused only long enough to snatch up Black Fox's musket and powder horn.

An arrow arched over the fugitive and quivered in the ground at Denis's feet. "Onondagas," gasped Black Fox as he passed.

Loutray whirled and followed. An arrow caught one of the fleeing Hurons between the shoulder blades. The man stumbled, flung out his arms, and pitched to the ground. Denis crawled behind a rock.

One of the Onondagas swerved toward him, knife in hand, but a grunt from the leader drew him back, and all five disappeared up the valley. The Huron lay with his face in the pine needles. A streak of sunlight fell across him, lighting the colors in the feathers on the arrow.

Ineffectually Denis attempted to work his hands free. His first impulse was to hurry up the hillside and lose himself in the thickets. But any Indian child would be able to follow such a trail as he would leave, and if they saw him fleeing he might join the dead Huron.

He did not have long to wait before the five Iroquois returned. One had a new scalp at his belt. Ignoring him, they clustered around the body on the trail. One stepped from the circle, drew out the arrow, wiped it on his breech clout, and returned it to its quiver. He drew his knife, and putting his foot on the neck of the dead Huron, grasped the scalp lock. The knife flashed in the light as it circled. There was a tearing sound. When the Onondaga straightened the scalp lock dangled from his hand.

Then they all turned to look at Denis.

One made a movement forward, war club upraised, but was stopped by a companion, a young warrior who had shaved half of his skull and had bound the remaining hair into a towering knot held in place by thick grease and two black feathers. He stalked forward, circled Denis completely, and returning to his place began a speech to his companions.

To his surprise Denis could understand a little of what he was saying. Between Chastaignac and Le Sueur he had picked up a few words of both the Oneida and Onondaga dialects of the Iroquois language, but of more help was the similarity of Iroquois to Huron. The young brave was recounting how the party had left the town of Onondaga to intercept strays from the expedition against their brothers the

Senecas. The spirits had not smiled. Denis lost some
of the next words, but he understood the phrases "two
scalps, two guns" and the look of gratification that
accompanied them. Then the young orator was pointing at him and looking very pleased. He made the
motion of scalping and shook his head. Apparently
he was saying that it would be too bad to convert a
valuable French prisoner into a mere scalp. The other
four grunted approval and Denis began to breathe
more easily. He was sure, as he looked at them more
closely, that they were all under twenty years of age.

The one who had spoken began to search him for
valuables. There was nothing he seemed to think in-
teresting until his fingers struck the snuff box La Hontan had given Denis during the fight at Gannagaro,
which he had since carried in an inner pocket of his
belt. The Indian drew it out. His eyes widened at the
sight of the pretty blue enameled toy.

"*Ganoron*—it is valuable," said Denis in Huron.

The other held the box gingerly, turning it over and
over, smelling it, shaking it against his ear. At last
he set it upright on his palm and gazed long and solemnly at the portrait of Louis XIV on the lid. The
gaping warriors crowded about him.

Denis tried to tell them how to open it. Finally the
leader understood that he was to press the spring.
As the lid flew back the Indians grunted in alarm
and gave ground. Inside the lid was the portrait of a
lady in pink flounces and white wig. After an awed
inspection of this picture the young warrior, looking
rather like a curious small boy, glanced inquiringly at
his prisoner.

Up to this time Denis had had no purpose in mind
other than a vague hope that interest in the box would

soften his captors' hearts. But now a brilliant idea popped into his mind. Turning his back so he could pinch some of the snuff between the forefinger of one bound hand, he sniffed loudly. "Smell," he commanded.

Obviously torn between a desire to impress his comrades and reluctance to tempt the unknown, the young leader set the box upright on a nearby stump. He extended his right hand cautiously and took a tiny pinch. The others watched intently as he lifted it to his right nostril and gave a loud sniff. His sneeze was so violent and sudden that it nearly threw him backward off his feet. His companions retreated to safety, but continued to watch with horrified interest. The warrior shook and sneezed as though he could never stop. Tears ran down the red stripes of his war paint.

"Magic," said Denis, underlining the moral. "Great magic."

The warriors looked at him with vast respect.

"Magic," agreed the leader weakly. "Smell."

Each warrior in turn cautiously took a tiny pinch, and each sneezed until he was weak and crying. Through it all, remembering Perrot's advice, Denis had not moved a muscle of his face.

When the last warrior had recovered, the box was snapped shut and tucked into the breechclout of the leader. With Denis in their midst, two Indians holding the cords, the party loped down the valley.

It was nearly dark when they stopped to eat. Denis's hands were untied. He was given a handful of a mixture of twice-parched ground corn and maple sugar, the only food carried by Iroquois warriors on the warpath. Then he went to sleep between two of the Indians. Any attempt to escape, even the slightest movement, would have roused the others, for the cords were tied firmly to their wrists.

All day they trotted through woods where squirrels flashed in the sun, shattering the stillness with cascades of chatter, and deer snorted their surprise. Just before sunset they halted where a stream had eaten into a clay bank to form a shallow cave. After the unvarying meal the snuff box was brought forth again and set in their midst.

Then began one of those long slow Indian discussions, where each speaker must trace his family history and detail his own prowess before he can arrive at what he really intends to say. Denis appeared to drowse. From the words he knew and others he could guess he decided they were arguing the advisability of showing their magic box to the elders of the tribe. One felt the elders might confiscate it for their own uses; another argued that the possession of two scalps and a prisoner was glory enough; while a third maintained that their discovery of the magic box would give them vast and lasting importance. Finally it became apparent that the leader, whose name was Atotarho, was for hiding it temporarily. The others agreed.

It was nearly noon the next day when they crossed a wide creek and mounted a little hump of a hill covered with maples and elms. On the crest they halted. With infinite care, Atotarho wrapped the snuff box in a piece of birch bark, cut away a square of moss at the foot of a slender elm. He hollowed a space beneath and deposited the box in the hole, then replaced the moss and tossed the handful of earth into a hollow tree. Denis fixed the spot in his mind.

Ten minutes later they came out of the woods into fields of tasseled corn where squash and pumpkin vines lay thick underfoot. In the midst of the fields stood a hill crowned by the palisaded town of the Onondagas. A stream ran around two sides of the stronghold and was lost to sight among the fields beyond. A well-worn trail led up a steep narrow spur of the hill. Terror of what might await him in this savage town made Denis falter for a moment, but he forced himself to note each detail in case he could by some miracle escape from the stockade.

The five young warriors halted. Atotarho called "Ko-he" twice, and then repeated the words twice more, telling the people how many scalps the party had brought back.

Naked children ran out of the gate and down the hill. They were followed by women, a few warriors and several old men. Other women came from the fields, carrying the long pointed sticks they had been using to cultivate the corn.

Atotarho called out something Denis did not understand. The Indians looked pleased. Warriors drew their clubs; women sought sticks; children scrambled eagerly for small stones. They began to line the path. Atotarho turned to Denis and pointed to the gate of the village. *"Haugh,"* he grunted.

He was to run the gantlet! Denis caught his breath. There was no chance to bolt now. Better to risk the gantlet and wait. He shook a lock of hair out of his eyes. He dropped his head on his chest and hunched his shoulders as high as his bound hands would let him. He started to run.

Sticks thwacked his back. A stone numbed his right arm. A glancing blow from a club sent him spinning dizzily off his course. A child squealed with pleasure. He ran on, staggering when the blows landed solidly. The stab of pain as a sharp stick gashed his thigh cleared his head. He choked back a cry as something struck the shoulder Loutray's rapier had scratched at Gannagaro. His ears rang with shouts, jeers, laughter, the shrill cries of women and children.

Then it was over, and he was leaning against one of the gateposts, drawing his breath in panting sobs. Through sweat-dimmed eyes he saw the five young warriors proudly approaching with the two scalps held aloft on a pole, saw the people surge around them.

Quick fingers untied the hard knots at his wrists. Someone urged him through the gate and steered him toward a bark hut. Hands pushed him down. He slumped to the ground, his back against the wall of the lodge.

A middle-aged woman clad in a shapeless skin garment gave him water in a bark bowl. He drained it eagerly. Next the woman brought a bark dish heaped with corn mush and bits of tough venison. When he had finished he said *"Hineaweh—I thank you."*

In an open space beyond the rows of lodges the men of the village had seated themselves in a big circle around the five returned heroes. The young warriors stood in the center of the circle looking rather self-conscious but delighted with the attention they were receiving. In turn each intoned his account of the expedition, giving, it seemed to Denis, the details of practically everything that had happened to them—except the finding of the magic box.

He listened dully for a time. The older warriors sat immovable and silent. In order to hear better Denis got up and walked to the hut nearest the council circle.

The woman who had fed him followed a few paces in the rear, but no one offered to stop him.

Atotarho began to speak, pacing back and forth as he chanted and gestured. He was showing his youth and inexperience by speaking too quickly, and his gestures lacked the flowing quality of good Indian oratory.

After some moments a warrior in a dirty loin cloth arose from his place behind Atotarho and began in solemn dumbshow to imitate the youth. His tall, thick-set body swayed grotesquely as he minced back and forth, making awkward gestures with his pipe, exaggerating the speaker's nervous eagerness. On his square hook-nosed face was an expression of droll earnestness as he silently mouthed his imaginary oration. Some of the Indians were watching him with broad grins of appreciation. One laughed outright. Atotarho pretended not to be aware of what was going on, but by the way he stammered and lost the thread of what he was saying it was plain to see that his dignity was suffering acutely.

As more and more of his hearers turned their attention to the mimic the young Indian's gestures grew more frantic. He pointed to Denis, raised clenched fists above his head, beat on his breast, stamped on the ground, made the motions of piling fagots for a fire. All of which was duly copied by the other, while the circle roared with laughter.

Denis turned to the woman. "Who?" he asked pointing to the joker.

"Otreouatie," she chuckled.

Denis was astonished. So this middle-aged ungainly comedian was the renowned orator whom the French called Big Mouth! The wisest and wiliest of the Iroquois warriors! Perrot had spoken with admiration of how boldly he had defied Governor LaBarre three years before, and how astutely he played the English against the French to the advantage of his nation.

Atotarho sat down sullenly. Otreouatie slapped his leg and bellowed with mirth at his own joke. A chief stepped into the cleared circle. Their young brother, he said, was not a skilled speaker, but there was sense to what he said. The French made war on the Senecas and by so doing made war on all Iroquois. . . . The black eyes of the seated warriors turned to Denis expectantly.

With a determined effort he squared his shoulders and walked into the circle. Inwardly he was in a panic. How could he hope to sway them? How would Perrot go about it? . . . He folded his arms and began to speak in halting Huron, hoping most of them could follow.

The Onondagas were wise people, he began. They had not hated the French like the misguided Senecas. They had received the Black Robes and allowed them to set up the Cross in this very town. He was trying to speak slowly, impressively. He avoided gestures lest he make the wrong ones and ruin his cause at the start. He stole a glance at Otreouatie, fearing mockery. But Big Mouth was squatting on the ground, smoking vigorously. His bright eyes watched, unwavering as a hawk's. . . .

Denis went on, making the speech last as long as possible. He described the beauties of the Onondaga country, extolled the bravery and honor of his captors. . . . Grunts of "That is reasonable" helped. . . . He had long admired the Onondagas. He knew they would care for him as for a brother and send him back to Onontio, the great chief of the French. Then the

French and the Onondagas would smoke the calumet.

There was a pause as he ended. A warrior chief stood up to answer.

"I am Garakontie," he announced with dignity. "You know that I do not speak falsely. Our prisoner has said words as soothing as the wind in the Month of the Ripening Corn. He has told us truly of the Black Robes, of our country and our warriors. But he has forgotten that we do not take orders from Onontio. We are free people. If it pleases us to destroy the nation of the Andastes, to scatter the Eries like leaves before a storm, that is our affair. Onontio has taken the side of our enemies. He has burned the towns of our brothers. He has killed Seneca warriors. So our prisoner here has become as the white dog. He must bear the sins of Onontio. By slow death we will avenge our brothers and honor this youth who has no fear. I have spoken."

"That is right. . . . That is reasonable," chorused the warriors.

Denis could think of nothing to say. It took all his will power to remain standing. He did not want to die at the stake. He knew what the Iroquois could do by way of torture. Nails pulled out one by one, ears wrenched away, eyes burned out, body stuck full of blazing splinters . . . How could he make them change their minds? . . . His shuddering brain could think of nothing.

Then Otreouatie got to his feet with a grunt. He rubbed his bare stomach with one hand and yawned elaborately. "Garakontie, the wise and powerful, has spoken words of wisdom," he said negligently. "I am neither wise nor powerful. But I am hungry. The sun nears the tops of the trees. I can smell cooking meat.

My belly is like the inside of a drum." He gave a comical skip toward the row of huts and called back over his shoulder, as if in afterthought, "Maybe the prisoner can sing and dance for us tonight. We'd be foolish to burn him up too quickly, if he can offer other amusement. But do as you wish. I go to eat." He lumbered away.

The chieftains conferred together. "Let us eat," announced one after the conference. "Then the Frenchman will sing for us."

Denis's self-appointed servitor tapped him on the shoulder and pointed to one of the lodges. He followed her dully.

The house stood near the center of the village. It was about thirty feet long, twenty wide and fifteen from floor to apex of the roof. The walls and roof were of long strips of elm bark laid against an inner framework of poles and held in place by outer poles, to which the bark strips were lashed with tough vines. The only openings in the walls were the two entrances at either end. Across the top of the doorway was a slab of wood on which a creature resembling a turtle had been carved, showing that the families living within were members of the powerful turtle clan.

Inside the house it was very dark. Denis choked on the overpowering smell of drying fish, smoked meats, coarse tobacco and stinging woodsmoke. Three fires burned on the earthen floor. Above each was a small hole in the roof, altogether inadequate as a chimney. Men and boys squatted by the fires. Women stirred the contents of iron kettles. Around the walls of the lodge ran two sleeping shelves, like a row of double bunks in a barracks. From the rafter poles hung strips of fish and venison, dried squashes, bundles of herbs, war clubs, tomahawks, bows and arrows, hides, bowls of bark.

The woman's hand guided him toward the center of the place. He was conscious that every eye was fastened on him. She gave him a bowl of succotash with a large piece of meat in it. He seated himself on the lower sleeping shelf. She brought him a bark cup filled with a sort of tea made from hemlock tips and flavored with maple syrup. When he had had all he wanted he looked into space and said, *"Hineaweh,"* as was the custom. Then there was nothing to do but wait.

The Indians let him alone, either out of politeness or indifference. The food was warm inside him. He wouldn't have been here to eat that succotash, perhaps, if Otreouatie had not intervened.

He wondered if Otreouatie had done it on purpose. He began to clutch at the fantastic hope that the orator for some obscure reason was trying to help him. But why hadn't he spoken out in council? Perhaps because he didn't want his people in their present mood to suspect him of favoring the French, for that would weaken his position. Maybe the subtle savage wanted to save him as a hostage. Perhaps he realized that in the present state of affairs the killing of a Frenchman by his tribe would be disastrous to his future plans. He needed the French to counterbalance the English. Otreouatie was not one, from what Perrot had said, to carry all his eggs in one basket. . . .

With new hope in his heart Denis waited to see what would happen. If he was spared tonight he must think of some way to escape.

Chapter XIII

"BIG MOUTH"

It grew dark. He could see people passing toward the council ground. The men in the long house rose and went out. The woman motioned to Denis to follow them. At the door he looked back and saw her watching him.

He stepped around two dogs that were voraciously licking the inside of an overturned kettle and walked slowly toward the gathering place. His hands were shaking. The roof of his mouth was dry as dust. He saw the gleam of a fire. He rounded the last hut and the tenseness left him as he saw there was no pile of brush at the base of the pole where captives were tied.

"Sing," commanded a chief.

Denis stood alone, his arms folded on his chest. The firelight gleamed on a red-bronze ring of smooth limbs, hard bodies, intent eyes. Silent as foam drifting on water, women and children pressed in to stand close-packed behind the waiting warriors. Hard stars looked down from a velvet sky.

What should he sing? He seemed to see old Giles seated by the hearth polishing an ancient halberd. As he polished he sang. What the song had originally been Denis never knew, but Giles had said it came down from the Northmen who had settled in Normandy centuries ago. It was a rollicking, triumphant account of a knight's foray on his rival's lands.

Denis began to sing. He put lots of vigor into it and did not worry when he lost the tune, for the Indians' idea of music was very different from that of white men. He sang all of the song he could remember, shouting the chorus twice into the night. When he ended there were scattered grunts of approval.

After that he sang everything that came to mind—nursery jingles like "Au Clair de la Lune," ballads he had picked up from the coureurs, snatches of the "Chanson de Roland." He sang until his voice became a croak. Then he danced—part of a dance some Ottawas had performed before starting after the white fish of Lake Superior, a Pottawattomie war dance he had seen at Fort St. Antoine, a harvest dance from the Norman fields. At last his knees gave way from sheer weariness and he sat down abruptly. A warrior brought him a cup of water sweetened with maple sugar.

"Didn't I say the prisoner would give us a lot of entertainment?" Otreouatie's pipe spilled little flakes of burning tobacco as he waved it in the air to emphasize his words.

"It is true," said the audience.

Denis got to his feet. He must sing one more song, something for them to remember. A hymn he had heard at the cathedral in Rouen came to him, a solemn, rolling anthem, as resonant as the Latin it carried. He lifted his hands above his head. Somewhere he found enough voice to carry him through the first stanza. He dropped his hands, and holding his head high, marched across the space toward the lodge where he had eaten. The circle of Indians opened for him.

Denis was awakened early the next morning by the whimpering of a peevish baby. He shifted wearily, trying to ease his aching arms and legs. His captors had taken no chances; they had bound him securely to one of the posts that held up the hard bunks.

Through the smoke vent overhead he could see the sky was a faint gray. The air in the lodge was stifling. The sleepers grunted, snored, gurgled. Two warriors lay across the entrance.

Wide awake now at the sense of the peril the new day would bring, Denis tried to think of some way to escape. They might want to start torturing him at once. How he wished Perrot were here! He would know what belief, what superstition, to play upon to gain freedom. Denis frowned up at the dried fish hanging above his head.

At the far end of the long house someone began an indistinct babble, as though protesting in his dreams. Slowly the hole in the roof turned from gray to blue. As it changed color the idea came to Denis.

From beneath lowered eyelids he watched what he could see of the preparations for breakfast, the stirring of live coals, the mixing of corn meal with water for the eternal mush called sagamite. He felt a touch on his shoulder but he lay still, eyes obstinately shut. Later someone untied his bonds and shook him gently. Still he pretended sleep. At last the men finished their breakfast and left. The sun was high now. He could hear laughter and talk outside.

Keeping his eyes tight shut, he said loudly, *"Orenda,"* which he knew meant "The magic one." The lodge fell silent around him. *"Orenda,"* he said again and swung his feet to the floor. Moving stiffly as though waking from a trance, he strode out of the long house.

At the entrance of the opposite lodge he saw through half-closed eyes Otreouatie squatting in the dust, telling some story to a group of admiring youngsters, while his blackened pipe smoked in his hand. Denis moved haltingly to the center of the street and said once more, "*Orenda.*"

Otreouatie rose to watch him. "How does it happen that our prisoner who last night knew no words of our tongue has now found one?" he asked.

Some of the older warriors, Garakontie in their midst, drew near, watching suspiciously. Denis shivered violently and rubbed his eyes as though awaking.

"An eagle told me," he answered in Huron, making his voice as deep as possible. "An eagle brought me a few words of the People of the Hills, but not many, for the words which roll like the waves on the shore cannot be learned in one vision." He raised his arms before him, palms down. "My brothers," he began, "a dream came to me, a dream which showed me the way to great magic." He dropped his arms. "But I did not learn enough words in my dream to tell you the way," he added in his normal voice.

Otreouatie waved his pipe. "Speak in the tongue of Onontio, my brother. There are many of us who have learned it from the Black Robes—or from prisoners," he added with a grin.

If they had as hard a time understanding his French as he did theirs it might be difficult, thought Denis.

"I was asleep in the lodge of the Turtle," he began, speaking very slowly. "In my dream I saw an eagle, golden as a poplar tree in autumn, fly through the door of the lodge. It spoke and said to me, 'Magic. Come with me.' Then the eagle turned and flew from the lodge of the Turtle. I rose from my bed and followed.

I went out of the door, out of the fort, following the gleaming eagle. The night was black as the head of the loon, but the bird shone like the golden sun. Across the fields of corn I followed into the forest. The bird rose upward. Still following, I rose upward, too."

He did not dare open his eyes to see the effect of his words. "On the branch of a tree, straight as an Onondaga arrow, the glittering bird halted. 'Beneath this tree,' it said to me, 'lies magic in a painted box.' Its voice was as sweet as water over white pebbles. It said, 'Show my people the magic in the painted box.' I looked at the ground beneath my feet. I looked up. The eagle was gone. The light was gone. Again I was in the lodge of the Turtle. All was darkness. I slept."

He opened his eyes. Had it worked?

Otreouatie removed the pipe from his mouth. "Our brother has been fortunate, favored beyond all. He has told us a story as wonderful as that of our own Hiawatha when the Great Spirit spoke to him alone. But can our brother show us this magic?"

Garakontie took the hint. "Will our brother guide us to this magic?"

"I will," Denis answered in Onondaga. He turned firmly toward the gate of the fort. The warriors fell in behind him.

Down the hill, through the corn fields, into the woods he went, his heart pounding for fear he would not be able to find the right hill, the right tree. He climbed one hill, watching narrowly for landmarks. He must show no hesitation. Ah, there it was. He remembered it by the forked tree on the near slope and the creek beyond.

"It was here," he said.

At the top of the hill he made surely, but without

haste, for the elm where the snuff box had been buried.

"There lies the magic in a painted box."

Garakontie's deep tones rang out behind him. "Let one of the warriors of the Turtle Clan search."

A young man, who would obviously have preferred to face a Huron tomahawk, knelt at the foot of the elm. The square of moss lifted easily. The youth hesitated, then began to paw out the loosened earth. He held aloft the snuff box.

Denis, his arms folded, watched, fairly shaking with fright. Now that the hoax was successfully started, he began to fear that their knowledge of tobacco would ruin his plan. Had they ever seen snuff before?

"Open the box," commanded Garakontie.

The watchers drew closer. A spring lid was new to the finder's experience. By accident he struck the catch and the painted lid flew back, spilling a little snuff on his hand.

"It is powder," he exclaimed. He raised his hand to his nose and sniffed.

It was Otreouatie who plucked the box, unspilled, from the young man's hand as he fell into a paroxysm of sneezing. He pranced; he doubled up as though in a war dance; he wept; he coughed. Motionless, the Indians watched. At last he leaned against the tree, sniffling.

"It is strong magic," announced Garakontie.

As his eyes left the stern old face Denis caught the expression on Otreouatie's. It was blank, even more blank than usual, but his glance flew from the box to Denis, then back to the box, then inspected the younger warriors. In his eyes was a gleam of amusement. Neither Atotarho nor any of his four comrades was present. Denis paled as he realized that Otreouatie understood everything that had happened.

"Our brother has indeed spoken truly. It is great magic," he agreed smoothly. Denis relaxed. "Our brother is a mighty youth. Our young men who made him captive should be proud. We have seen a thing that requires long thought."

"That is reasonable," assented Garakontie hastily. "We must hold a council. We must consider carefully what shall be done."

The rest of the morning Denis sat in the sun in front of the lodge of the Turtle. As a magician he had a certain dignity to uphold; besides he could think better by himself. He was sure now that Otreouatie did not want him to die; but the orator could not be counted on to try openly to save him. The diversion created by the magic box might be temporary. The snuff couldn't last very long, with everybody taking a pinch of it. If he were going to get away he should do it before another sunrise.

At noon the woman brought him food and water and seated herself beside him while he ate. After some moments of silent inspection, she pointed to herself and said in broken French, "Me, Royannah."

Denis pointed to his chest and replied, "Me, Denis."

The woman nodded and smiled and said in a mixture of bad French and Onondaga, "Brave man ought to live with other brave men. My brother dead three moons. French brother take his place, live with Onondagas."

She was offering to adopt him into the tribe to take the place of her dead brother. All Indians, men or women, had a right to save prisoners by adoption. It would mean life and safety. For a moment he was tempted, then sorrowfully he shook his head. He would have to live always with the Onondagas—actually become one of them—or break a solemn pledge of friendship and allegiance. While there was any other hope for life he could not do that.

"Denis thanks Royannah," he said. "It is a great honor. But he would sicken and die so far from his own people."

She smiled regretfully. "The eagle is brave, and so is the wolf, but they do not live together," she admitted with resignation. She rose and reentered the lodge.

Hours passed. The shadows of the long houses were slanting far across the hard-packed earth when Denis felt a tug at his belt. He looked around quickly. A hooked stick disappeared into the lodge. Behind it he saw Royannah's face. She beckoned.

With a glance at the women pounding corn, at the somnolent warriors sprawled in the shade of the neighboring houses, he yawned, stretched, rose lazily and strolled into the Turtle lodge. Royannah crouched beside the sleeping shelf. She had snatched up a deerskin and was busily chewing the edges, pausing to take a stitch with a bone needle, and then chewing again to make the hide pliable. How she had contrived to get rid of the other occupants he did not know, but for the moment they were alone.

He sat down. The skin slipped from her lap. In recovering it she crept closer until she was almost beside him. Something cold and hard slid into his hand. His fingers closed on the handle of a knife.

"Tie on belt. Hide down leg," she whispered.

There was a long rawhide cord attached to the haft.

He slid the knife inside the left leg of his trousers. A soft skin pouch filled with parched corn found its way into his hand and disappeared down the other leg. He tied the ends of the strings to his belt and pulled his shirt out so that it hid the knots.

"*Hineaweh*," he said huskily.

"Otreouatie," she whispered. "He send. He say you go away tonight. Maybe we fix. Maybe not."

Denis grunted to show he understood. His smile was grateful.

Royannah moved away and went on with her sewing. Denis rose and walked to the door, where he leaned against the wall for a time, then, with another yawn, threw himself on the nearest shelf. The knife and the bag of corn nestled snugly against his legs.

Since he might not have another hot meal for a long time, he ate as much venison and rabbit as he could at supper. There was an air of excitement in the lodge. He was treated with a studied deference in which there was much caution, a little fear and some hatred. In the dimness he could feel black eyes watching him. Children planted themselves in front of him, staring at every mouthful he took.

The warriors finished their suppers and left the hut hastily for the council ground. Obviously they did not want to miss a word of the long discussion of the prisoner and his magic. The women and children gobbled what the men had left, tipped over the kettles for the dogs to clean, covered the fires. One by one they disappeared after the men. As Royannah left she brushed by him. He felt the touch of her hand on his arm. It was a timid caress, light and fleeting, that seemed to say a little sadly, "Good luck." He rose to follow.

At the door a young brave, tomahawk in hand,

barred the way. "Prisoner stay here," he said in a French that Denis could scarcely understand. "They talk magic . . . bird . . . Onontio. Black Robes . . . Garakontie and Otreouatie, they say you no hear. Me watch . . ." He shook his head regretfully. "Me no hear, too."

He indicated that Denis was to sit down beside the door. His manner was sullen, whether from personal dislike, or disappointment at being given a task that kept him from the meeting, Denis could not fathom. He was obviously somewhat afraid of his prisoner. Denis resolved to be careful, knowing that a false move might result in the guard braining him out of panic.

Already the town had emptied itself into the circle around the council fire. Yellow flames leaped high against the dusky blue of the evening skies. The young brave sat facing Denis. Most of the time he kept his eyes on his charge. Sometimes he glanced quickly toward the show he was missing.

The speeches had begun. The present speaker sounded like Atotarho, but the words were an indistinguishable murmur. Denis grinned to himself. Atotarho would not dare tell about hiding the snuff box now. Otreouatie was probably enjoying himself hugely listening to the youth's fabrications.

An hour later, when it was quite dark, Denis recognized Otreouatie's bellowing voice. He could almost make out the words. The guard, torn between duty and desire, rose to hear better.

Denis had been growing more and more impatient. He wished he knew what plan the orator had made. Perhaps he had no plan. Perhaps Otreouatie was merely holding the crowd, trusting that the prisoner would act for himself. Denis leaned back slowly.

With infinite caution his right hand stole behind him, groped inside the door. The guard was intent on the council. Denis pushed himself back inch by inch. His fingers touched the pile of utensils they had been searching for—a bowl, some wooden spoons, a bear skin. They groped on until they felt the cool, gritty roughness of a stone mortar and pestle used for pounding corn. They closed over the handle of the pestle. Slowly he gathered his feet under him. Quick as a panther he sprang.

The young warrior's head swung round as Denis leaped. His mouth opened. Denis struck. The Indian went down with a gurgle scarcely louder than a whisper.

It took but a moment to drag the unconscious brave into the long house and heave him onto the sleeping shelf. Another to tie him with thongs cut from hanging joints of meat. A piece of deer hide served as a gag. The whole business was over so quickly it scarcely seemed real. Otreouatie's voice still rolled from beside the fire.

Denis crept out of the back door of the hut and slid as soundlessly as a ghost toward the gate of the palisade.

At the last house he flattened himself against the wall until he could be sure, by the glow from the great fire, that the gate was unguarded. He had counted on the overpowering appeal of eloquence and he had not been mistaken. With a little prayer of thankfulness, he sped across the intervening space and out of the gate.

As fast as he dared he ran down the spur of the hill and through the fields. In the east a faint glow, translucent as mother-of-pearl, heralded the moonrise. A little breeze rustled the leaves of the corn. His ears strained for the sudden roar that would tell him his flight had been discovered. But behind him he could hear only the voice of Otreouatie diminished by distance to a faint murmur.

The forest closed around him.

Chapter XIV

PERILOUS TRAILS

LONG before he was out of breath he slowed to a walk. Although he must put as much distance as possible between himself and the town before daylight, he had to decide at once which way he was to go. The west was out of the question because of wandering bands of Senecas. South, the Onondaga lands stretched away toward the doubtful safety of the English colonies. To the east lived the Oneidas and Mohawks. Beyond them, along the Hudson, were the English. The Onondagas would expect him to make north for the end of Lake Ontario and Canada. He would go east for several days and hope to throw them off his track before turning north for Montreal.

Ruefully he went over his equipment. His moccasins had been new at Michilimackinac and were still in good condition. His buckskin trousers were dirty but whole. He had a knife, and a little food, but no tinder, no gun, no ax. It was a long way to the St. Lawrence. He shrugged his shoulders. The next thing would be to hide his trail.

After half an hour of swift progress he heard the gurgle of a small stream. He plunged joyfully into the chill water and waded with the current. Even in the stream bed he moved cautiously lest he scrape moss from exposed stones or leave footprints in the shallows where the water was too quiet to wash them out.

He realized the difficulty of eluding the painstaking Iroquois trackers, but if he waded far enough he might at least delay the pursuit. Otreouatie could be counted on to hold the warriors for several hours. His greatest danger was that someone meanwhile would accidentally discover the bound guard.

The moon was touching the western treetops when he came to a long sloping shelf of bare rock where his footprints would dry out quickly. The dawn glow warned him that he must soon find a hiding place for the day. On his right was a rocky ridge overgrown with spruce trees. Spruce would be ideal; it was thick, and its ladder-like branches were easy to mount. Halfway up the ridge he came to a large tree and began to climb.

Fifty feet above the ground four branches spread out side by side like the sticks of a fan. He swung himself over them, hooking a foot under the farthest. Then he tied himself to the trunk by the leather string on the bag of corn and passed his belt under a branch, buckling it over his legs. With his head against the trunk, he went to sleep.

Sunlight in his eyes woke him. His foot, still twisted beneath its branch, was numb. He was instantly alert, but only forest sounds—the murmuring of a brook, the distant mew of a hawk, squirrel chatter—could be heard. With a sigh of relief he flung his arm back along the branch. His hand touched a face.

Time stood still. He could not have moved if the forest had been full of shrieking Iroquois. But nothing happened. His hand groped over the face. He felt nose, cheekbones, cold and strangely dry. He snatched his hand away, found his knife, slashed the cord that bound him to the trunk and swung around to face the menace.

He saw a still figure bound to the branches, an Iroquois, perhaps a chief, for he wore a collar of white wampum. He was dead—had been dead so long that he had turned into a mummy.

Wiping his forehead on his arm, Denis slid back against the tree trunk. His first impulse was to get to the ground and run. But he realized as the shock passed that he could have found no better hiding place than a burial tree. He climbed as high as he dared and spent the day there above the old Indian. Sometimes he dozed. Much of the time he tensely watched the forest, seeing in every movement of leaf or branch a creeping enemy. Once he examined the knife he clutched so tightly. It was not very sharp and the point was broken. It was no prized possession Otreouatie had sent him!

At sunset he munched some of the parched corn. It was not very filling, but a handful a day sufficed an Indian hunter, and it would have to do. Then he came down, took a long drink at the brook, and set off at a fast walk. As darkness came on he was forced to go more slowly. Ages later the moon rose and he was able to make faster progress and correct his course. Before dawn he crossed a wide Indian trail running east and west. He decided that it probably led to a village of the Oneidas, whose towns were not far from those of the Onondagas, so he followed it until it dipped into a spruce-choked valley, where he left it to find a stream and eat before climbing another tree.

Sun and a squirrel woke him again. Stiff though he was, he stretched and yawned luxuriously, Onondagas forgotten in the warmth of the sunlight and the scent of the spruce. If he only had some way of carrying water aloft with him he would ask nothing more. He glanced below to where the stream should be. Instead of dark water his eyes fell on a narrow ribbon of brown needles—the Indian trail. Last night he had walked in a circle and returned to the trail he thought he had left. Now he would have to stay in spite of the danger. His face reddened at the thought of what Chastaignac would say about his stupidity. An hour passed without incident. He began to feel sleepy. He moved up to the next ring of branches, as much to keep awake as for any other reason. He didn't dare go to sleep now.

Hardly had he settled himself in the new position when an Indian, moving in a long easy stride, came around a bend in the trail. Another followed him. They were so close when Denis discovered them that he could see every line on their paint-daubed faces. He remembered having seen the first one around the council fire in Onondaga. He clung to his perch like a leech, scarcely daring to breathe lest the keen ears of the warriors should hear.

To his horror the leader stopped squarely beneath the tree. Denis prepared to sell his life as dearly as possible. But neither of the warriors raised his head. The leader said something and pointed down the slope toward the brook. They were thirsty.

They came back in a few minutes, wiping their mouths on the backs of their hands and sat down for a rest. Despairingly Denis waited for the moment that seemed inevitable, the moment of discovery when he would have to choose between surrender and hopeless battle. But luck was with him. The warriors got up soon and followed the trail to the east.

Half an hour later Denis dared to move again. Even then his hands trembled so that he nearly lost his hold.

For four nights he pressed on, snatching bits of sleep in trees by day, growing more starved and weary with each mile. His store of corn was nearly gone. He grew so weak that climbing trees was hazardous. On the last morning he did not even attempt to hide in the usual way but lay down in a thick covert of ferns. When he awoke he realized dizzily he must have meat. His skill at making deadfall traps was of no use without a hatchet. So, careless of danger, he began to throw rocks at the chattering squirrels.

But he gave up after an hour. Either his aim was faulty or the squirrels were too nimble. He began to look for rabbits, chipmunks—anything. At last, toward sunset, he managed to creep close enough to a browsing rabbit to knock it over with a stone. Even had he had means of making a fire he would not have dared to light one. So he cut up the rabbit with the knife and devoured the flesh raw. He did not attempt to travel far that night. When he awoke it was noon.

The next dawn he stood on a low cliff overlooking a river, wondering dully if it were the stream marked on Perrot's map as the Mohawk, which flowed east into the Hudson. If so, it was time for him to turn north. Wriggling down through the bushes, he reached a little copse of elders and birches.

He had taken off his moccasins and tied them around his neck, preparatory to swimming the stream, when he saw four canoes paddled by eight Iroquois warriors. He ducked into the bushes and watched. The canoes turned toward the opposite bank and were beached on a sand bar where Denis had planned to land. The warriors stepped out, raised the canoes, and bore them to a fringe of bushes beyond the bar. Two Indians returned and brushed away the marks of landing with branches. Then the whole party climbed the opposite ridge and disappeared toward the northeast.

Now he would have to make new plans, for with a wandering band of Iroquois ahead of him the route was closed. Eastward lay his only chance, and that meant the river. He peered from his covert. There was no sign of life except for a doe drinking daintily upstream.

He swam across slowly, risking the chance that a guard had been left over the hidden boats. The cold water chilled him; the current carried him beyond the sand bar to a thick growth of alders. He drew himself slowly up the bank and picked his way carefully, with many stops to reconnoiter, toward the thicket.

The canoes were hidden better than he had expected, but he found them, at last, in a little swale. He chose the smallest of the four, and shouldering the two maple paddles, dragged it to the river. It was a heavy, clumsy, unstable boat, made of elm bark cut in one piece, with the ends sewn together—not nearly so good a craft as the birch-bark canoes of the Ottawas.

At first, with the sun in his eyes, his muscles aching, and the canoe unresponsive to his paddle, he was acutely miserable. But as the steady flow of the river carried him past steep cliffs and green banks his spirits rose. It was better, at least, than groping his way through dark forests.

Late in the afternoon he sighted an Indian village on a high hill above the south bank of the river. He ran the canoe into a marshy creek and waited anxiously for night. When it was quite dark he drifted down with the current, steering noiselessly past the glowing campfires on the hill. From what Perrot had told him he judged that the village was the westernmost of several Mohawk towns. If so, it might be better to quit the river now and strike out north. But drifting with the current was so much easier than walking that he decided to go on until daylight.

For hours he drifted through the inky blackness, dozing in spite of himself, rousing when the canoe grounded on sand bars or was caught by snags. Once the sound of rapids awakened him just in time. With a frantic shove of his paddle he beached the craft. He tottered out and fell asleep sprawled on the river bank.

The next morning he devoured the last grains of his corn and set out in broad daylight, desperate now in the realization that he must get past the hostile villages and find food before another dawn. . . . Sometime that afternoon the sight of a second Mohawk settlement on the southern bank roused him from his lethargy. A single spark of determination to live made him automatically swing the canoe toward the north shore.

A sunken log, lodged by some freshet, ended his voyage. The bright sun and the tiny waves kicked up by an east wind made the water almost opaque. Too late he glimpsed the dark shadow beneath the surface. A pointed branch pierced the fragile bark and slit it like a knife cutting cheese. The canoe filled and rolled clumsily on one side. Denis threw himself out. His head struck the log. A last flash of moving water and bright sunlight, then darkness.

A voice had been speaking unintelligibly above him for several minutes before he opened his eyes. He didn't want to open them at all; he had no desire to come back to harsh reality. But open them he did. He perceived a pair of high moccasins and above them stained buckskin trousers. As his gaze traveled upward he saw a shirt, a grizzled beard hacked to a point, and a narrow face with high forehead and strange gray eyes.

The white man nodded with satisfaction and said something to the Indians who stood beside him.

"I don't understand," said Denis. "I am sorry."

To his surprise the man answered in French, an accented French, but much better than the poor attempts of the Onondagas. "I thought so," he said. "I was sure you were French, though what you are doing here is beyond my understanding. Never mind. We will talk of that later." He smiled suddenly. "I am glad you do not speak English, since it gives me an excuse to speak your language, the most elegant of tongues, Greek always excepted."

One of the Indians touched him on the arm. The man heard him through, shook his head mildly, and answered in one short phrase. The Indian protested, then lapsed into sullen silence. The man dropped to his knees beside Denis.

"We reached you just in time. But there is no injury save a slight bump on the head. You look starved. Can you sit up? There, that is better. Now take a drink of this rum; it will put new life into you."

It all sounded very queer to Denis. Perhaps the man was mad. But the promise of food drove all other thoughts from his mind. He choked down a swallow of fiery liquid. With the help of the stranger's arm he rose to his feet and stood rocking uncertainly.

"I thank you, sir, for saving me from the river," he said. "If you will give me a bite of food I'll be ready to go my way."

The man shook his head. "Food you shall have," he

smiled, "but not freedom. It grieves me to tell you
that you are a prisoner of war. Look you, these two
Mohawks of mine have recognized your French speech
and are all for scalping you. If I left you alone they
would get word to the village and you would not live
a day. I am going to take you to Albany, where Governor Dongan can assure you of protection in accord-
ance with the rules of civilized warfare."

"But—but I want to go to Montreal, sir," protested Denis.

"You would never get there," replied the bearded
man. "Come, my boy, believe me when I say I am
doing this for your safety."

Denis grasped at his knife. A thin, strong hand
clutched his wrist. With the utmost good humor the
man took his knife away.

"Food is better for you than fighting. Come, get in
the boat."

Meekly Denis walked to the long birch-bark canoe.

When the canoe was well out in the stream the stranger cut a generous slice off the roasted hind quarter
of a bear that lay in the bottom of the canoe and
watched with approval while Denis ravenously chewed
it.

"It is high time we introduced ourselves," said the
other, when Denis had finished the slice. "I am Horace
Alexander Kirk, once classical tutor of Magdalene
College at Oxford, in England, now trader-at-large.
These two tawny—er—gentlemen whose Mohawk
names are too discordant for ordinary use, I have
nicknamed 'Meum' and 'Tuum,' or 'Mine' and
'Thine.' " He leaned forward suddenly with a pathetic
eagerness. "You have not, by chance, studied Latin?"
he asked. Denis admitted that he had. "Ah, then, you

will recognize the conceit," chuckled Kirk. "When you consider that the Indians have no sense of property rights and are always purloining anything they may happen to desire at the moment, don't you think 'Meum' and 'Tuum' are rather good? A little joke, you know. 'What is thine is also mine.'" His laughter was pleasant to hear.

"That is amusing," said Denis politely. "Perrot would like it. My name is Denis de Lornay."

Kirk bowed as formally as he could in his cramped position. "Perrot did you say? Not Nicolas Perrot? . . . I should like to know him. Too bad politics keeps such as us apart."

The food in his stomach and the soft slap of waves against the canoe lulled Denis into a drowsy state of resignation. The English did not seem so bad, after all.

He was confirmed in this opinion as he grew to know Kirk better. On the second day the scholar told him why he had left his sheltered life at Oxford. He had grown tired of pale living, he said, and having read accounts which pictured the redskins as noble children of nature who lived a glorious life of freedom, like Man before the Fall, had decided to cast his lot among them. "Alas," he smiled, "though they have their virtues, the picture was not quite accurate. Still, I am content."

Late that day the canoe grounded beside the palisade of the little Dutch settlement of Schenectady. Denis, almost himself again, returned with interest the curious stares of the people. They left before daybreak the next morning and toward the middle of the afternoon passed out from the Mohawk, now grown broad and placid, into the Hudson.

A mushroom of wood smoke, pale blue against the

yellow of the evening sky, was the first indication of the English town of Albany. Under the straining efforts of the Mohawks the canoe swept downstream. A wooden palisade bordered the river bank and climbed a hill to join the walls of a fort which stood out blackly against the sunset. In the shadows below steep roofs, a church belfry, a large house, loomed indistinctly above the palisade. Here and there a window opened yellow eyes into the dusk. Two lights appeared on the wall. A rusty axle squeaked. A cowbell gave forth an intermittent, mournful clank.

Kirk beached the canoe deftly. He shouldered one pack and Meum took the remaining two, while Tuum swung the canoe over his head. The trader led the way to the gate, now easily distinguished by its lanterns. A soldier was standing on guard. Kirk conversed with the man at some length.

As they passed through the gate Denis was conscious of small houses crowded closely together along the narrow street. The lighted doorways showed people sitting on little stoops.

"The Governor is at the Stadt House with Peter Schuyler, our Mayor. We shall go there at once," Kirk explained.

The Stadt House, not far from the gate, was three stories high. In the hall, dimly lighted by two candles set in sconces, Kirk and Denis waited until they were announced. Governor Dongan was seated at the head of a sturdy table so long it nearly filled the room. A pair of five-branched silver candlesticks, sturdy as the furniture, threw light on the white walls. But Denis had eyes only for the man at the head of the table, the blustering enemy of his people who, it was rumored among the habitants, sent the painted Iroquois

to massacre French women and children on isolated
farms.

He saw a thickset solid figure dressed in a suit of
dark plum-colored satin. White lace bloomed at wrist
and throat, in odd contrast to the stubby red hands
and fleshy chin. The features were large and heavy.
The nose was straight, the forehead broad. It was a
stubborn, irascible face—the face of a man accustomed
to command, but it was not mean or vicious. Peter
Schuyler, sitting at the Governor's right, was soberly
dressed in black. He had a long straight nose and
thin lips.

Kirk made a half-bow to both men at once. "I beg
Your Honor to pardon the intrusion at this hour, but
I have here a prisoner whom I wish to put under your
protection immediately. He is a Frenchman, strayed
from Denonville's forces. I trust you will hold him
safely, sir, until an exchange can be arranged."

The Governor shook his head impatiently. "That
means added expense for the town. A ransom, now—"

Kirk translated the speech, and Denis assured him
there was no one who could afford to ransom him.

"Well, we'll hold him until something can be arranged." Dongan drew a piece of paper toward him.
"Tell him to give his parole he will not try to get
away, and he can have the run of the town."

Again Kirk translated, adding that he advised giving the parole, as the cells in the guardhouse were
small and dirty. Denis hesitated. If he gave his parole
he could not escape.

"Tell him," he directed finally, "that I will give my
word that I will not try to escape during the day, but
I make no promise from sunset to sunrise."

"Od's blood!" exclaimed the Governor, staring.

"This young pigeon talks as if he were King Louis, or better still, our stubborn old enemy Frontenac himself." He laughed, summoned a guard, and making Denis an ironic salute, said, "As Your Honor pleases. Take this boy to the guardhouse, Jenkins."

Kirk was troubled. "Come tomorrow morning to see me," he told Denis. "My house is in Maiden Lane."

"Gladly, sir," replied Denis and followed the trooper to the street. They turned soon at right angles and climbed a steep hill, crossed a ditch, and entered the gate of the fort. Other soldiers showed him to a black and odorous cell.

Chapter XV

SKONAKOA

ON THE muster ground before the blockhouses Denis stood with his face to the morning sun. The gate of the fort lay invitingly open, but he hesitated, not knowing the regulations governing prisoners. A young officer saw his perplexity and yelled unintelligible directions, waving his arm toward the town. Denis walked out. He was halfway down the hill before he realized he had not been given breakfast.

Two rows of sturdy neat houses stepped down the hill toward the river. Some were built of logs, others of weathered boards. Tiny dormer windows peered from roofs of thatch or colored shingles. From the lower corners of the roofs large water spouts projected far over the streets below. Each door gave onto a wide stone step. There was a pleasant air of Dutch stolidity and order about the place.

At the foot of the decline Denis paused until he saw a man come out of one of the houses. "Maiden Lane? Kirk?" he said inquiringly.

The man pointed to the next street and held up four fingers.

Alexander Kirk opened the door. "Come in, my boy," he cried. "I was about to begin breakfast. Will you join me?"

Denis murmured his thanks and slid onto the narrow bench by the table. Kirk filled a pewter plate with corn-meal porridge from the iron kettle in the fireplace. Next he forked thick pieces of ham out of a skillet and poured two mugs of beer.

When he had finished eating Denis examined the home of his strange friend. The great stone fireplace with its blackened andirons and kettles filled much of one end of the room. A massive chest of drawers, a high-backed settle covered with a bearskin and a four-poster bed with canopy and curtains were the principal pieces of furniture. On shelves above the chest pewter and copper gleamed dully. The floor was of scrubbed brick. From the rafters hung strings of peppers and corn, hams, slabs of bacon. Through a small window he could see a vegetable garden and a bark lodge beneath an elm.

"Meum and Tuum live there when they are in town," explained his host. "Some families keep their Indian retainers in their attics, but I prefer a certain distance between us. Do you like my home? I bought it complete from a worthy burgher named Gerritse."

He detached a long clay pipe from the wall, filled it with tobacco, and lighted it with a coal from the fire. Crossing one leg over the other, he puffed meditatively.

"From the way you spoke last night you evidently entertain some thought of escape," he remarked at length. "Let me warn you against trying to cross the mountains in the north. Heaven knows how you got as far as you had when I found you. It would be better to wait patiently until you are exchanged. Your name goes to Quebec tomorrow in a dispatch the Governor is sending to your Governor. They often correspond, albeit," he added dryly, "their letters to each other are usually hot enough to burn the hands of the messengers."

"But I don't want to be exchanged," blurted Denis, thinking only of what would happen to him once he was delivered to Denonville. "I mean," he went on hastily, "I want to go back west to my friends."

Kirk gave him a quick penetrating look. "Very well, we'll say no more about it," he agreed. "Meanwhile, I will try to make your stay pleasant. Would you like to see the town?"

Denis replied that he would. The more he learned of the place the better it would be. "You are very kind, sir," he said. "I will always remember."

"Tush, lad," grumbled Kirk, knocking out his pipe. "Repay me by telling your people that we are not all wild Irishmen like Governor Dongan."

The morning was spent in loitering about the small city. They repassed the Stadt House, largest building in Albany, its gabled roof a landmark to voyagers on the river. They strolled by the Lutheran Church, with its tiny burying ground, and back by the Dutch Reformed Church, which stood like a blockhouse in the middle of Yonckers Street at the foot of the hill below the fort. Returning to the river bank, they lingered before inns with swinging signboards and watched the soberly dressed people. The men wore round woolen caps, breeches and stockings, buckled shoes and blouses with wide linen collars. The colored skirts of the women were covered with broad aprons, and their sleeveless bodices were topped with small white ruffs. Kirk was greeted with respect by all.

At the end of Handlaar Street stood one of the city gates, guarded by a brass cannon. The palisade,

which entirely surrounded the city, was made of pointed
pine logs planted upright in the ground.

Kirk suggested that the study of English and Mohawk might help to pass the time. Denis was more
than willing. He really liked learning a new language,
for strange tongues seemed to come to him easily. The
trader began the lessons that very afternoon. Within a
fortnight Denis had acquired enough Mohawk to speak
a few simple sentences and enough English to understand some of the conversation that went on around
him.

The hot summer days passed quickly. Denis could
have enjoyed them if he had not been constantly worried about how to make his escape. He had been unable to think of any plan, for each night he was locked
securely in his cell in the well-guarded fort and he was
not yet reduced to the thought of violating his parole.
But each day his sense of impending fate deepened.
Surely the messenger would soon return from Quebec,
and then it would be all up with him.

The white people, whether Dutch or English,
treated him kindly, but he had to be constantly on the
watch for trouble from the Indians, who, at this season, came to Albany in great numbers, sleeping at
night in log houses built for them outside the walls
and loafing about the streets during the day.

He spent as much time as possible with his scholarly
friend, who was never too busy to give an hour or so
to lessons or to discussion of lands and peoples and
the countless books he had read. By the latter part of
August, when he had been in Albany four weeks, he
began to feel fairly at ease in both English and Mohawk, so diligently had he pursued his studies.

Then Kirk and his Indians left for a trading trip among the Oneidas. They would be back, Kirk said, before the first snow. But something told Denis it would be a very long time before he would again see the kindly man, so incongruous and yet so happy in his frontier life. For days after he left Denis wandered forlornly about the town, dreading the return of the Governor's messenger.

One afternoon about the middle of September he was strolling aimlessly up Yonckers Street when he became uneasily aware that he was being followed by a young Indian. Turning into Handlaar Street, he quickened his pace. He glanced back and saw the Indian rounding the corner. There was something vaguely familiar about him. At first Denis thought he had seen him in the Onondaga village, but then he was not so sure. He doubled on his tracks and entered the lane which led past the Lutheran Church to the Indian burying ground. There, in the shadow of the stockade, he wheeled and waited. The Indian stopped twenty paces away and raised his hand in the gesture of peace.

"My brother is brave, but his eyes do not remember," he said in Huron.

Denis caught his breath.

"My brother does not know me," stated the other placidly. "Does he remember this?"

From the folds of his breechclout he produced a sheath and drew out a knife. The sunlight flashed on the metal. With a start Denis recognized his own silver dagger that he had given to the Huron chief on the French River to ransom the Mohawk captive.

"Skonakoa!" he cried, for the stranger was indeed

the young warrior he had first seen chanting his death song in the bow of the Huron canoe.

"I give my comrade back his knife," smiled the Indian. "The Huron dog does not need it any more. He has gone," he added more explicitly, "to the land of spirits."

Joyfully Denis took the knife and sheath and slipped them on his belt. It was good to have the heirloom back, regardless of the means Skonakoa had taken to recover it.

"How did you know I was here?" he asked in Mohawk.

"We have ways of knowing what goes on in the town of the English," stated Skonakoa in his own tongue. "Five nights ago I came back from the Huron lands and heard of the new French prisoner. The winged words of my people told me you were that captive. I came to see. Now I will help you through the forests to your own tribe. I am glad you are learning the speech of the People of the Flint."

"I am glad my brother has returned," said Denis. He halted, wondering how to explain the matter of the parole. "When chiefs make a treaty," he began, "they swear by their manitou to keep it."

"That is true."

"I have made a treaty with the Corlaer, the white chief in the Stadt House, that I will not leave Albany while the sun shines. When the sun is asleep I could go—except that then I am locked up in the fort."

"Treaties should not be broken, but I did not know the white man had such respect for them," observed Skonakoa ironically. "We will leave in the dark. My brother is locked in the blockhouse? I will have to think about this matter. Let us meet here tomorrow when the sun is as high as it is now."

"I will be here," agreed Denis.

Skonakoa raised his arm in salute and stalked away.

Buoyantly Denis climbed the hill to the fort. He was a trifle early, but he wanted to be alone to think. It was wonderful to be able to hope again.

The guard at the gate informed him that Captain Moore, the spare New Englander in command of the little garrison, wished to see him. Puzzled, Denis entered the Captain's cabin. The Captain received him gravely and spoke through his French interpreter.

"The messenger has returned from Quebec," he said. Denis turned pale. "I am sorry to have to give you bad news," the other continued. "The Canadian authorities did not offer an exchange. Instead, I am ordered by the Governor to keep you locked up day and night."

"But—but why, sir?"

The Captain shifted in his chair, hesitated. "All I know is that those are my orders. They evidently don't want you in Quebec. I don't know why. Do you?"

Denis didn't, at first. He was stunned. But he had plenty of time to think about it. Some hours later he reached a conclusion. Pezzard was undoubtedly to blame. He had somehow prevailed on Denonville to refuse the exchange. Pezzard was in traitorous correspondence with the English, LeRoux had said. He had probably sent a private message to Dongan—that would explain the new orders. But why had the merchant changed front? Denis could think of only one logical explanation. It was that Pezzard had begun to fear that he knew too much to be allowed to come back to Canada. The merchant might be planning

some new villainy. If such were the case, he would try
to keep clear even of accusations by an apprentice. Oh,
why was Denonville so blind?

His cell was one of four in a stoutly built log house
which stood between the barracks cabin and one of
the six-gun bastions of the fort. Its single window
faced the parade ground where a sentry walked beat
at night. The opening was quite small, and its three
iron bars made it impossible for him to wriggle out
as he had in Quebec. The door gave on a narrow
passage between the cabin and the barracks. It was
securely barred outside.

The next day dragged endlessly while Denis racked
his brains for a plan. He wondered what Skonakoa
would do when he failed to appear at the appointed
place. Everything now depended on the Indian lad.

After eating his meager supper Denis passed some
time in reviewing his Mohawk vocabulary. Later he
took stock of the few possessions he had bought with
money Kirk had insisted on lending him. He had a
blanket, new moccasins, new leather breeches, a flint
and steel. He had not tried to buy a hatchet for fear
of arousing suspicions. Outside the sentry called the
hours.

The midnight change of guard had just taken place
when a dim glow through the window attracted his attention. From his window he could see that it came
from the red reflection of flames against the stockade
wall. He heard shouts and the sound of running feet
on the hard earth. The reflection brightened.

Fearing that the fort was burning, Denis hastily
rolled up his blanket. What if they forgot him! He
tugged at the door, began to pound on it. He gave it
up after a moment and started back to the window

when he heard a scraping sound beyond the door, then the clank of metal and a little screech like that made by a staple as it is drawn out of wood. The door swung open. An invisible hand grasped his wrist.

"Come, my brother," whispered a voice.

A shadow fled down the passageway toward the parade ground. In the shelter of the blockhouse it paused, pointed to the right, and darted out into the ruddy glare. Like a flash it slid along the wall and vanished into the next lane. Feeling as conspicuous as the Stadt House, Denis darted after it.

Without an instant's hesitation Skonakoa led through the gloom to the base of the stockade. His hand groped along the face of the wall.

"It is a rope," he grunted. "Climb."

The rope tightened as Denis trusted his weight to it. In a moment he had one leg over the wall. He felt the rope grow taut again as Skonakoa followed. He jumped, and landed with a jarring impact on the soft earth of the ditch. His Mohawk friend dropped silently as a cat beside him. Together they made off into the darkness.

Chapter XVI

HUNTING LANDS OF THE IROQUOIS

UNTIL dawn they sped through pine forests. There had been only one pause. Skonakoa had stopped a short distance from the fort to pick up a bow and some arrows, a hatchet and a bag of parched corn from a cache near a spring. For the rest of the night he had led at a tireless pace over the smooth carpet of pine needles. The sound of wind through the treetops was like the steady march of rain up a lake. In the graying light of the new day they came to the Mohawk River.

They stopped to rest before attempting the crossing. Skonakoa searched along the bank until he found a flat piece of driftwood large enough for his purpose. The blanket, weapons and pouch of corn were tied on top of the slab, and the two companions, each taking one side of the makeshift barge, waded into the chill water and began to swim. On the other bank they shook themselves like dogs, regained their breath and set off at a slow trot toward the northwest. Denis was brimming with questions, but there was no time for them now.

At noon they dropped wearily beside a stream fully thirty miles from Albany. They ate a few grains of corn and snatched a brief nap. When they awoke they drank from the brook and silently resumed their journey. Knowing that they were not yet safe from Mohawk trackers Governor Dongan might send after them, they pressed on, with short rests, all that night. At dawn they stopped in a fern-grown valley. Here they ate a good deal of their corn and curled up for a long sleep among the sheltering fronds.

They did not waken until late afternoon, but Skonakoa was no longer in a hurry. Leisurely he helped himself to some more corn and observed that they would do some hunting soon. Though they said nothing about it, they were both rather proud of themselves. Denis asked his companion how he had managed it all.

Skonakoa grinned. After their talk in the burying ground he had gone to an Indian outside the city wall and bought the bag of corn which, with the weapons, he had stowed in the cache. Early the next morning he had come back to the city and had managed to steal a small keg of whale oil, a rope and a crowbar. They had come, Denis learned, from the shed of the trader Rondevoort while that worthy Dutchman was at breakfast. Skonakoa said that had been easy, but the difficult thing had been getting them through the streets to Kirk's garden. Fortunately he had not been challenged. The stuff had been hidden in the empty lodge of Meum and Tuum. After that he had gone to the fort, loitering inside the palisade until he memorized the details of the place.

He had been somewhat puzzled at not seeing Denis on the streets during the afternoon. When Denis failed to meet him he had made inquiries and had learned of the Governor's orders.

After it had grown thoroughly dark he had carried the keg of oil to the ditch beside the palisade, some distance from the gate of the fort. Next he had gathered a number of dry sticks. When the opportune moment arrived he had broached the keg, poured oil on the sticks and on the logs of the palisade and started a roaring fire with a spark from his flint. While the soldiers came running to put out the blaze Skonakoa had fled to the farther bastion, where he had lassoed the point of one of the logs with his rope and pulled himself over. He had pried off the staple of the door with the crowbar. The whole thing had been easy.

Denis concealed his wonder that the Mohawk had done all this for him. He knew enough not to thank him or show undue admiration, so he merely said, "It was well done. My brother is as resourceful as the beaver and as brave as the wildcat."

The tone of Skonakoa's grunt showed that he was pleased.

In turn, Denis told of his adventures since they had parted on the shore of Lake Huron—his travels in the west, the expedition against the Senecas, and his captivity in the Onondaga town. When he described the magic snuff box the Indian boy slapped his thigh and laughed.

"I will call you Orenda, 'the magic one,' " he chuckled. "Besides, it is easier to say than 'Den-ee.' "

He rose and pried off some spruce gum that had oozed from a lightning-made scar on a nearby tree. Denis took one of the nodules and began to chew. Soon the dustlike particles welded into a smooth mass which would long retain the sharp aromatic flavor of the spruce.

"Where does my brother lead me?" he inquired.

The Indian boy replied that he did not know. Where did Orenda wish to go

"But surely you will return to your own people?"

The Mohawk waved his hand carelessly. "When it is cold," he said. "A Mohawk goes where he pleases. I will see you safe among your friends."

By this time Perrot, Chastaignac and DuLhut had probably given him up for lost, reflected Denis. They would be needed more than ever to keep the western Indians in line. On the other hand, if his suspicions about the reason for Dongan's orders were valid, he might be able to do some good in Quebec. Perhaps LeRoux could hide him and help expose Pezzard.

He decided to ask Skonakoa's advice, so he told him enough of the story to make the problem clear. The Indian's keen eyes watched him until he had finished. Afterwards Skonakoa remained silent for a long time. At last he spoke.

"A cunning warrior does not make the same mistake twice," he said. "A wise man does not try to fight a whole tribe. The English are not yet ready to take the warpath against Onontio. There is no hurry. My brother can learn patience and craft from the fox."

"That is wise counsel," admitted Denis. He would do what he really wanted to do—go west. But how? The Huron country would be dangerous for them either singly or together. The southern route by Niagara and Lake Erie would, it seemed to him, have fewer hazards. Skonakoa at least would not be in danger from his Iroquois kinsmen along the shores of Ontario. From Niagara Denis could go on alone. They might even encounter a coureur flotilla on Lake Ontario. The best thing to do was to strike for the eastern end of the lake. . . . He told Skonakoa what was in his mind.

"It is good," was the reply. "But we must go to the northwest to avoid the Onondagas. I know the trails through our hunting grounds in the land of the lakes and high mountains. But first we must have meat."

They surprised a deer drinking at the edge of a small pond at sunset. After stuffing themselves as full as they could, they cut off some of the hind quarters to take with them.

The next day's march brought them into high broken country where Denis occasionally sighted mountains away to the north. There was an invigorating crispness about the air. At night it was cold, so that they were glad to supplement their one blanket with a bed of balsam boughs.

Although the country was uninhabited, there was still danger from hunting parties, Skonakoa said. Once he pointed to a series of scratches on the north side of a birch tree telling of an Oneida party of twenty warriors which had passed two days before. Once they heard the echo of a musket shot and increased their pace to a long, distance-devouring lope. The country grew rougher and wilder. It was filled with lonely little ponds where trout jumped with sudden plops, where deer browsed placidly on water lilies. A lovely country of rocky precipices, towering tree-clothed hills and tumbling brooks as cold as ice.

One morning they came to a hill higher than its fellows, bare on top where fire had burned the trees the year before. Denis determined to climb it to see more of the rugged land to the north. The sky was so deep a blue that he imagined if he stared at it long enough he could see the stars beyond. His skin tingled in the chill air. There had been a frost, and the birches had turned to gold.

Disapproving but acquiescent, Skonakoa led the way up the steep incline, dropping to hands and knees as the trees gave way to blackened stumps, the white flower called immortelle and tufts of charred moss that crumbled at the touch. On the very crest they crouched beside a bare rock, careful not to show themselves against the skyline.

Denis stared as if he could never look his fill. Directly below lay a lake like a sheet of blue glass. Around it stretched the rich carpet of the forest—the dark green of spruce and pine, flaming patches of hard maple, red as a cardinal's robe, and splashes of birch and beech, yellow as candles burning before an altar. Beyond, mountain after mountain, dappled with cloud shadows, rolled up like ocean waves, rounded or sharp, green at first, then dark blue, and finally, far to the north, into peaks such as he had never before seen, misty in the distance.

The soft sound of scraping pebbles caused him to turn his head. Skonakoa's hand had closed over a stone, clenching so tightly that the knuckles showed white. "Our land," he said, and his voice was deep. "The hunting ground of my people. The white man tries to snatch it. But it is ours, and we will hold it until our warriors are ghosts. If we lose it, we will lose our strength, like a burned and blackened pine."

With a single movement he stood upright and tossed into the air a handful of the precious corn, saying something Denis could not understand. For a moment his bronze body stood outlined against the sky, then he was once more crouching tranquilly against the rock.

Denis looked into his eyes. "You are right, my brother. When the hunting lands are lost, all is lost. May you keep them as long as these hills stand."

Silently they began to descend.

There was little trouble now about food, or at least about meat. Deer, rabbits, squirrels, were plentiful, and could be killed with arrows. Trout could be caught with grubs on the bone fishhook the Indian had brought with him. A pole and a bit of rawhide string was the only tackle necessary.

At sunset they would find some hollow, near a lake if possible, where the glow of the fire would be hidden. Skonakoa would use dry branches so there would be no smoke. Meat would be roasted in the coals, and though it was never quite done enough to suit Denis, he would eat all his share and wish for more. They would sit quietly until dusk deepened to night and stars glimmered between branches and trout ceased to rise for their evening flies. This interval of silence grew shorter each day. Sometimes the talk would turn to how people live, and Denis would tell the Mohawk as best he could of life in that other world of France. Sometimes it would be Skonakoa who would talk of Mohawk ways and point out how much superior they were to French ways, since all Mohawks are equal and all are free. Then, when the fire was only crumbling white ashes, they would fall silent, rise and seek a nearby place to sleep. Often the last sound Denis would hear would be the long and lonely wail of a loon.

One night they camped early, for they had come to a small lake and the water, shining under the setting sun, demanded a swim. Afterwards Skonakoa started the fire, then left to see if he could catch some trout. Denis fed pine sticks to the tiny blaze. This was a good life. No wonder the Indians had been happy before the coming of the white men!

Back of the fire was a dense, shoulder-high clump

of small spruces. Idly Denis noticed a sudden movement among their spiked tops. He sprang to his feet
as a horrible face appeared among the upper twigs. It
was oblong and dark brown, with staring red eyes
and mouth and black streaks on cheeks and forehead.
The red sunset flushed it to a horrid pink. All Skonakoa had told him of the sorcerers who have magic
powers, of the spirits who live in trees and rocks, of
the False Faces who visit huts by night, came to him.
He drew his dagger and moved backward, slowly, a
foot at a time, until he felt a tree behind him.

"Ha-e-e, ha-e," cried a soft high voice.

It was the call of the Little People of the Onondagas—elves who live in a secret valley filled with
boulders. Dagger in hand, he jumped forward.

The young spruces shook violently. The face disappeared. Skonakoa, doubled up with laughter, came
out of the thicket. Denis lowered his knife sheepishly.
"I wish," gasped the Indian, "you could have seen
your face. If you had not jumped so hard I would
have given you more strange sounds."

Denis laughed, at first uncertainly, then whole-
heartedly. When they had recovered from their mirth
he examined the face. It was a smooth slab of hemlock bark on which features had been drawn with
charcoal and blood. From behind the clump Skonakoa
produced two trout and a porcupine which had supplied the blood. Denis knew that according to Indian
custom he should play some trick on the Mohawk, but
he owed his comrade so much that he could not bring
himself to work out a practical joke.

That night they feasted on trout and porcupine
liver broiled over the coals.

Chapter XVII

TOWARD THE SETTING SUN

Slowly they made their way westward, lingering by each pond, sometimes spending the whole of a crisp autumn day hunting or fishing, so loath were they to quit this mountain land. Denis learned much Iroquois lore. Now he walked up hillsides with his toes turned in, measured time by the passage of the sun and referred to the North Star as *iacte ouattenties*—"that which does not move." If only Perrot and Chastaignac were here he would be content to remain in this land forever.

He was thinking of this as they followed a knife-like ridge late one afternoon. The sun slanted through the crowded pine trunks and fell in bright bars on the round leaves of the scarlet bunchberries that carpeted the ground. Suddenly Skonakoa stopped and pointed to a flicker of light below. Without a word he began to descend, sliding under the low branches, steadying himself by the trunks of trees. Denis followed.

The flicker came, he soon saw, from a pond. Dead alders stood branch deep in the water. On the opposite ridge the steep incline bore bright straight gashes, as though someone had made slides down through the poplars to the pond. For a moment he puzzled over this, then he laughed at his own stupidity. It was, of course, a beaver pond.

Skonakoa smiled companionably. "Tonight, we will not eat rabbit." He turned at right angles and crept along the face of the slope toward the head of the pond.

A cool grayness filled the little valley. On top of the ridges above them the sun still turned the tips of the pines to a golden green. Denis's eyes followed Skonakoa's pointing finger and saw, not twenty feet away, a sleek brown head moving rapidly across the water, leaving a smooth ripple like the bow of a canoe. It was carrying a stick in its mouth.

On a flat stone near the tiny stream that fed the pond Denis built a fire. It was hardly well started when Skonakoa returned with the dripping body of a beaver. "They are tame," he said. "That is because no one hunts them here. This one had just come out and was beginning to gnaw a tree."

After they had skinned and cleaned the animal Skonakoa cut off the head, remarking, "With this we may catch an otter, as with an otter's head we could catch a beaver, for the beaver people and the otter people are always at war."

They lopped off the flat, oval tail and buried it beneath the coals to be served as a final delicacy. The rest of the carcass was roasted over the fire.

The Indian boy slipped away, taking with him the head and a strip of rawhide to make a snare. Denis carried the skin to the edge of the pond and, carefully weighing it with stones, immersed it in the water, so it would keep soft.

Later, while they ate, they could hear the faint

squeaks of the beaver as they went busily about their work. At the other end of the pond a tree fell, with a sound like tearing paper. "They make their dam stronger," said the Indian. Once there came an echoing *smack,* like a paddle blade slapped down flat on the water, as a diving beaver warned his companions of something that had alarmed him. The boys held their breaths, but relaxed when, after a moment of silence, the squeaks were resumed.

That night around the fire they talked for a long time about this animal on which so much of the life of New France depended. Skonakoa did most of the talking, for Denis's knowledge of the creature was small by comparison with that of his red friend.

"The beaver is one of the animals whose spirit survives after he is dead," began Skonakoa. "This must be so, or why should the beaver be so wise? They can fell a tree exactly where they want it to fall. They are more expert in this than men. Their dams are sound and strong and can only be destroyed with great effort. What man pursued by enemies would think of making a lake around his lodge as the beaver does? The beaver know how to make the water run as they wish; in low lands where streams wind in loops I have seen ditches dug by them between the loops so that they can float poplar logs to their lodges. They do the same when they want to move a log too large to drag; they dig a ditch and float it."

"That is true," said Denis.

"I know an old man who says the beaver have their own language. I have heard him tell that he fell asleep one night beside a pond and awakened in the moonlight to see a council of beaver sitting in a circle around one who was the sachem. He was speaking to them in the beaver language and they were squeaking, 'That is reasonable.' "

He settled himself more comfortably on his back. "There is a tale I have heard about a beaver," he continued. "As my brother knows, by dreams do warriors live or die, and what they dream must come to pass. . . . There was an Oneida warrior named Howetaho who dreamed one night that he had been changed to a beaver. He woke frightened, for the beaver had been old and sick and had not long to live. He set out at once to look for himself."

"For what?" interrupted Denis, hiding his smile.

"For himself," replied Skonakoa severely. "For the beaver he had been in the dream. He searched for a long time and finally found the sick old beaver. He built it a home near the village and fed it, and in time it grew strong and well. The stronger it became the stronger and more successful grew Howetaho. Each day he would talk with it and it would advise him.

"Then, one morning, he told the elders that he must go against the Twightwies, the tribe you call the Miamis, and that he would receive his death wound in the raid. So he left. Back in his village the women saw that the old beaver had suffered a wound in his right paw. Day by day he grew more feeble. Howetaho came back at last, and the elders saw that he had been wounded in the right hand by an arrow. On the third day the beaver died. Howetaho laid himself down beside the beaver and in the morning he too was dead. Dreams do not lie."

The fire died down and the night crept closer. Denis dreamed of beaver, but he did not tell the Mohawk.

Before starting on their way the next morning they

inspected the beaver dam. From the stream bed, on the outer side, it measured a good ten feet in height. Although it appeared a haphazard jumble of rocks, logs, branches and dried mud, not a drop of water leaked through except at the bottom where seepage through the face of the dam came out as a small stream. From the crest of the dam he could see the round mass of sticks and mud that was the beaver house. Among the poplars on the bank lay peeled logs, their ends pointed and marked with strokes as though they had been cut by a small dull hatchet. Denis would have liked to spend the day watching the animals at work, but it was a long way to Fort St. Antoine on the Upper Mississippi.

Then the mountains and the lakes were behind them and they were in a country of rolling hills. Now their caution returned, for this region was frequented by Onondaga hunters.

One day they stood on a little knoll overlooking the blue waters of the lake. Without loss of time, for the nip in the air warned them of winter's approach, they set about making a canoe. Denis burned down a large birch tree and with infinite patience stripped off the bark. Skonakoa sewed it together with strings of buckskin made by cuting up the left leg of his trousers. Denis made ribs of cedar, bent into shape after soaking. While he melted spruce gum in the shells of freshwater clams to seal the seams, Skonakoa fashioned the paddles. For six days they labored at their boat building. The result was a craft they would not dare to take out of sight of land but which would do for their purpose.

They slipped, as the days passed, along the southern shore of the lake, by the country of the Onondagas and the Senecas. Skonakoa's ability to read warning into the most trivial forest signs kept them out of trouble. Only once did he fail. That was when, by accident, they encountered a small Cayuga party. Denis was burned so brown that it was easy to pass as an Iroquois, but, lest his accent betray him, he kept silent, and Skonakoa explained to the strangers that his brother was dumb. Since the Cayugas were a friendly people, somewhat removed from English pressure and French invasion, they were incurious. The two boys accompained them westward for three days. The strain of remaining quiet all that time was nearly more than Denis could bear. He relieved his feelings by laughing frequently, which made the Cayugas pity him as simple minded.

They hastened by Irrondequoit, where stood the blackened remains of Denonville's fort, and came, five days later, to the mouth of the Niagara River. Here Denis proposed that Skonakoa turn back, but the Mohawk boy said he was enjoying himself far too much. Denis was very glad of the decision. It influenced him to avoid the fort Denonville had built there after the expedition, for the presence of an Iroquois traveling companion might have involved explanations difficult to make to a strange commander.

So they stole by the fort at night and paddled up the river until they came to the foot of the rapids. There they began the long and laborious carry around the cataract. Long before they reached the chasm a heavy rumbling, as of loaded wagons passing over cobblestones, filled their ears. The noise increased to a continuous roar. . . . Denis stood again on the brink of the cliff beside the great falls that had filled him

with awed wonder on the trip to fight the Senecas.
The majestic plunge of the waters, the foaming tur-
moil below, the whirlwind of sound, made him feel
his unimportance as even the gray wastes of the Atlan-
tic had not. Silently they picked up the canoe. . . . Late
the next day the heaving waters of Lake Erie lay
before them.

Fort St. Joseph, built by DuLhut the previous year
to guard Lake Huron from the English, stood on rising ground commanding the St. Clair River at the southern end of Lake Huron where that stream began. It
lacked both towers and bastions, which gave it a singu-
larly impermanent look, like a toy block dropped by a
child and forgotten. The country roundabout was
beautiful, even though it was late in November.

Denis beached the canoe as soon as he sighted the
palisade. Twenty paces from the gate a voice hailed
him, and the black muzzle of a gun appeared through
one of the loopholes. Suddenly conscious of his Indian
appearance, he threw up his hands. But he had said
only a few words in French when the heavy gate was
thrown back, and a young officer came running out to
embrace him.

"But I remember you," he cried. "The protégé of
Perrot. You saved me from a Seneca tomahawk. Mon
Dieu! how come you here? I thought you were in
Quebec. Did that canaille with the drooping lid turn
you loose, after all? Chastaignac was like a crazy man.
I have not seen him since he was freed and set out on
your trail."

The officer was the Baron La Hontan, who had
given Denis the snuff box.

Laughing, yet with a curious lump in his throat,

Denis put off the questions. "I will tell you everything, sir, but first I must know if it would be safe to
bring a young Iroquois friend into the fort. I owe him
my freedom."

"As safe as in his own village," La Hontan assured
him largely. "I have a secret admiration for the Iroquois. I wish they were our allies. By all means let us
have a look at him."

Skonakoa, who had remained hidden in a clump of
bushes by the river, demurred at first, saying that he
trusted no Frenchman save Denis, but at last yielded,
and the two presented themselves at the gate. La
Hontan received the stranger with a courtesy as dignified as that of any Mohawk chief. Within the fort
they found some twenty soldiers and four huntsmen,
whose duty it would be to provide meat for the garrison through the winter.

As briefly as possible Denis told the Baron what
had happened to him since they parted.

"I shall not ask you what is behind this business
with Pezzard," said La Hontan, "but if you want my
advice, my boy, I would stay in the west with Perrot
until Count Frontenac returns. He is bound to come
back, for he is the only one who can keep New France
from dissolving beneath our feet. I knew him slightly
at Versailles. He is fiery but just, and he will listen to
your story, I think, with an open mind. That is what
I would do, if I were in your moccasins. But do not
rush off tomorrow. Wait here two or three days. The
rest will do you good. And the delay may be worth
your while."

From the twinkle in his eyes Denis knew he was
concealing something, but he would admit no more
than a desire to entertain them.

For two days Denis and Skonakoa lived in La

Hontan's cabin. The Indian boy had agreed it was better for him to turn back to his own tribe now. They had said nothing further on the matter, but each was oppressed by the thought of parting.

On the third day, returning sadly from a last hunt together, they heard voices in La Hontan's hut. Denis flung open the door. A tall figure loomed in the candle-light. Denis blinked. With a shout of "Perrot!" he unashamedly threw himself into his friend's open arms.

La Hontan beamed on them. "A nice surprise, eh? The last voyageur through here told me Perrot had been detained in Montreal and would pass by the southern route because of the lateness of the season. Perhaps I should have told you sooner."

With a full heart Denis perceived, through the formal words of greeting that Perrot and Skonakoa exchanged, that they approved of each other.

After supper Denis repeated his story in more detail. Perrot's brief, "It was well done. You have used your head as a true coureur should," was all the accolade he could have desired. Skonakoa's eyes gleamed with pleasure as Perrot praised his courage and resource.

Perrot took up the tale from his angle. Chastaignac had grown thin under the weight of remorse. The two of them had sought out Loutray in Quebec. He had told them that Denis had died of an Onondaga arrow. Chastaignac had wanted to kill the man. In spite of the wealth of detail in his story, Perrot had not quite been able to believe it. He had sent word to the Onondagas that he would pay well for news of the missing one. He had intended to return to the Iroquois country himself in the spring and learn the truth. He hoped Skonakoa would take word to Kirk—who sounded like a man he would like to meet—of Denis's safety.

The Mohawk's prowess was recognized more tangibly the next morning with new trousers, moccasins, knife and a splendid musket newly come from France. Although Skonakoa was almost overwhelmed by the magnificence of the gifts, he refused to take them. Denis was his friend, he said, and one did not accept such great gifts for helping a friend. Perrot tactfully pointed out that the gifts were not payment for help but were such tokens of esteem as great chiefs might be proud to receive from their beloved comrades. At that Skonakoa gravely accepted them.

By the canoe they had built together the two friends said good-by, their hands on each other's shoulders, hazel eyes looking into black eyes.

"We will meet again, my brother," said Skonakoa. "No matter what happens between our people, you and I will meet in friendship. When next you pass beyond the land of the Hurons I will hear and I will find you." He turned and walked away among the leafless trees.

La Hontan's farewell was considerably more emotional than Skonakoa's. He had vague plans for a journey beyond Lake Superior in the spring, "to stretch my legs after being cooped up all winter," and surely he would see them.

Perrot and Denis set their faces to the west. Overhead hung gray snow clouds. Ahead of them lay more than two hundred leagues of wilderness—across the Michigan peninsular, around the foot of Lake Michigan, past the portage of the Chickagou, and on to the mouth of the far Wisconsin—a journey of well over a month. And it was already winter. But Denis cared naught for that. He was going home.

Chapter XVIII

FRONTENAC RETURNS

Nicolas Perrot agreed with La Hontan that in the present state of affairs Denis should remain as far from Quebec as possible. During his short stay there he had seen that the anti-Frontenac party, headed by the Intendant and with Denonville under their influence, was completely in power. If Pezzard ever succeeded in getting Denis into his hands he would use every method possible to discover the whereabouts of the papers which he suspected Mersan had hidden.

From Quebec Perrot had sent some money to Giles, through a facteur at Honfleur, with a message that it came from Denis. Next year, if trade prospered, there would be more.

But for the French of Canada there now began a long series of misfortunes that brought the colony to the verge of ruin. The fur trade had come to a complete stop. The former allies of the Great Lakes had turned sullen since the failure of the Denonville expedition to wipe out the Senecas. Between Montreal and the west hovered a cloud of infuriated Iroquois. Their canoes patrolled the eastern lakes; their warriors overran the land. Only an occasional coureur could slip through the web.

The year passed uneventfully at the post, for Perrot kept matters in hand in the region of the Wisconsin, although he was frankly worried about the future. Once he mentioned that he was glad Denis had chosen to come back instead of going to Quebec; every man was needed now to keep the tribes quiet. Eastern Canada might survive an English attack, but if the fur trade was killed the whole colony might as well be abandoned.

Rumors reached them from time to time of more trouble in the east. Dongan, still angry at Denonville's attack on the Senecas, encouraged the Iroquois in their forays. He demanded abandonment by the French of their western forts along the Great Lakes. At the trading post the winter was passed in an atmosphere of uneasiness that was not relieved by splendid luck at the traps. Of what use were furs piled high in the storehouses if there was no way of getting them to Montreal?

In the spring of 1689 a coureur arrived from Michilimackinac with more bad news. Denonville had torn down the fort at Niagara. La Hontan had abandoned Fort St. Joseph. The Indians at Michilimackinac were no longer trustworthy. Dongan had been recalled to England and Sir Edmund Andros had taken his place, but the change of English Governors had not brought a change in policy.

From the messenger Denis learned that Otreouatie, the same "Big Mouth" who had saved him from the stake, had appeared at Montreal, pursuing his policy of not allowing either the French or English to obtain too strong a hold on his people, and haughtily offered Denonville peace on terms favorable to the Five Nations. A truce had been drawn up, but the envoys, returning with the agreement to the Iroquois, had been ambushed by a certain Huron chieftain who saw disaster for his own people in the terms of the peace. That had ended the truce. Now the Iroquois were more implacable than ever.

That summer and fall Denis and Chastaignac, sometimes by themselves, sometimes in company with a small band of coureurs, traveled far and wide, seeking, in addition to furs, new alliances and renewal of old ones. When necessary, Chastaignac could conduct himself with the dignity of a sachem. He did much to uphold what was left of the French reputation.

They journeyed north to the tribe of the Saulteurs on the shores of Lake Superior and on into the far northern lands of the Assiniboines and Winnipegs, where there were many lakes and the days were long. With the coming of the fall they turned south and made friends with one of the many branches of the great Sioux nation. These were tall, strong people, much dreaded for their fierceness and their skill in war. They told of vast treeless plains to the west, black with countless buffalo, and of mountains beyond so high they scraped the sky, of plains kinsmen who rode on horseback and of rumors of a great sea beyond the mountains. Denis would have liked to see these marvels for himself but realized it was out of the question then. Instead, they descended the Mississippi to the mouth of the great muddy river called the Missouri. They wintered at Perrot's fort.

His three years in the wilderness had so changed Denis that old Giles would hardly have recognized him. He was nearly as tall now as Perrot, and though he would never have Chastaignac's bulk he was able to win at least one out of three falls in the friendly wrestling bouts with the Gascon.

"My faith," exclaimed the Gascon, arising one day

after Denis had pinned his shoulders to the ground, "you are no longer a protégé. The alder sapling has changed into a hickory. Our mutual acquaintance with the drooping eyelid will note the difference if you ever come to clutches with him."

"I hope so," returned Denis quietly, his eyes narrowing at the thought.

That winter came word of the massacre at La Chine. Fifteen hundred Iroquois warriors had surprised the little village near Montreal one night in August and butchered the inhabitants. The people in Montreal were terror-stricken. The country people had flocked to the towns, abandoning their farms to the enemy torch. . . . At Michilimackinac the western tribes were preparing to make overtures to the English and the Iroquois. DuLhut and La Durantaye could do nothing against the terror and despair of their former allies.

In the middle of the winter Perrot and three sturdy companions set out from Michilimackinac for Quebec with La Durantaye's message begging help from the Governor.

Late in the spring of 1690 the Pottawattomie Nayonsay turned up at Fort St. Antoine with extraordinary news. The Great Father had come back to Canada! Frontenac had reached Quebec the previous fall, replacing Denonville as Governor. More than that, the English and Iroquois had already felt his heavy hand, for his troops had invaded New York and surprised Schenectady, even as La Chine had been ravaged a few months before. Perrot was on his way westward, bringing soldiers for the garrison at Michilimackinac and words of encouragement from Frontenac for his "children."

When Denis and Chastaignac, with an escort of Pottawattomies and Malhominies, reached Michili-mackinac, they found that Nayonsay had spoken truly. Perrot was there with Louvigny, the new commander, and his eloquence, backed by the message from Frontenac, had revived the allegiance of the tribes. After four years of interruption the fur trade was to be resumed. A flotilla was even then about to start for Montreal. . . . It was as if a bad dream had come to an end. Frontenac had returned!

Despite the vast bustle and the incidents, amusing and otherwise, that accompanied the journey of three hundred coureur companions and five hundred red warriors across the top of the lake and eastward along the remembered Ottawa River, the trip seemed very long to Denis, so impatient was he to get to Quebec and end the suspense. Frontenac would have the Mersan papers by now, and perhaps the lawyer LeRoux had already told the Governor of Denis's own part in the matter. At last he would be able to walk the streets of the city without fear of Pezzard and Loutray. His furs would bring many gold louis to send to Giles. All his hopes seemed nearing fulfillment.

It was a golden afternoon late in August when they arrived in Montreal. Their flotilla had halted at the lower end of the last portage while the Indians prepared themselves for the ceremonies ahead by painting their faces in every color and design imaginable. In the same festive spirit, the coureurs bedecked their caps with wild asters and the prows of their canoes with pine boughs.

On the beach they were welcomed by a shouting, joyous crowd of townspeople headed by Champigny, the Intendant, and de Callières, Governor of the town. Some of the women were crying from sheer relief at sight of the bundles of furs, the first such cargo seen in three years.

Perrot, Chastaignac and Denis were assigned an attic room over one of Hertel's storehouses. There, when the furs had been packed in place, Perrot took a moment to wash his face and comb his hair before going off to one of the inevitable conferences. Denis seized the opportunity to try to find out what he had learned from the merchants. Was Frontenac here? Had Perrot seen him? When would they go to Quebec?

Perrot's eyes crinkled affectionately at the corners. He remarked that Denis was acting like a small boy. Frontenac was here, but he was very busy. He would see the Governor about Denis's affairs as soon as possible.

The name Frontenac was on every tongue. Still dazed by their troubles, the people seemed unable really to believe in the good fortune that had brought him back to them. Denis heard them tell again and again of the greeting the Governor had received when he arrived at Quebec—how men and women had wept for joy as he stepped ashore that chill October evening, how candles had blossomed at every window and torches had lined his path up Mountain Hill. In spite of his sixty-nine years, the courageous Governor had set out within the week through the cold autumn rain for Montreal. Ah, but there was a man for you!

Not until three days had passed did Denis get a glimpse of the old hero. It was at a feast given for the Indians as the signal for the opening of trade.

Many oxen and dogs had been slaughtered for the savage gourmands. In the fields beyond the town great caldrons of prunes and meat were aboil over the fires.

Freshly painted and feathered, the Indians, grouped by tribes, sat in a motionless circle arond the bonfires, not caring whether they waited minutes or hours. Night had fallen when Denis and Miscoue arrived and made their way by the light of the blazing logs to the front rank of the Pottawattomies. The air was filled with the sweetish smell of steaming prunes.

Hardly had they found seats before there was a stir at the farther end of the field, and a number of officers were seen making their way through the dark ranks of the warriors. Striding at their head was a well-knit, military figure in a white uniform. There was no need for Denis to inquire who he was. A low murmur rose, like the soughing of the first breath of a storm.

Frontenac was dressed for the occasion in a white uniform with wide blue sash, high boots and a wide hat with sweeping plume. From the golden baldrick that crossed his breast hung a great sword with a golden hilt that flashed in the firelight. His thick gray hair fell in curls about his shoulders, and he wore a mustache that emphasized rather than obscured his large determined mouth. But most striking of all were the piercing eyes that looked out indomitably from beneath their heavy brows. Beholding those eyes Denis understood at last the reason for Frontenac's reputation. They were the eyes of a keen and restless soul to whom action was as necessary as breath.

The chief of the Hurons of Michilimackinac arose and welcomed their father. Ouabautchet, of the Algonquins of Lake Nipissing, echoed the first speaker's words. Scattered "Houghs" of approval greeted the end of these preliminaries.

But the tribal jealousies that inevitably cropped out in such a variegated gathering made their appearance with the next speaker. Louis Ateriata, chief of the Christian Indians living around the Long Saut, stalked to the center of the council and turning on the Ottawas began to accuse them, with very good reason, of plotting with the English and the Iroquois. An Ottawa replied hotly that the proposed alliance had been for their own protection, since the French had shown themselves unable to defend their own. As Ateriata continued his accusations, another Ottawa took up the gage of battle, and in a moment Christian Mohawks and pagan Ottawas had sprung to their feet, glaring at each other like tigers. An ominous muttering drowned out the words of the disputants.

"Halte!" rang out Frontenac's voice commandingly. Amid a dead silence, the Count stepped forward to face the glowering tribesmen.

"I, your father, wish to speak." The words were in Huron. "I have returned to my children. I am pleased at my welcome. You all know I have come to fight the Iroquois, hence this clamor is strange in my ears. I am astonished," he continued, turning to the Hurons and the Ottawas, "to learn that you had forgotten the protection I always gave you. Did you think that I was no longer alive? Or that I had a mind to stand idle, like those who have been in my place? Did you think that if eight or ten hairs have been torn from my children's heads while I was absent I cannot put back ten handfuls of hair in the place of every one that was pulled out? You know that before I protected you the

ravenous Iroquois dog was biting everybody. I tamed
him and tied him up; but when he no longer saw me
he burst his bonds and went howling through the forests. Now that I am back again he will be chased into
his kennel. Already he has felt the weight of my hand.
That was but the beginning."

He paused. His eyes darted over the dark faces
before him. "I sent my children a hatchet by Perrot.
It was to be used against our enemies, not to be buried.
If you have forgotten how to use it I will show you."

With one stride he was beside Ateriata and had
snatched the tomahawk from the Indian's belt. Three
times he brandished it about his head, and burst into
a Huron war chant. For a moment he stood like an
image, his voice rolling out the sonorous syllables,
then, slashing the air with the hatchet, he bounded
forward into the war dance, with its regular rhythm
of stamp-shuffle, stamp-shuffle—like the beat of a tomtom.

A spontaneous yell went up from the watching warriors. La Durantaye and de Callières, quick to per-
ceive the change of mood, had seized hatchets, and
were performing their own dances. Ateriata fell in with
a whoop behind Frontenac. Western chiefs, their
grievances forgotten, sprang forward to join. High
above their "Sassakouies" could be heard the ringing
chant of the Governor. With a forward sweep, the
excited savages threw themselves into the council space,
prancing and stamping, throwing their bodies from
side to side, brandishing tomahawks and knives. Denis
found himself beside Nayonsay, waving his dagger and
screeching at the top of his lungs.

Half an hour later the dance was brought to a halt
by its instigator. Denis was limp with excitement and

exhaustion, but Frontenac, despite his age, seemed quite fresh. The warriors milled about like leaves slowly settling to earth after a whirlwind.

The Count raised his hand for silence. "Now that my children have shown they are ready to fight the Iroquois, let them eat the feast their father has provided. Tomorrow we will buy the furs you have brought. Then we will talk again of the war. I have spoken."

As Frontenac was escorted from the field by his officers the Indians began a wild scramble for the kettles.

CHAPTER XIX

PLANS GO ASTRAY

TRADING began the next day. Hertel had already pur-
chased Denis's skins and was holding the money until
some means of sending it to France could be arranged,
so Denis had his time to himself. He wandered over
the town watching the bargaining. Chastaignac had
sold his supply to half a dozen merchants and, although
the prices he had received varied, he maintained that
the pleasure of trading had more than made up for
any losses he might have incurred. Perrot was off for
his first interview with the Governor. Denis waited
impatiently for him to come back.

Toward noon he picked up Chastaignac in a tavern
by the waterfront where the Gascon had been cele-
brating the return of wealth in numerous tankards of
his native wine. Together they made their way to the
house of de Callières to meet Perrot.

"A great man, our Governor," was Perrot's greeting. "He understands our Indians and our problems as
no one else can."

"That means he's pleased with you and is going to
keep you trotting from one tribe to another until your
feet drop off," said Chastaignac with a hiccup. "And
I suppose I'll trot with you," he added resignedly.

Perrot eyed his devoted companion and grinned.
"From the looks of you a little trotting wouldn't do

any harm. It would clear your head of the fumes of that third-rate Gascon wine."

Chastaignac reared like a wounded horse. "Third-rate Gascon wine? If any other man had said that to me, Nicolas Perrot, I'd slit his gullet like I'd clean a fish. Nothing's third-rate in Gascony. I'm—"

"Come, you lout," said Perrot, drawing his arm good-humoredly through Chastaignac's.

"Did you have a chance to say anything about me?" inquired Denis as they gained the street. "Did you tell him about the—" He had been about to say "papers" but, at Perrot's warning glance, changed to "anything." Indians were all about them.

"I told him nothing, for it is only you who can tell the story. I merely asked him to hear you. I am to bring you tomorrow morning."

Denis shuffled his feet in a war dance.

The afternoon was spent in patching and repairing the bark shells of the canoes, weakened by the rocks and rapids of the Ottawa. After supper Chastaignac grew restless and dragged Denis off for an hour's visit with friends. Toward ten o'clock they turned their steps homeward. By this time most of the townsmen had gone to bed, but here and there groups of drunken coureurs gathered to sing or fight; and Indians who had already exchanged their furs for brandy slept in the streets wherever stupor had overtaken them. In one of the groups where a tenor warbled uncertainly of the charms of Nannine of Normandy, Chastaignac recognized yet another long-lost friend. Impatiently Denis pulled at his sleeve.

"It's Yves," explained the red-haired man. "Old shipmate of mine in the West Indies. Haven't seen him in years. Got to say hello. Go on. I'll catch up."

Glad to be spared another long exchange of reminiscences, Denis strolled ahead. He was wondering how Frontenac would thank him for saving the packet from Mersan and planning what he would say in reply. He was torn between something like "It was only my duty, sir" and the proud humility of "No risk is too great to run for Count Frontenac and King Louis" when suddenly a sixth sense warned him of danger.

Automatically he whirled, ducking his head. By the dim light of the stars he saw a black object hurl itself at him, saw a hatchet split the air where his head had been.

"François!" he yelled and drew his knife.

A black shadow, detaching itself from the gloom in the lee of the house, sprang at him. He struck, and felt his knife plunge into a body. He could tell it was an Indian by the smell of grease and paint and the feel of oiled skin against his fist. He pulled his knife free and whirled to meet the first assailant. He struck and missed and leaped from beneath the descending hatchet.

Out of the shadows sprang yet another figure and then a fourth. . . . Glittering lights burst before his eyes, whirled like pinwheels and were extinguished in deep soft darkness.

It seemed to Denis that his head was as big as a house—a house that rocked like a ship in a storm and was filled with streaks of red light. Rapidly it dwindled to the size of a pea. A sound rolled in his ears like the booming of surf. There was something familiar about it. He listened carefully. It was Perrot's voice.

When next he woke his head seemed normal in size but it was all one throbbing ache. He opened his eyes,

closed them to shut out the glare of light, opened them
again. He found that he was lying on his own pallet
in the attic of the storehouse. Sunlight fell in a stream
through the dormer window. Cross-legged on the floor
beside him, Chastaignac dozed, chin on chest. Beyond
Chastaignac he glimpsed another figure, prone on a
pallet.

The familiar form of Perrot swam into view. "I'll
take your place, François. Get some sleep."

"No," replied Chastaignac. "I must know if he is
going to live."

With great effort Denis managed to speak. "I am,"
he said.

Both men, their faces alight, bent over him.

He tried to nod reassuringly, but the pain of the
effort jerked a grunt from him. He lay still and tried
to smile. He must have succeeded in a measure, for
Chastaignac began to laugh and cry at the same time.

"You look so funny, my Denis, with the white bandage around your head, like the Grand Turk, without
his mustache. . . . Yes, yes, Nicolas, I will get the
broth."

He was back in a moment with two pewter mugs.
Gently, almost imperceptibly, Perrot raised Denis so
he could drink. The hot broth was delicious. Denis
stayed awake long enough to see Perrot turn to the
other pallet, then dropped off into a good sleep.

The sun was shining again when he awoke. This
time he knew his head was firmly in place, though it
still ached. Perrot brought him more broth.

Sometime later—he could not tell whether it was
days or hours—he regained enough strength to rebel
at so much babying and demanded to know what had
happened.

Perrot replied that there was little to tell. Chastaignac had borrowed a torch from his friend and started on his way. In a moment he heard Denis cry for help. He rounded a corner on the run and saw three struggling men. One, a young Indian, was warding off the attack of the other two. The light disconcerted them. In the confusion the young Indian was hit by a tomahawk. Chastaignac drew his sword and rushed in, whereupon the two strangers took to their heels. He had recognized one of them as Loutray. Beside the wall of the house he had found the body of the man Denis had knifed, an unknown Huron. The fight had taken place ten days ago.

Denis strove to collect his wits. "Who was the young Indian?" he asked.

"Someone you know," replied Perrot with a smile. "Turn and see."

Painfully Denis shifted his position to follow Perrot's glance. Sitting tranquilly on the opposite pallet, his head bound in a white rag, was a stalwart young warrior. "Orenda, my brother," he said, and grinned.

"Skonakoa!" cried Denis joyfully.

"Lie still," commanded Perrot, "or you'll get no rabbit stew."

Denis sank back. "I welcome my brother," he said, finding that the Mohawk came easily to his tongue. "I am grateful. How did you happen to be here?"

"I came to Montreal to find you," Skonakoa replied. "I saw you at the council where Onontio led the war dance. The next day I followed you. I had to be careful in this city of my enemies. I saw a Frenchman and a Huron watching you and the man with red hair. While my brother was talking with Metaminens I saw those two listening. I took up their trail. But I was like a stupid porcupine. I should not have waited until they laid a trap."

"You saved my life," protested Denis. Now he understood. Loutray had heard Perrot's words about the appointment with Frontenac. "They're frightened," he exulted to Perrot, "or they wouldn't have taken such a risk to stop my mouth."

"I don't believe that they know all that you discovered," Perrot said, "but they decided to take no chances."

"It's lucky I don't have to worry about the papers. LeRoux has already given them to the Count, I'm sure."

Perrot agreed that undoubtedly this was what had happened. Had Denis been well he would have perhaps noticed that his friend spoke almost too cheerfully.

Denis and Skonakoa recovered rapidly. The intervening three years had not, they found, dimmed their friendship in the least. Being together again seemed the most natural thing in the world. There was much to talk about. The Mohawk had seen Alexander Kirk, who had been delighted to hear of Denis's safe arrival in the west. They talked over everything that had happened since their parting.

It was nearly the end of September before they were strong enough to walk in the tiny garden behind Hertel's house. Chastaignac told them of all that had happened during their convalescence. The booming of cannon they had heard, which at the time had been explained as salutes to Indian allies, had been in reality an alarm sounded to the outlying garrisons on reports that an army of English and Iroquois was approaching from the direction of Lake Champlain. The troops had gone out to meet the enemy, but had returned without finding him. The western Indians had departed for the Lakes, agreeing to fight when called upon. Some Mohawks and English under John Schuyler, of Albany, had descended on La Prairie, killed the reapers in the fields and retreated with prisoners. Frontenac was hastening preparations to strike the Iroquois.

September ended and October began in a riot of flaming colors. One morning Perrot found the two boys wrestling in the garden. Later he drew Denis aside. "Don't be too disappointed. I was with Count Frontenac while you were ill," he began abruptly. "I spoke, quite casually, of the lists which the lawyer LeRoux had given him. He looked at me as though he thought me mad. He has not received any such lists, nor has he seen the lawyer. I did not feel free to tell him all. He said I might bring you to him when you were strong. When I saw you throw Skonakoa I knew you were well. We are to go to see the Count this evening."

Denis sat down quickly on the garden bench, his head in a whirl.

"It is evident," went on Perrot in a troubled voice, "that something has happened to prevent the lawyer from communicating with the Governor. We will have to find out what it was. In the meantime, tell the Governor your story."

But before Denis had his long-sought interview Montreal was in an uproar. At three o'clock that afternoon an exhausted messenger had arrived from Quebec with a letter from the major in charge of the city's fortifications begging Frontenac to return at once. The letter said that an Abenaki runner had come from

Acadia with the startling news that a large English fleet had sailed from Boston to take Quebec.

Chastaignac brought the word to Perrot. The Governor, he said, had set off promptly in a canoe.

Denis and Perrot exchanged glances. If the English laid siege to the capital Pezzard would be more dangerous than ever.

Perrot rose from his stool and gathered up his accounts. "Take these to Hertel," he directed. "Tell him I will be back, but that business takes the three of us—"

"Four," corrected Skonakoa in his guttural French.

"The four of us," amended Perrot, "to Quebec."

Driving rain slanted into their faces as they passed the cove beneath Cape Diamond. It had rained steadily throughout the four days they had driven their canoe down the St. Lawrence. They had risen before daybreak each morning and had paddled on far into each night without ever catching up with the Governor. At Three Rivers they had learned that the English fleet had been sighted at Tadoussac.

Through a rift in the mist they glimpsed the huddled roofs of the lower town and on the heights above the spire of the Cathedral. The river lay empty before them.

"Faugh! I have worn out my shoulders for nothing!" exclaimed Chastaignac, dropping his paddle. "Where is this English fleet they talk about?"

They landed to find the town in a state of wild excitement. The Governor had preceded them by only a few hours, and the townspeople were still in the throes of patriotic fervor. Levies from nearby villages and bands of friendly Indians were arriving hourly. The people were working like beavers to complete the palisade thrown up along the banks of the St. Charles and along the landward side of the city. Frontenac, they said, was everywhere at once, directing the labors, enrolling habitants in companies, assigning troops to their places in the hastily devised fortifications.

They secured the last available room at the tavern of the Drinking Stag in the lower town. Denis was all for seeking the Governor immediately, but Perrot pointed out that first he should see LeRoux. Frontenac was too busy at the moment to spare time for interviews. A hot supper and a good night's sleep, and in the morning he could look up his friend. He advised Denis to keep close to quarters that night and go directly to the upper town in the morning.

"I do not think, as things are now, Pezzard would be able, even if he learns you are here, to lodge charges against you. But we must have no more ambuscades in dark alleys. Seek out the lawyer, by all means. Don't, however, be disappointed if the papers prove of less value than you had imagined. I don't know how else to account for LeRoux's silence."

Accordingly, after breakfast the next day Denis buckled on a pistol Chastaignac lent him and set forth, accompanied by Skonakoa, who carried an exceedingly efficient-looking tomahawk. His memory of the streets of the lower city was better than he had expected. Avoiding that part of the Rue Notre Dame adjacent to Pezzard's house, he made his way without difficulty to the foot of Mountain Hill and up the steep street to the Place d'Armes.

The rain had stopped. The bright sunlight glinting on the roofs gave the town an air of festive gaiety. The streets were full of armed men, habitants and coureurs, Indians from Lorette and militia from the south bank of the river, all hurrying from one place to another with more enthusiasm than order.

The Rue St. Louis, sheltered by the walls of the Jesuits and Ursulines, seemed tranquilly remote from the feverish bustle of the other streets. Denis stepped briskly to the door and raised the remembered brass quill. It fell with a flat clack against the metal guard.

The door was jerked open. A slatternly, red-faced woman peered at him. "What do you want?" she demanded in a surly tone.

The sight of her stirred some vague memory which Denis could not place. "I want to see the lawyer LeRoux," he replied.

She looked at him in dull surprise. Her mouth cracked open, showing yellow teeth. "You knock at the wrong door," she cackled. "You will have to seek either above or below, and only the Saints could tell you which."

"But this is his house," protested Denis in bewilderment.

"It was his house," she retorted. "You must come from the back of beyond. The lawyer LeRoux has been dead these twelve months. He was killed in some street fighting between a bunch of Indians. Like as not he was mixing in something that didn't concern him. Yes, it has been all of a year. I remember it happened just before the Count came back to Quebec. It was only the next week that my master moved in."

A terrible certainty crept into Denis's mind. "Who is your master?" he demanded.

"The good merchant Zacherie Pezzard," was the reply. "D'ye want to see him?"

"No," said Denis, turning quickly away. He remembered her now. She was Marie, Pezzard's cook, who had grudgingly given him the bread and cheese that eventful day four years ago.

CHAPTER XX

"CANNON WILL ANSWER"

DENIS strode on, scarcely conscious of where he was going, until he had turned the corner where the brick wall of the gardens began. Now he understood why Frontenac had not received the papers from LeRoux. A street brawl between Indians, she had said. That meant Black Fox and Loutray. Those two scoundrels had added still another score to the long tally of their crimes.

Skonakoa touched his arm. "There was a Huron in that lodge," he whispered. "I smelled him when the squaw opened the door. He was watching in the shadows. He is the one I saw in Montreal with the Frenchman whose eye is half shut."

Denis nodded. He was so dumfounded at the turn of events that he couldn't think. The death of the poor lawyer made the problem ten times more difficult than before. By some means he must get his hands on the papers. But how?

Without noticing where he was going, he had taken the path which led to the Saut au Matelot, or Sailor's Leap, the name given to that part of the Rock which, like the prow of a ship, overlooked the junction of the two rivers. Here the line of the cliff turned abruptly, towering, on the one hand, above the St. Charles, on the other above the lower town and the beach of the

St. Lawrence. A battery of three guns had recently
been mounted there. Half a dozen laborers were still
spading up earth to protect the cannon.

Skonakoa, who had been pacing beside him in silence,
touched his arm. "The English will not take this town
easily, brother," he said admiringly. "They are terrible weapons, these that speak with the voice of
thunder."

Even the bravest of Indians were deathly afraid of
cannon, for the great noise and the clouds of smoke
savored too much of magic. The Iroquois had known
small arms for two generations, but artillery was still
a dreadful novelty.

The path turned to the left along the top of the
cliff bordering the St. Charles. Below the cliff, along
the edge of the mud flats, a new palisade stretched a
quarter of a mile in the direction of the Intendant's
Palace, which stood a short distance outside the new
line of fortifications constructed by Frontenac to guard
the upper town. The tide was out now, and the St.
Charles was little more than a broad creek wandering
through the flats. At high tide water came almost to
the foot of the stockade.

They arrived soon at another path that crossed
theirs at right angles. It came from the gardens and
buildings of the Jesuits and led, with many turns, down
the face of the cliff to a small gate in the palisade. Beyond the gate several canoes lay on the muddy shore.
A priest, his robes lifted halfway to his knees, was
making his way across the beach toward the gate
where two soldiers sat idly watching.

"What a convenient path for the good Fathers when
they go to the Huron villages up the St. Charles," remarked Denis.

Skonakoa grunted disinterestedly, his eyes on the habitants who were making the dirt fly on barricades at the entrance known as the Palace Gate.

As they worked the habitants talked excitedly. Rumors were flying as thick as starlings. "The captains of the militia in the neighboring villages had been ordered to stand at arms in case the English should try to land and plunder outlying settlements. De Vaudreuil had taken a hundred men to watch the enemy; maybe he would capture the fleet. . . . Nonsense, the fleet would be too large. . . . The English were terrors. . . . On the contrary, they were cowards. . . . The Count had sent two canoes behind the Isle d'Orleans to warn the merchant ships expected from France. Soon the Montreal men would arrive and then Quebec would be saved. . . ."

Denis joined the work, but his mind was still on his problem. By noon, when the barricade was finished, he had decided what he was going to do. He was going to find the Governor and try to convince him that something should be done about the papers in the black box.

With Skonakoa trailing, he walked purposefully toward the upper end of Mountain Hill. Here more townspeople were laboring on barricades, throwing up trenches across the street so the upper town could be defended in case the English gained possession of the lower part of the city.

The sentry at the door of the Chateau St. Louis halted him. When he demanded to see the Governor the soldier grinned. "Come back next month," he advised. "Do you think he has time for every complaint you people can think up? He's a busy man, is our Governor. Get along with you."

"Listen to me," snapped Denis. "I have an important matter to talk over with him. Call an officer."

The man scowled. But he called the officer, a harried young lieutenant. Denis explained that he must see Frontenac. What, asked the other, was his business with the Governor? Denis replied that that was a matter for Frontenac's ears. It had to do, he added, with the defense of the city.

The lieutenant looked him up and down superciliously. "I think the Governor is fairly competent to handle that without advice from a woods ranger," he replied.

Denis made the mistake of losing his temper. "Don't be a fool," he said rudely. "This can't wait. I tell you—"

The lieutenant's face flushed angrily. "Throw him out," he shouted.

The sentry lowered his bayonet until it touched Denis's breast. "On your way," he barked, full of assurance now that the lieutenant had accepted the responsibility.

Skonakoa slipped his knife out of its sheath and crouched, ready to spring. The officer drew his sword. "Guard," he called.

Before other soldiers could come Denis intervened. "It's no use, brother," he said. "We'll have to think of something else. Let's go back to the inn."

Gloomily he led the way toward Mountain Hill and thence down the cliff to his lodgings. He would have to contrive to meet Frontenac outside the Chateau. That would not be too difficult, for the Governor spent much of his time supervising the work of defense. But what then? The only way he could convince Frontenac that the supposed papers were important was to show them to him. He could scarcely count on Frontenac's ordering a search of Pezzard's house on the strength of his unsupported word. It would be necessary, somehow, to get the papers.

At the inn, Perrot listened to his story sympathetically. He advised him not to worry. The Governor was much too busy to concern himself with documents the very existence of which could not be proved to him. When the English were defeated he, Perrot, would again bring about an interview. The delay would not cause any harm.

De Vaudreuil returned that afternoon with word that the English fleet was anchored only three leagues below the city and would reach the basin the next morning. All afternoon and evening the men labored on the fortifications, strengthening barricades, carrying shot to the batteries, filling fresh bags of sand. Just let the English try to storm their fortress, then they would see what a job they had undertaken, said the townspeople. But the officers, who knew more of war, were silent.

The next morning, when thirty-four ships anchored in front of the town, the people, too, fell silent. There were four great ships and four smaller ones, the remainder ketches, barques and sloops. From his place by the battery of the Saut au Matelot, Denis looked uneasily across the bright water at the enemy decks crowded with men. Above the Chateau, at the edge of the cliff, the white flag of France with its golden *fleur-de-lis* flew defiantly in the breeze. The guns of the batteries on the cliff and in the lower town waited like black dogs on the leash. The wharfs, the beach, the streets, were crowded with people watching the approach of the enemy. In the long shadows of early morning that enemy was formidable.

Perrot came into the room as they were snatching breakfast. "A boat with a white flag is putting out from the admiral's ship. Frontenac has sent for all the leaders to come to the Chateau. You and Chastaignac might find place among the spectators." He laughed briefly. "I am told I must put on my new clothes to impress the English."

Denis and Chastaignac had new hunting shirts they had bought in Montreal, and Chastaignac had a bright blue scarf he wore across one shoulder. He gave Denis the wide piece of red silk he had worn as a sash. Denis left the silver dagger in his leather belt under his tunic and drew the brilliant stuff tightly around his waist.

They had struggled through the barricades and the anxious crowd and reached the top of the cliff when they heard a shout from the waterside. The English envoy, an officer, had been landed from one of the canoes and a white handkerchief had been tied over his eyes. Now, his arms held by two sergeants, he was being led up one street and down another. He was being forced to climb barricades and jump ditches in order to confuse him and make him think the fortifications were stronger than they really were. Around him a group of men jostled and pushed to give him the impression of passing through a vast crowd, while from the houses women and children screamed and shouted. At the top of Mountain Hill Chastaignac led the way toward the Chateau. Once there he managed, by bluster, flattery and main strength, to worm his way into the great hall, with Denis tight on his heels.

They had hardly secured a place inside the doors

when the English envoy was brought in and his bandage whipped off. Denis could read the astonishment on the man's face. At the end of the room on a slight dais stood Governor Frontenac, splendid in his white and gold uniform. On either side stood the officers and leaders of New France. Never had Denis seen so many suits of red, green, plum or blue velvet, such brilliant uniforms, such plumes and ribbands and so much gold and silver lace and braid. All eyes, haughty and defiant, proud and implacable, were fixed on this representative of the enemy who had dared make his way to the stronghold of His Majesty Louis XIV, the falcon's eyrie of Quebec. It was a good bluff, thought Denis, if it worked.

The enemy recovered himself and saluted Frontenac punctiliously.

"I deeply regret, sir, that the duty which my commander has assigned to me is not of a more agreeable nature. I bring you a summons to surrender from Sir William Phipps, Commander-in-chief of Their Majesties' Forces of New England." With a flourish he drew out a beribbanded scroll.

"What does he say?" Frontenac demanded bruskly, looking like a hawk about to swoop. "Read it, Lesancourt."

One of the officers stepped forward, took the scroll, and began to read aloud in French. Denis tried to follow, but lost himself in the maze of words. He was more interested in watching the scene. As his eyes wandered over the crowd, he saw standing near the black-robed group that surrounded the Bishop and the Intendant the heavy figure of Pezzard. Denis moved back into the shadows.

Words of the message droned to his ears across the

stillness of the listening hall. "I, the aforesaid William Phipps, Knight . . . demand a surrender of your forts and castles . . . other stores . . . persons and estates . . . you may expect mercy from me . . . if you refuse I am come by force of arms to revenge all wrongs and injuries . . . make you wish you had accepted the favor tendered. Answer—in an hour."

As the officer began to roll up the scroll the Englishman pulled out a large gold watch.

"Hang him," shouted the crowd.

Frontenac's raised hand quieted the tumult. His eyes were flashing and his left hand gripped tightly the gold hilt of his sword.

"Your answer," he barked, "shall be given now. It is No. If that does not suit your master then let him seek another answer at the mouths of my cannon. Let him learn that this is not the way to summon a man like me. Let him do his best and I will do mine."

At the Governor's abrupt gesture of dismissal the two sergeants seized the envoy's arms and hurried him from the hall. A swelling murmur outside told of his return trip over the barricades. When he saw that Pezzard was talking to the Intendant, Denis slid through the entrance and dropped behind a group of coureurs.

Little work was done in the town that morning. Along the fortifications people watched the little rowboats scurry back and forth between the ships of the English fleet. Small boys, for once forgotten by their parents, scrambled over the heights of Cape Diamond, their shrill voices floating thinly down over the town like the mewing of gulls.

Early that night a great shout and a ruffle of drums were heard at the western gate. A long line of torches,

bobbing like a procession of fireflies, was pouring into
the city. Singing, shouting, eight hundred coureurs and
soldiers, habitants from tiny stockades and gentry,
were pouring into town behind de Callières, Governor
of Montreal. They had followed Frontenac in canoes
but, hearing at Three Rivers a false rumor that the
English were attacking, had hurried overland to be in
the fight.

Chastaignac mingled with the newcomers, shouting
greetings to friends, dragging Denis after him as he
plowed through the crowd at the Place d'Armes. Frontenac had just appeared to welcome the arrivals, and
now oxen were being roasted over hastily built fires.

"Ha, Miscoue, do you still strangle bears for pleasure?" asked a merry voice.

Chastaignac whirled and threw his arms around the
tall laughing young man. "Sainte-Hélène! I saw you this
morning, looking like a peacock. Now you are dressed
like a human being again. So you remember the bear?
Poof, that was nothing."

"If you had not had nearly a barrel of brandy inside
you it might have been something. Those were great
days, my Miscoue. I often think I will leave exploring
to my brothers and return to hunting."

"Denis," Chastaignac drew his arm inside his own,
"I have the honor to present you to M'sieur de Sainte-
Hélène, who can drink, hunt and fight nearly as well
as though he had been born in Gascony."

White teeth gleamed in the bronze face as Sainte-
Hélène gave a shout of laughter. "Even the Sioux have
not been able to tame you, François."

While the talk skipped from Indians to hunting and
back to drinking bouts, Denis studied the young man
whom he had glimpsed once at Irrondequoit. He was

tall and slender, and his dancing eyes showed that for him life was ever an amusing and exciting adventure. Denis had heard great tales of Charles Le Moyne of Montreal and of the ten famous sons who each added luster of his own to that name—Longueuil, Serigny, Assigny, Maricourt, Chateauguay, Le Moyne d'Iberville, Le Moyne Bienville—young men, yet known by reputation from the frozen sea to the north to the warm waters of the Spanish Main. For them the life of the coureur was too quiet, too circumscribed. On land or on sea, each sought new lands, new peoples, new adventures.

"There will be fighting soon, make no mistake about that," Sainte-Hélène assured Chastaignac. "The Governor has said I may take out some of the coureurs. We will see where the English land, then worry them. When you hear my horn come here to the Place d'Armes." Over his shoulder was slung the coil of a small horn such as huntsmen had carried at home. "You are included in the invitation," he bowed courteously to Denis. "But I see Maricourt is beckoning. Good night, François."

Even after he had disappeared in the crowd they could still hear the sound of his laughter.

Chapter XXI

QUEBEC STANDS SIEGE

IT WAS late in the morning when word flew around the
city that the English were mustering aboard their
ships. Denis opened his window and looked out across
the St. Lawrence. The wind brought the tattoo of
drums, shrilling of fifes and confused shouts. Many
little figures were piling from the decks into the landing boats. The first set off toward the shore of Beauport, more than a league down the river. Ah, so their
plan was to circle up the St. Charles and attack from
the landward side!

To the high sweet notes of Sainte-Hélène's horn,
Denis and Skonakoa set off through the hurrying
crowds in the lower town toward the Place d'Armes
where the coureurs would be gathering. Denis pushed
his way past soldiers and Indians, impatient of even
an instant's delay. His eyes were alight and his face
was flushed with excitement. The red glory of war
filled his imagination—not the slinking war of the
wilderness, but something he supposed to be thrill-
ingly spectacular, like Giles's stories of battles in
Europe, of desperate charges led by romantic cavaliers
on white horses. He knew little of that sort of war.
He did not realize the grim fact that death in a glorious charge was no different from death in an Iroquois
ambush.

Skonakoa trotted beside him, his face expressionless.

They found the Place jammed with a horde of coureurs, habitants, Indians. Sainte-Hélène marshaled them in a semblance of order and led them across the upper town to the Palace Gate. They crossed the St. Charles, now at ebb tide, by the ford, and made their way through the forest where they were joined by a band of Hurons from Lorette. Half an hour later they halted while Sainte-Hélène and his scouts made a reconnaissance.

"It is perfect," he announced when he returned. "There are many, many English, twelve or thirteen hundred, I think, against our three hundred, but we have more trees than there are Englishmen—nice thick trees directly in front of where they are landing."

So, thought Denis, with a certain disappointment, it was to be woods fighting again, instead of a charge. But doubtless Sainte-Hélène knew what he was doing.

From the screen of scrubby bushes, still covered with brown and yellow leaves, they watched the English disembarking from their shallops on the muddy shore. Denis cuddled his musket against his shoulder. Chastaignac was whistling softly, tunelessly.

"Do not give them time to form ranks," called Sainte-Hélène. "Fire at the count of three. One. Two . . ."

At the crashing volley the English began to form ranks. "Too far," muttered Chastaignac disconsolately. A ragged volley was heard on the left. "That's the Sieur de St. Denys and his tenants from Beauport," called Sainte-Hélène. "Give it to them, now, in your own way. If they charge, scatter and contest every foot. When I blow my horn, retire."

In spite of the hidden fire the English did charge, wading clumsily through the mud but coming on grimly. The coureurs abandoned their line of bushes and disappeared, each to his own tree or rock. On firm ground the English stubbornly formed ranks again.

But they were obviously not accustomed to dealing with an enemy who persisted in remaining invisible. Each rock and tree spat forth its bullet, and the charge netted them only deserted bushes. A young officer ran up and down the ranks, begging the men to stand. Turning, he shook his fist at the woods.

"Come out and fight like men," he taunted.

Sainte-Hélène's laughter answered him.

Once more the English charged. Denis sprang from his rock as a bullet chipped it. Around him dislodged men were dashing back to the safety of other trees, pausing to reload and fire, and retreating again. More English were pouring into the wood. On the left the fire drew nearer. Sullenly the English returned to the beach. Sainte-Hélène's horn echoed through the woods.

As they neared the St. Charles, grumbling because they had been called off, they met militia from Three Rivers, marching out to hold the English to the shore.

At the Place d'Armes Frontenac awaited them. "With three thousand men like you the English will never reach the town," he proclaimed. "Tomorrow I will lead you myself."

An officer hurried across the Place. "The English ships are moving, sir. They are anchoring before the town."

Sainte-Hélène stepped forward. "The Le Moynes do not often ask favors, my Governor, but now I ask one. Would you permit me to send the first cannonball against the enemy?"

Frontenac smiled grimly. "If all the favors which came to me were of this nature my life would be easier. Fire the first shot, by all means, as your reward."

Sainte-Hélène bowed and spun on his heel. "Dismissed," he called. "And tomorrow, when I summon you, meet me once more in this place and we will tweak their noses again."

He started at a run for Mountain Street, Chastaignac and Denis at his heels.

The two batteries in the lower town had been planted at the water's edge; one beyond the unfinished church in direct line with the end of Mountain Street, the other halfway between this point and the mouth of the St. Charles. Sainte-Hélène raced to the first, the *Batterie Royale.*

In the river before them the four largest ships were maneuvering stiffly in the fitful breeze, their half-raised sails sheets of gold in the light of the setting sun. The *Severn,* which bore the blue flag of the rear-admiral, was dropping anchor directly in front of the Saut au Matelot, with the admiral's flagship, the *Six Friends,* between the two batteries, and the *John and Thomas* opposite the *Batterie Royale.* The fourth ship, with the commodore's pennant, was working for a place a little above Cape Diamond.

A black-frocked schoolboy tugged at Denis's sleeve. "Look! They have hoisted the picture of the Holy Family from the Ursuline Convent on the spire of the Cathedral," he cried. "That will protect the city."

Denis tore his gaze from the spire as Sainte-Hélène aimed a gun at the admiral's ship and pulled the lanyard. For a moment the smoke hid the ships, but they heard the dull *thump* of metal on wood. Someone cried, "Hit! The center of the hull!"

Sainte-Hélène grinned and wiped the powder from his face. "Is not this more fun than your western forests, François? Me, I would not have missed this fight. Are you ready?"

Another shot boomed across the water and was followed almost instantaneously by one from the other battery. Suddenly red flames darted from the dark hulls. There was a crashing roar. The ships heeled over ponderously under the impact of their broadsides, then slowly righted themselves.

Now the batteries by the Saut au Matelot and the Chateau St. Louis opened. Toward Cape Diamond the commodore's ship and the lonely battery of Vaudreuil on the beach below the redoubt were dueling vigorously. The four ships were joined by the smaller ones, each firing in turn. The roar of the cannon and the booming echoes from the cliffs and Cape Diamond kept Denis's hands to his ears. It was as if the whole sky were breaking to pieces.

A shopkeeper hurried up, a wicker basket in his arms. "This fell in the garden of the convent of the Ursulines," he panted. "The Sisters send it to you with their blessing." It was an English cannonball, still warm.

"We will return it to its parents," chuckled Sainte-Hélène. "Do you thank the good Sisters for me. I'll send it, for luck, at the flagstaff on the admiral's ship."

Denis thought he was jesting, but as he watched through the smoke he saw the pennant jerk sharply and topple into the water. A ragged cheer went up.

The batteries in the upper town were no longer firing. He turned to ask Chastaignac the reason, but Chastaignac had disappeared.

"The upper batteries cannot reach the ships," explained a Breton gunner. "It is too far. If you seek your friend, look there."

Denis's glance followed the pointing finger. A canoe, white against the darkening water, was crossing toward the flagship. In the stern knelt Chastaignac, his red hair catching the last of the daylight. Another coureur knelt in the bow. Denis started for the shore, but Sainte-Hélène jerked him back.

The English had seen the canoe. One gun was being depressed to aim, but already the craft was too near the ships. The townspeople fell silent, watching with open-mouthed intensity. Even the guns slowed their hoarse duel. Amid the crackling of English muskets Chastaignac threw the canoe into a graceful curve toward the drifting spar. The man in the bow leaned over and grasped the flagstaff. He shook the ensign above his head, for all to see, then dropped it into the boat and bent over his paddle. Cheer after cheer, punctuated by shots from the ships, burst from the watchers on the shore. In ten minutes Chastaignac and his friend pushed their way through the admiring mob toward Sainte-Hélène.

"For you, my friend, to take to the Governor."

Sainte-Hélène threw his arms around the Gascon. "It is for you, François."

"Together," shouted someone. "Take it to Frontenac together."

Good-natured hands pushed the three in line, Sainte-Hélène in the center, carrying the trophy, the other two with arms linked on either side. Sainte-Hélène lifted the flag above his head. "So may all the enemies of New France fall into our hands," he cried.

Denis knew he would never forget that proud figure, his white shirt torn and blackened, arms upstretched, eyes dancing. . . . The crowd followed toward the Chateau. The English were silent.

Chapter XXII

AT THE HOUSE OF PEZZARD

THE bombardment had caused very little damage to Quebec, but Quebec had punished the English ships severely, as the watchers from the walls could see. At nightfall the enemy fleet drew off down the river out of range.

In the back of Denis's mind was a still, small worry. His own affairs were in no better shape than before. The English were a dogged folk; they might succeed on their next try. In the forests toward Beauport their army still threatened from the landward side. If they should capture the city the black box containing Mersan's disclosures would do not a whit of good. Maybe Frontenac would have time to hear him tomorrow. He doubted, however, that an interview would help much unless accompanied by such a striking proof that the Governor would be immediately convinced. And that meant recovery of the black box.

He beckoned Skonakoa away from the group of coureurs to whose boastful stories of the day's fighting they had been listening. Retiring to a secluded spot along the shore he whispered his thoughts to the Mohawk. Skonakoa nodded, his eyes gleaming in the moonlight. "It is good," he muttered. "This is something I understand. I do not understand all these thunderings of guns. Lead, brother."

Approaching Pezzard's second house, where the un-
fortunate LeRoux had lived, the two companions held
a hurried consultation and separated. Denis scaled the
walls of the Recollect garden and made his way to the
brick wall which divided the land of the religious order
from the garden in the rear of the dwelling. Skonakoa
circled toward the front of the place.

Denis lay patiently watching by the faint light of
the moon. The house, although somewhat larger than
most in Quebec, was of the same design as many others
in the city. It was built of stone and was two stories
high. Its longer side faced the street. There were two
double chimneys at either end. Dormer windows peering from the slate roofs showed that there were additional living quarters in the attic.

He remembered that he had entered a narrow hall
and turned to the left into the study where LeRoux
had heard his story. That would be the room where a
light shone, for the window of the study had looked
directly onto the garden. The other lighted room,
where he occasionally glimpsed Marie's dark bulk
moving about as she finished her evening's work, would
be the kitchen. Should he slip across the garden and
into the study by way of the window, or should he go
through the kitchen, which, he judged, was across the
hall from the study? He could not do either until the
lights went out.

At last the kitchen was dark, and a glow in one of
the dormer windows told him that Marie had gone to
her own room. Still he waited, for what seemed like
eons.

Actually it was perhaps only an hour later that he
heard a faint hiss behind him. Skonakoa's hand
touched his shoulder. "The man with the drooping lid

left by the front door a long time ago," whispered the Indian. "The Huron followed later. Now another has gone—one who wore a broad hat and walked with quick, heavy steps."

"That would be Pezzard," muttered Denis. "The three we most fear have gone. The light still burns where the box is hidden, but I am growing tired of this. We must take a chance. Are you with me, brother?"

For answer Skonakoa slid over the wall.

Denis crept through the garden to the window of the study, which, to his great disappointment, he found to be effectively barred by three iron rods set into the stone. It was Pezzard's work; the bars had not been there when he talked with the lawyer. A candle guttered in its holder on the table, but the room was empty. He turned toward the kitchen door.

To his surprise the door was unlocked. Marie had forgotten her final duty. With his heart in his throat he raised the latch and slipped into the room. A faint glow from the fireplace gave enough light for him to pick his way past the hazards of tables and benches toward the door that opened into the hall. He remembered that this was partly masked from view by the stairway leading to the upper floor, a stairway that began some feet back from the front door and filled about half of the passage. So eager was he to reach his goal that he was about to grasp the latch when the Mohawk seized his wrist and pointed to the thin line of light beneath the door.

They stretched side by side flat on the floor listening intently for a space of several minutes, but could hear nothing save an occasional faint movement which seemed to come from the room above. Denis rose and with infinite caution raised the latch. An inch at a time he opened the door. On hands and knees the two crept out and peered around the stairway.

What they saw made them jerk back their heads. A man sat in a chair tilted against the wall a few feet away. In a dish on the floor beside him stood a lighted candle. He appeared to be dozing, for his chin was on his chest, but Denis could tell by his breathing that he was not sound asleep.

With a longing look at the door of the study, almost within the reach of his hands, Denis drew back into the kitchen. Together they could probably knock the man out before he could utter a sound. But what about the two front rooms? He had no way of knowing whether other guards were on duty there. He could not even see if the doors were closed. A single sound might bring half a dozen men boiling out into the hall.

He made his decision. Motioning Skonakoa under the angle of the descending staircase where he could leap on the guard if the man stirred, Denis started for the door of the study. Now came the real test of his training in Indian craft. He scarcely dared to draw breath as he moved across the hall and raised the latch. If it creaked on its hinges! . . . But he could trust Skonakoa. . . . It opened without a sound.

He waited until the Mohawk joined him, then closed the door as cautiously as he had opened it. Skonakoa, knife poised, took up his post behind it. Denis tiptoed to the fireplace.

He had repeated LeRoux's instructions so many times that they had long since become as much a part of his memory as the sound of his own name. As his hands touched the handle of the damper he paused and said a wordless prayer. Gently he pushed the handle to the right. His groping hands found the stone, removed it, began to turn the knob of the compartment. Fourteen times . . . His fingers touched the box. All atremble, he pried open the lid and seizing the packet stowed it carefully inside his shirt. So great was his relief that he had difficulty making his hands replace the box and reseal the compartment.

He had moved the handle of the damper to its former position and was on the point of turning away when he heard the clump of feet on the stoop of the house. A peremptory knock sounded at the front door. For an agonized instant his eyes met Skonakoa's. Then his glance fled about the room, searching for a hiding place. He heard the scrape of the guard's chair, a yawn, the slow shuffle of feet. The banging at the door grew more insistent.

There was not a second to lose. The window was no good. Even if he could break the glass he could not get through the bars. There was the chimney, but it offered no holds for hands or feet. In the corner behind the door stood a bulky cupboard some six feet high of the sort known as an armoire, used for storing clothes. Like a flash he sprang across the room and opened the cupboard. Together the two pulled the doors closed behind them and burrowed into the mass of hanging garments.

They heard footsteps in the hall. The study door was flung open. Beyond it someone was protesting. "But, Master, I wasn't asleep. I opened as soon as I could."

"You took a long time about it, friend Jacques," retorted a high-pitched voice. "It is always well to avoid the appearance of evil if one is to come off with clean hands. I pay you to watch, not to sleep."

Denis recognized the voice immediately. He couldn't

have forgotten it in a thousand years. Unctuous and piping, it represented to him all imaginable hypocrisy and villainy. Had it not come back to him and set his blood to boiling a hundred times as he trod the forest trails? He did not want to hear it, but he could not escape it, for there were wide cracks at top and bottom of the armoire doors. Through the apertures he now heard another voice.

"Do you have any orders for me?" asked Loutray. "If not, I'll snatch an hour's sleep before I go to meet the messenger."

"Very well," replied Pezzard. "I will stay here. I have some work to do. Tomorrow—or today, rather, since it must be all of three o'clock—will be a busy time. But don't forget that you are to meet the messenger at the foot of the cliff above Cape Diamond half an hour before dawn. Jacques will have the clothing ready. He will wake you in time. It's great news, isn't it, my good Loutray?" The speaker cackled with merriment.

Denis parted the clothing in front of his face to hear better. He heard Loutray depart, heard his footsteps on the stairs. For a brief moment he thought that Pezzard had been left alone, and was forming a plan to spring out and knife the merchant before he could call for help. But Pezzard spoke again.

"Black Fox, I want you to stay here with me. You, too, Anton. I may need you for messengers as soon as I have written some letters. Jacques, you will stand guard in the hall, but you'd better keep awake this time—if you value your skin. In an hour wake up Jules and Marcel and bring them here."

"Yes, Master."

There was a long silence, broken only by the occasional scratching of a pen. Not daring to move, Denis suffered torture in his cramped quarters. He and Skonakoa stood like statues, side by side, drawing in their breaths slowly and quietly lest even that be heard by the three so near at hand. He listened for the sound of Loutray's return, hoping that the merchant and his companions would leave the room then. He heard Jacques mount the stairs to wake Loutray, heard footsteps descend the stairs and the front door slam.

Several hours later the same steps returned. "Here he is, Master," called someone from the hall.

Pezzard's chair scraped as he arose. "Go, Black Fox. You also, Anton. I'll speak with this man alone."

Their feet patted the floor as they left. Heavy boots clumped across the room. The door closed firmly. A chair squeaked under a man's weight.

"You are the merchant Pezzard?"

At the sound of the English Denis pressed his ear against the crack of the door.

"At your service, Captain Chaddock—I believe that is the name. You have credentials? Good. Yes, they are satisfactory." Pezzard's voice was suave. "Let us continue in English, for safety. I am glad you got here without trouble."

There was a rather pleasant chuckle in response. "It is fortunate you speak English since I have no French. As for getting here safely, that is largely your doing, Mr. Pezzard. When the fight was over I sent you word, as you know, that I would await your man. First we ran two of our little boats up the river to that cove behind the high cliff you call Cape Diamond. Well after midnight we went downstream again, and I sent mine as close to the point as I dared. There I went over the side. Brrr, that water was cold enough

to be Boston harbor in midwinter. Your man was waiting for me with these clothes. A good disguise they
proved to be. We came right into town with some of
the country people."

"After your swim, Captain, you might like some
brandy. I brought it in myself." There was a clink of
glass and a faint gurgle.

"Just what I needed. And good brandy it is. But to
get down to business. If I am to reach Walley's men
on the shore I will need all the time I can get. I am
to tell you that your offer is accepted. Your terms are
high—devilish high. If we had come sooner, before
your old wolf of a Governor got back from Montreal
and the walls were finished, we might not have needed
you. But no use thinking about that. . . .

"It is agreed," continued the same voice, "that I am
to meet you and your men at ten o'clock tonight at the
foot of the little path which goes down the cliff between the place you call Sailor's Leap and the Palace
Gate. You are to dispose of the guards. I am to come
alone and see if the way is clear. If it is, I signal for
our men. Walley has fifteen hundred, and boats for
them all. Ostensibly they will be returning to the ships.
At my signal they will turn in the mouth of the St.
Charles. The tide will be high. Meanwhile our ships
will create a diversion by drawing in close to the beach
below Cape Diamond, beyond the town, and make as
if to send a landing party.

"For your share I am to pay you here and now one
thousand of your gold louis, and glad I am to get rid
of them. Here is a receipt for you to sign. When the
town is taken you will receive two thousand more. In
addition I have here a written guarantee that you will

be made deputy for the English Governor in charge of the fur trade."

"My figure was four thousand louis," interrupted Pezzard.

"By King Charles' head it was three, and three it stays!"

"Oh, very well. I will take the three. You will see that nothing happens to the receipt? Where is the guarantee? Ummmm. Ummmm. All seems in order. Our bargain is sealed, Captain Chaddock. You wish to start right away? We'd better have breakfast first. Ho, there, Jules. Fetch Loutray from the kitchen."

Denis sniffed as the aroma of hot stew came into the cupboard. It had been a long time since supper. At last the Captain pushed back his chair.

"I must be going. You'll doubtless want a word with Loutray, Mr. Pezzard. I'll wait in the hall. Until to-night, then." The door closed.

There was a momentary silence, then Denis heard the soft hateful sound of Pezzard's laughter. "All is settled, my Loutray," he snickered. "See, here is my promise of the management of the whole fur trade. You shall be my second in command. In five years we'll be millionaires."

"Splendid. Let's have a drink to that." Glasses clinked. "I'd like one of Frontenac's ears to nail on the wall," mused Loutray.

"Maybe it can be arranged," chuckled the other. "But right now we must hide this paper safely. Where should it go? I have it. Be so good as to put it in the pocket of my blue coat in the armoire. No one would think of looking there."

Denis stiffened as Loutray's chair scraped the floor.

He grasped his knife. Loutray's footsteps approached the hiding place. Skonakoa stirred uneasily. In another instant—

"On second thought perhaps the document is safer in my own hands," said Pezzard. "Let's have it back. . . ."

The footsteps turned, receded. Denis breathed again.

"Now see that the Captain gets to Major Walley on the Beauport shore. Take him out by the Palace Gate. You have a pass. Be careful to circle far enough to miss our forces. I leave the rest to you, but meet me tonight at the bottom of the cliff."

Pezzard fell into a feverish activity as soon as Loutray and the Englishman had gone. Various men were summoned and sent off on errands, some to mysterious tasks connected with the storehouse in the lower town, others about jobs that Denis supposed had to do with making ready for the expected capture of the city.

For Denis the situation was desperate. Something worse than even Mersan had feared was about to happen. Were it not for the precious packet from the chimney he might have dared to spring out and try to fight his way out of the house. But he couldn't risk that now. No, even without the papers, he couldn't take the chance, for he suddenly realized that if he were killed Quebec would be taken. There would be no one else to warn the garrison. Patience.

Cannonading started during the morning, boomed irregularly for a time and died away. Once the window was opened for a moment and Denis heard the faint sweet chanting of the Ursuline nuns. Pezzard remained at the desk.

It must have been about noon when the merchant stepped into the hall to order Marie to bring his lunch. But he returned at once. The smell of hot soup and roast meat nearly roused Denis to a frenzy.

Ages passed. Finally several of the merchant's henchmen came in and settled down to a game of dice. The merchant left. The game went on and on. Denis began to fear that the click of the dice against the boards would drive him crazy. Even Skonakoa, with a patience far greater than his own, was growing restless. At last Denis could tell by the fading of the light through the cracks of the cupboard door that the day was waning.

At dusk Pezzard returned. "I thought the Intendant would never let me go," he grumbled to the men. "There is much to do yet. Go to the kitchen for your suppers. I will send for you later. Anton, stay in the hall."

Denis leaned wearily against the wall of the armoire. He was stiff from inaction and faint with hunger. He had to get out! Why couldn't he think of something. But all he could see was the tiny gate at the foot of the cliff where the English would land. . . . If only Perrot and Chastaignac knew where he was!

Sometime later the men returned. He heard Pezzard say, "I must go now to the lower town. Anton and Jules will stay here on watch and to carry messages. Marcel, you come with me."

Feet tramped into the hall. The front door closed. At last the room was empty!

It was several minutes before Denis dared open the door of the cupboard. Save for the banging of pots as Marie washed the supper things the house was quiet. Skonakoa peered into the hall, motioned Denis to follow him. The hall was empty, but the door opposite the foot of the staircase was open and light streamed from it across the passageway. Inside the room they heard two voices.

They crept as silently as shadows. Skonakoa reached the edge of the patch of light and rose to dash for the front door. Denis heard a grunt of astonishment from one of the guards. The man's eyes must have been on the hall. At any rate, he flung himself out of the room, knife in hand. Skonakoa met him, feet braced. The man tried to swerve, but too late. He fell heavily sideways with the Mohawk's knife in his heart. The second man rushed out. Denis whirled up the chair that stood by the staircase and brought it down with all his might on the fellow's skull.

They dragged the two into the vacant room across the corridor and closed the door. A moment later they were out in the deserted street. Now to warn the Governor!

CHAPTER XXIII

THE FIGHT AT THE GATE

AT THE Chateau a sentry tried to bar their way. Something of Denis's desperation must have shown by the torchlight, for at last the sentry grudgingly turned the two over to another soldier inside. He also maintained the Governor could see no one.

"But I must see him." Denis raised his voice. "It is on business of state. It is vital information for his ear alone."

"What's this?" A door on the corridor opened suddenly and a sturdy figure stood outlined against the glow of candles. "Who speaks with such authority?"

"Your Excellency, it doesn't matter who I am. The news I bear is what is important."

"All right, speak, and be quick about it."

"The English are going to land tonight. A traitor is going to let them into the city. I have proof. You will understand when you read these papers by one you know who served you faithfully. I got them from the house of LeRoux, the lawyer, who also died in your service." He could fairly feel the probing stare of the Governor.

"What is this? You speak in riddles, young man. What have your messages to do with the landing of the English?"

"Sir, the merchant Pezzard plans to open the gate

237

to the enemy—the gate below the cliff near the Saut au Matelot."

"What! A Quebec merchant? You are mad!"

Despairingly Denis whipped out the packet and held it out to the Governor. "Please read this, sir. Then you will understand."

Frontenac took the packet and turned it over in his hand. The door was flung open. "Lieutenant Valcour, sir," announced the sentry breathlessly.

"Excellency, the English boats have been discovered moving up under Cape Diamond," gasped the officer. "They are filled with men. They are making for the little beach beyond the battery where the path leads up the cliff."

Frontenac whirled. "Hola, Barbeau. My cloak. My sword. My hat. Lieutenant, run to Provost. Tell him to meet me at the beach with three hundred men. Have the alarm sounded. Rouse the garrison. Station three hundred militia on the walls by the windmill. A hundred coureurs as scouts beyond the walls. We'll give them a reception they won't forget."

The Lieutenant saluted and dashed out of the door.

"Here, Barbeau, take this packet. Put it in my safe. Help me buckle this sword belt."

"But, Your Excellency, listen to me," cried Denis. "This is a trick—a diversion. The English are going to land at the Saut au Matelot."

The cloak was already about the Governor's shoulders. Denis flung himself in front of the door.

"Out of my way, lad," rumbled Frontenac. "Your information can wait. Come back tomorrow."

Propelled by the orderly, Denis found himself outside in the deserted Place. Frontenac was already striding off, lighted on his way by four soldiers with pine torches.

"Onontio is like an angry panther," observed Skonakoa disapprovingly. "He is a great chief, but no one can see everything."

"What time is it?" Denis demanded of the orderly who lingered, watching them suspiciously.

"Near ten of the clock, to judge by the last call of the sentry," replied the soldier.

Denis caught Skonakoa's arm. "Come," he cried and raced across the Place d'Armes.

At the farther side of the parade ground he gasped, "You must go for Perrot and Chastaignac. They'll believe us. Bring them to the gate where the Jesuits enter. You remember. I'll go ahead and watch. *Hurry.*"

As the Mohawk vanished toward Mountain Hill Denis turned and dashed up the path toward the Saut au Matelot. It was very dark on top of the cliff. The moon, which the evening before had furnished a certain amount of light, was now hidden by a blanket of clouds. Here and there a yellow window gleamed through the night. Tiny pinpoints of light far out in the river showed the position of the English fleet.

He reached the edge of the cliff above the St. Charles and, throwing himself flat on his stomach, peered down. A small bonfire burned beside the gate of the palisade. By its light he could see two sentries lounging against the outer wall. A faint glimmer of the firelight on water told him that the tide was well in. Below him the path wound down the face of the cliff.

He pressed himself tight against the rock and waited. Several minutes passed and nothing happened.

At last he heard moccasined feet approaching. Four shapes appeared at the brink of the cliff, were outlined momentarily against the firelight, then disappeared into the darkness below. Far out on the black waters of the St. Charles there was a very small splash. It might have been a fish—or it might have been a cautiously wielded paddle. From the Jesuit chapel behind him came the tinkle of a bell.

His straining ears heard the sound of a faint rattle, as if a pebble had been dislodged from the path. His eyes tried to pierce the blackness of the river, but he could see no sign of waiting boats. A rush of feet toward the sentries below jerked his eyes back from the river. Black shapes leaped into the firelight. The soldiers were overpowered before they could utter a sound. The stocky figure of Pezzard flung open the gate.

Denis listened in anguish for the sound of approaching aid. What had happened to Skonakoa? Surely by this time Perrot and Chastaignac could have come from the tavern! But behind him all was quiet. He wormed his way to the path and began to crawl down it. His ears caught a sound from the beach.

At the foot of the cliff the path curved behind a rock. Denis crouched in its shelter. It was scarcely thirty feet to the stockade. Through the open gate Denis saw a man in a cloak approaching from the water's edge. Behind him stalked Loutray. Pezzard rushed out to meet them. The stranger stood for a moment looking carefully in each direction and then to the cliff above. He nodded.

One of Pezzard's men lighted a lantern with a brand from the fire. He stood holding it while Pezzard and the stranger whispered. Denis tried again to see into the darkness beyond. Though he could neither see nor hear anything he was certain that the English boats lay somewhere offshore within a few moments' row of the gate. A signal from the officer and they would dart in. Once the invaders had gained the top of the cliff they could take the garrison in the rear and Quebec would fall. The cloaked figure took the lantern and turned toward the beach.

As he turned Denis screamed the Huron war cry and raced toward the Englishman. One of the half-breed followers of Pezzard rushed between. Denis slashed at the man's throat. The Englishman whipped out his sword. "Treachery!" he yelled and began to lay about him lustily.

But if the English officer was confused, Pezzard, Loutray, Black Fox and the other half-breed reacted promptly to the surprise. With a muttered curse one made at Denis with a hatchet. Denis sprang back into the shadow of the cliff. The hatchet clattered on the rocks by his side. The next instant he was locked in the fellow's arms and the two of them were rolling toward the gate, each seeking the other's throat.

"Turn him loose," screamed Loutray. "Marcel, let him go, I say. I'll finish him."

He heard the shrill chatter of Pezzard, seeking to explain to the English officer, offering advice to the others. Despairingly he clung to his adversary.

Suddenly a ferocious yell rang out at the top of the cliff. *"Ouch'ka. Tenaouich' tenaga. Ouch'ka!"*

It was the dread war cry of the Iroquois that Denis had first heard at the Seneca ambush. Then it had screamed defiance to Denis and all his kind. Now it was the sweetest sound in the world. He heard the clatter of pebbles on the cliff. "Courage, Denis!" called Perrot. He heard Chastaignac's bellow.

He loosened his hold and sprang up. Marcel bounded to his feet. Three shadows catapulted from the base of the cliff. The lithe form of Skonakoa darted toward Black Fox, intent on the endless feud between Iroquois and Huron. Chastaignac's red beard flamed in the firelight as he leaped, swinging a great cudgel, toward the half-breed. Perrot's sword flashed like lightning as he engaged the English officer, now aware of what was happening.

Shaking his head to clear it, Denis sprang at Loutray. A fierce exultation filled him, blinding him to all else save that at last he was face to face with his enemy. He glimpsed Loutray's snarling face, like a heavy-lidded mask. It circled against the darkness of the cliff. It plunged toward him. He saw the flicker of the knife. He caught it with his own. He braced himself, straining, matching the strength of his right arm against the strength of Loutray.

He was dimly conscious of the click and slither of blades behind him, of the dull sound of a blow and a little cry that ended in a choked gasp. Loutray raised his arm and Denis ran in under it. He felt a searing pain in his upper arm. He felt his own blade meet cloth and leather and flesh. Loutray gave a hoarse cry and staggered. Again Denis struck, and Loutray went down writhing.

He whirled to see the Englishman throw down his sword. Chastaignac had turned his attention to Black Fox, for the half-breed was on the sand. But even as he circled for a chance to bring down his club, Skonakoa's tomahawk found its mark.

His eyes fell on a black figure running through the gate. "Stop him," he shrilled. "Keep him from the canoe."

Chastaignac bounded after the merchant. "I've got him," he yelled triumphantly. "The weasel was half-way to the water and trying to tear up a paper."

"Save it!" cried Denis. "It's the proof we need. It's his commission from the English."

"Oh-ho," answered the Gascon. "It's safe enough, my stout-hearted little Denis." He reappeared through the gate, one hand clutched in the collar of the struggling merchant, the other holding aloft the commission.

"What a fool," remarked the English officer, with a self-possession Denis could not but admire. "He should have hidden it. What do you propose to do with us?"

"I propose," replied Perrot, after Denis had translated, "to call the guard, see that this gate is properly manned against the chance that your boats will yet try to land, and then have you and your plotters escorted to the Chateau."

"As you will," said the Englishman.

Skonakoa stalked into the firelight. "Are you hurt, brother?" he asked. From his hand dangled a new scalp.

"No," said Denis. "It is nothing."

"See. At least I will not return to my people empty-handed," said the Mohawk.

It was Chastaignac who brought the guard from the Palace Gate. It was Perrot who superintended the herding of the prisoners to the Chateau St. Louis. There the comrades waited until Frontenac returned, grumbling because the English, instead of landing, had hovered offshore for hours, keeping most of the army watching helplessly.

He nodded to Perrot, looked at the prisoners and gestured wearily. "My guard will lock them up until tomorrow. Perrot, I am an old man. I feel my seventy years. Let me rest now. Come back tomorrow at eleven. Then I will hear all."

Reluctantly Denis saw the prisoners locked in separate cells in the barracks. He would have liked to sleep in the corridor, but Perrot would not let him. He had forgotten his wound until he stumbled going down Mountain Hill. Perrot's arm caught him.

"François, help me."

"I'm all right," protested Denis and knew nothing more.

Chapter XXIV

DENIS OF NEW FRANCE

"The English are leaving!"

Denis heard the words drowsily, repeated them to himself.

"The ships are going!"

At that he sat up in bed. It was the voice of the host of the tavern shrilling up the stairs. Skonakoa stirred on his pallet.

"It is late," Chastaignac announced. "There is breakfast to eat before we see the Governor. Yes, it is true. The ships are turning downstream. Let me help you dress, Denis. It would be an awkward business for you, with your arm in a sling."

They bolted some food and left. The streets were filled with weeping laughing people. From the top of the cliff, where they pushed their way, they could see the last of the sails disappearing around the bend of the Isle d'Orleans. A roll of drums sounded from the redoubt, and from the Cathedral came the triumphant strains of the *Te Deum*.

Frontenac turned from the window as they were shown into his study. "Good morning," he barked. "Well, my friends, they are gone, and they will not trouble us again. We have shown them we can hold what is rightfully ours. The King will be pleased." He smiled a little, but the next thought brought a frown.

245

"My only fear now is for the three ships long overdue. They bring the King's gold as well as goods. I have sent word to warn them."

He moved briskly to his desk. "But your chief concern is of more immediate matters, is it not? I have found time to go through these famous papers. There is much in them of interest. I wish to hear all of this affair. Be so good as to wait until the prisoners arrive; they have been sent for."

Denis glanced at his companions. Perrot was standing easily near the desk, his blue eyes contemplative, his right hand pulling at the lobe of his ear. Chastaignac teetered back and forth, his lips puckered in a soundless whistle. Skonakoa stood with his arms folded, his gaze fixed on Frontenac.

Steps rang in the stone corridor. Between a file of guards Pezzard, Loutray and the half-breed Marcel entered. A guard was supporting Loutray. Pezzard glared at the silent group, then twisted his face into a smile and stepped toward the desk.

"My lord," he purred. "I know not what misapprehension has caused our detention, but I am sure it may easily be settled."

Frontenac threw himself back in his chair. "What happened?"

"I and my servants here were returning from a call on M'sieur the Intendant and stopped to talk with the guard at the little gate below the cliff by the St. Charles. These four men sprang at us from the darkness below the cliff, killed the two guards and one of my men as well, and wounded M'sieur Loutray and Marcel. I am really at a loss as you to explain their actions." His voice was suave; his air one of tolerance.

"Is that all you have to say?"

"I know of nothing else, Your Excellency. You are not unacquainted with my name, my reputation. My friends will answer for me. If there has been an honest mistake I am not one to press charges."

"The sentiment is a noble one, Maître Pezzard," said Frontenac ironically. "I wish to hear, however, what this boy has to say." He turned to Denis, and his eyes were the chill blue of tempered steel. "Begin," he directed, "with how you came to New France. Tell me everything you know of Maître Pezzard."

Denis drew a deep breath and started, far back in Normandy, with old Giles and their grinding poverty. He reached the discovery of the dying Mersan in the attic of Pezzard's house.

"It's a lie," screamed the merchant. Tiny beads of sweat covered his forehead. He lunged forward to pound the corner of the desk with his fist. "It's a lie. I took this boy, out of charity, as an apprentice. He stole a silver mug the first day he was with me and ran away to join the lawless men of the woods. Now he tries to blacken my name to save his own skin—"

"Keep quiet." Frontenac's look would have silenced a stronger man than Pezzard. "Go on, Denis."

Perrot's fingers touched his arm, steadying him. Consciously he held his voice level as he summed up the rest of the story. He reached the events of the last days and the conversation he had heard from the armoire.

By now Pezzard had regained control of himself. He shrugged his shoulders, spreading his thick hands eloquently. "You see for yourself, Your Excellency, that the boy is unbalanced."

Frontenac turned to Perrot. "I take it you believe what Denis has said?"

"I do."

"Your Excellency is too patient." Pezzard's voice was suddenly hoarse. "Only a madman could believe such a tale on the word of a boy."

Slowly Frontenac shifted in his chair. "The Sieur Perrot is not mad, and does not give his trust lightly. Neither do I. As for the boy's tale, the dead, Maître Pezzard, speak for him."

His hand moved across the desk and rested on the packet. "I have gone through the papers which Denis de Lornay brought me last night. I find in them messages in the writing of Raoul Mersan, a devoted young friend of mine who disappeared four years ago. He has told me in these notes much of the activities of certain people in Canada, their correspondence with the English, their attempts to discredit me with my King, their efforts to inflame the people against me so I would not be returned as Governor. Your name is prominent, Pezzard. I have also found the papers of the lawyer, LeRoux, killed by some Hurons in a street fight last year, which report still further on the same matters and speak of his fear for his life. And again in the papers of the lawyer, I find your name."

Pezzard's face twisted into a snarl. "No matter what these spies may say there is nothing treasonable, Your Excellency, in what I have done. I have never pretended to be of your party or approve of what you did. The Intendant will protect me from your anger. A difference of opinion is not a criminal offense."

"No, but this is." From the inside pocket of his jacket Denis drew out the paper he had snatched from the merchant's hand and threw it on the desk. Frontenac looked at it frowning.

"I cannot read it. Hola, bring in Lesancourt to interpret. And bring in the other prisoner."

Again there came the tramp of feet in the corridor. The dapper young lieutenant appeared. Beside him strode the cloaked figure of the English captain. At a word from the Governor the lieutenant translated aloud the agreement between Pezzard and the English.

As he read, the merchant seemed to shrink inside his black clothes. Once he opened his mouth, but closed it at Frontenac's glance. When the paper was finished the Englishman spoke for the first time.

"Tell the Governor," he directed, "that this man guaranteed to deliver the city to us. Some of our people knew of him. We thought we might succeed by guile where we had failed by direct assault. But for these other men we would have succeeded. I will write out a statement if you wish. I throw myself on the Governor's mercy and hope that I may be treated as a prisoner of war. I took the precaution," he smiled wryly, "to come in uniform." He moved his cloak and showed the regimentals beneath.

The lieutenant translated swiftly. Frontenac nodded. "Take him with you, Lesancourt. Let him make out his statement. Tell him I bear him no ill will, since he failed, and that I will exchange him as soon as possible."

As the two men saluted and left the room Frontenac rose to his feet. It was the same stern, haughty Governor of New France who had faced the English envoy.

"Pezzard, I shall pass sentence on you here and now. You will be taken on the first ship to the West Indies and there sold as an indentured servant for a period of ten years. You will not return to France, nor any of her possessions, under penalty of death. Your money I shall endeavor to return to those from whom you swindled it." The merchant hid his face in his trembling hands.

Frontenac glanced at Perrot. "It would not be well for the people to learn of what he has done. It might shake their trust in honest men. I propose, if you gentlemen agree, to say nothing beyond these walls of what happened last night. You have saved Canada. Will you be satisfied with the thanks of your Governor?"

The four nodded.

"Loutray," Frontenac continued, "will go to the galleys. I know something of him. There are enough murders against his name to hang ten men, but in the galleys he will have more opportunity to regret his crimes than on the block. Five years should suffice to teach the other to avoid evil company. There should be another," he frowned, "a Huron."

Denis stepped to one side and pointed to the scalp hanging at Skonakoa's belt. Frontenac permitted himself a ghost of a smile.

"That is just as well. Captain of the Guard! Remove the prisoners."

Denis turned away as the four stumbled from the room. He made a move as if to follow, but a gesture from the Governor halted him.

"There is yet another packet of papers in the lawyer's box," he said. "It seems he became interested in the story you told him, Denis, of your life in Normandy. He thought there was much which needed explaining. He wrote to a friend in Rouen of what you had said, and the friend answered several times and at length.

"The friend went to your village of Cailly and found

Giles living at the farm with his son. There had indeed been a boy called Denis de Lornay who had disappeared. But that was not the boy's real name. This boy's father had had a younger brother, ambitious and ruthless. The father and mother both died of a fever when the baby was but a few weeks old. Giles did not trust this younger brother; it is easy to dispose of a new baby when the baby is sole heir. He took the child to his own niece, and when the brother arrived from Paris told him that the baby had died and been buried with its mother. This the brother preferred to believe, for he thus became the possessor of the title and the estates. Giles gave the baby the name of its mother, which was not known in the district, and said it had come to him from a distant cousin. The brother stayed in Paris, and the baby grew in safety. Giles did his best to teach him or to have him taught what he should know, for when the boy was eighteen he was resolved to tell him the truth and help him gain his estates. But one night the boy disappeared.

"The lawyer in Rouen kept the old man supplied with money and visited him in the hope the boy would return. One message came from him and later some money, and that was all. LeRoux himself could learn nothing of his whereabouts. Have you anything to prove you are that Denis de Lornay?"

Before Denis could answer there were voices in the corridor and a sharp rap at the door. "Word from the three ships, Your Excellency," called the guard.

Frontenac's face lightened. "Enter."

The burly figure was familiar to Denis. "Captain Marsollet!" he cried as it rolled across the room.

The Captain looked at him in surprise, then faced the Governor.

"I'm come to bring you word, sir, that the ships are

safe. Your messengers reached us in time for us to slip into the Saguenay River. With luck the English fleet will pass the mouth without seeing us. If they do see us, their big ships are too deep to enter, their small ones too feeble. We'll be safely at Quebec two days after they pass. I came ahead by canoe to tell you. But who called my name?"

Denis moved toward him. "Captain, do you remember your cabin boy?"

The Captain stared at him, frowning, for a moment. "Mon Dieu! It can't be. Yes! Denis! But no wonder I do not recognize you. And how glad I am to see you!" One red fist nearly knocked Denis gasping. "How I tried to find you! All I could learn was that you had run away from the merchant. I have long wished to make amends for the trick I played on you."

Frontenac motioned to Denis to keep still. "What trick, Captain?"

The weather-beaten Marsollet faced him frankly. "I must confess, though I am heartily ashamed. It was at Le Havre four years ago that a man came to me one evening. He offered me an easy way to make some money. He told me where I would find this boy. I was to watch until I could talk to him alone and then persuade him to come with me to Canada. It meant a hundred louis in my pocket as soon as he was on board ship. He said the boy was bad and better out of the country, so I did not mind. But I liked you, Denis, and I came to believe the man lied. I went to see Giles, but I dared not tell him. He was grateful for the letter you left with me. He gave me many messages I have forgotten. But one I have not. It was about your dagger."

"What dagger?" asked Frontenac quickly.

Denis slipped the sheath from his belt and laid it on the desk. Chuckling, the Captain picked it up. "You do not know even yet, hein? See, the top, here, turns. Let me see—first to the left, then to the right, and it comes off. And behold! Inside is the crest of your family. That is a surprise? But more. The handle is hollow and here is a paper giving your name and I know not what. Giles said to tell you the curé knew all he knew, whatever that may mean." He sighed deeply. "I am glad to have found you. It is a load from my conscience."

Frontenac had picked up the crest and the paper and was studying them. He handed them to Denis. "Put them back, my boy. That is proof enough. Captain, I thank you for your double message. You must be hungry. My men will give you food and drink. You shall have an escort back to your ship."

"And I'll be glad for all three. Denis, I'll see you again. Sir, your humble servant." He stumped from the room.

Frontenac leaned back again and looked at the four in front of him.

"I thank you again for what you did last night. The King himself shall hear of it." He pointed a sudden finger at Skonakoa. "What do you here? You are not a Huron, in spite of your Huron painting. You are not one of our Christian Mohawks. You are an Iroquois from the English."

"Onontio is half right," answered Skonakoa composedly. "I am one of the Iroquois, but not from the English. Denis is my brother. I stay with my brother."

The Governor nodded, smiling. "Some day I must hear how it happened. If anyone questions your presence here come to me."

"But, sir—" Denis could keep still no longer. "What —who am I?"

Frontenac smiled broadly. "Your name is Denis Michel Henri Brian de Valenceau, Baron de Montvaillant. I shall write to the King about you. I do not believe you will find it difficult to prove your identity satisfactorily and obtain your estates. I suppose you return on the next ship?"

Denis stared at him in bewilderment, then sought the faces of his friends. "Go back to France? But why should I?" He drew himself up and stepped back a pace. "Never, sir. Not if my friends will let me stay with them." He threw his right arm around Perrot, his left around Chastaignac.

Both looked at him without smiling. "It is your duty to go back, Denis," said Perrot gravely. "A young baron cannot remain a coureur."

"You must go back," agreed Chastaignac heartily. "Ho-ho, of course. You must go to court, live off the fat of the land, forget these hard years. You can even see Gascony. Yes, on my faith, I envy you." His tone was boisterous, his eyes very bright.

Frontenac echoed his friends. "You must go back, Denis, if only to see that justice is done. But you are of age. If you do not like Paris, and court life, there is no reason why you should not return. I must send you back, if need be, so that you can choose your own life. Afterwards you can do as you please."

Denis dropped his arms. "Very well, sir. If you send me. I should like to see Giles again, at least. It would be fine to tell him about everything. But," he straightened defiantly, "I'll be back on the first boat next spring. I belong in this New France with my friends. I will come back to stay."

"My brother speaks of what will happen," said Skonakoa quietly.

Frontenac was still smiling as the four filed from the room.

① Quebec.　② Montreal
③ Huron village where Denis
　saved Skonakoa ～
④ Mission and trading-post
　of Michilimacknac
⑤ Perrot's fort on the Mississippi
⑥ Seneca village of Ganagaro
　(Denonville's expedition.)
⑦ Onondaga capital where
　Denis was held captive.
⑧ Albany.　⑨ La Hontan's fort
⑩ Tonty's fort on the Illinois
⑪ Perrot's upper fort.
⑫ Three Rivers ⑬ Ft. Frontenac
⑭ Where Denis and Skonakoa
　built the canoe.

Assiniboines

Crees

Lake Superior

Otta

Ottawas

Pottawatomies

Malhominies

Sioux

Miamis

Lake Michigan

Illinois

George Carlson